CW01213828

Praise for the Mic
LARA

BOUND TO DARKNESS

"While most series would have ended or run out of steam, the Midnight Breed series seems to have picked up steam. Lara Adrian has managed to keep the series fresh by adding new characters . . . without having to say goodbye to the original ones that made the series so popular to begin with. Bound to Darkness has all the passion, danger and unique appeal of the original ten books but also stands on its own as a turning point in the entire series with new pieces to a larger puzzle, new friends and old enemies."

—*Adria's Romance Reviews*

"Lara Adrian always manages to write great love stories, not only emotional but action packed. I love every aspect of (Bound to Darkness). I also enjoyed how we get a glimpse into the life of the other characters we have come to love. There is always something sexy and erotic in all of Adrian's books, making her one of my top 5 paranormal authors."

—*Reading Diva*

CRAVE THE NIGHT

"Nothing beats good writing and that is what ultimately makes Lara Adrian stand out amongst her peers.... Crave the Night is stunning in its flawless execution. Lara Adrian has the rare ability to lure readers right into her books, taking them on a ride they will never forget."

—*Under the Covers*

"…Steamy and intense. This installment is sure to delight established fans and will also be accessible to new readers."

—*Publishers Weekly*

EDGE OF DAWN

"Adrian's strikingly original Midnight Breed series delivers an abundance of nail-biting suspenseful chills, red-hot sexy thrills, an intricately built world, and realistically complicated and conflicted protagonists, whose happily-ever-after ending proves to be all the sweeter after what they endure to get there."

—*Booklist (starred review)*

DARKER AFTER MIDNIGHT

"A riveting novel that will keep readers mesmerized... If you like romance combined with heart-stopping paranormal suspense, you're going to love this book."

—*Bookpage*

DEEPER THAN MIDNIGHT

"One of the consistently best paranormal series out there.... Adrian writes compelling individual stories (with wonderful happily ever afters) within a larger story arc that is unfolding with a refreshing lack of predictability."

–*Romance Novel News*

Praise for Lara Adrian

"With an Adrian novel, readers are assured of plenty of dangerous thrills and passionate chills."

–*RT Book Reviews*

"Ms. Adrian has a gift for drawing her readers deeper and deeper into the amazing world she creates."

–*Fresh Fiction*

Praise for LARA ADRIAN

"Adrian has a gift for drawing her readers deeper and deeper into the amazing world she creates."

–*Fresh Fiction*

"With an Adrian novel, readers are assured of plenty of dangerous thrills and passionate chills."

–*RT Book Reviews*

"Nothing beats good writing and that is what ultimately makes Lara Adrian stand out amongst her peers . . . Adrian doesn't hold back with the intensity or the passion."

—*Under the Covers*

"Adrian has a style of writing that creates these worlds that are so realistic and believable . . . the characters are so rich and layered . . . the love stories are captivating and often gut-wrenching . . . edge of your seat stuff!"

—*Scandalicious Book Reviews*

"Adrian compels readers to get hooked on her storylines."

—*Romance Reviews Today*

Praise for Lara Adrian's books

"Adrian's strikingly original Midnight Breed series delivers an abundance of nail-biting suspenseful chills, red-hot sexy thrills, an intricately built world, and realistically complicated and conflicted protagonists, whose happily-ever-after ending proves to be all the sweeter after what they endure to get there."

—*Booklist (starred review)*

"(The Midnight Breed is) a well-written, action-packed series that is just getting better with age."

—*Fiction Vixen*

The New York Times bestselling Midnight Breed series

A Touch of Midnight (prequel novella)
Kiss of Midnight
Kiss of Crimson
Midnight Awakening
Midnight Rising
Veil of Midnight
Ashes of Midnight
Shades of Midnight
Taken by Midnight
Deeper Than Midnight
A Taste of Midnight (ebook novella)
Darker After Midnight
The Midnight Breed Series Companion
Edge of Dawn
Marked by Midnight (novella)
Crave the Night
Tempted by Midnight (novella)
Bound to Darkness
Stroke of Midnight (novella)
Defy the Dawn
Midnight Untamed (novella)
Midnight Unbound (novella)
Midnight Unleashed (novella)
Claimed in Shadows
Break the Day
Fall of Night
King of Midnight

Hunter Legacy Series
A Midnight Breed Spinoff

Born of Darkness
Hour of Darkness
Edge of Darkness
Guardian of Darkness

Other books by Lara Adrian

Contemporary Romance

100 Series
For 100 Days
For 100 Nights
For 100 Reasons

Run to You
Play My Game

Historical Romance

Dragon Chalice Series
Heart of the Hunter
Heart of the Flame
Heart of the Dove

Warrior Trilogy
White Lion's Lady
Black Lion's Bride
Lady of Valor

Lord of Vengeance

GUARDIAN OF DARKNESS

A Hunter Legacy Novel

NEW YORK TIMES BESTSELLING AUTHOR

LARA ADRIAN

www.LaraAdrian.com

Available in ebook and trade paperback. Unabridged audiobook edition forthcoming.

GUARDIAN OF DARKNESS

CHAPTER 1

The smell of burnt timber clung to the warm, late-afternoon mountain air.

Even through his ultraviolet light blocking helmet and clothing, Razor's acute Breed senses recoiled at the stench. Whatever fire had been raging earlier in the day was over now. Its heat was extinguished, its smoke blown away, but that only meant he had arrived too late. The damage was already done.

Fuck.

Ignoring the sharp odor that scraped his throat with every breath, Razor ran faster up the side of the wooded incline.

After thirty hours on his motorcycle from Florida to this isolated corner of Colorado, impatience sizzled in his veins. He'd ditched his bike off a rugged dirt road about a mile behind him. He didn't need to draw unwanted attention on his approach. Besides, as one of the Breed he could make the rest of his trek much faster on foot.

His boots tore up the loamy ground as he sped for the small cabin he'd been surveilling remotely by drone for the past several months. He'd been watching the location as a favor to an old friend, but the dread he felt now was personal.

Too personal.

He didn't know how he'd let himself get so invested in a task, but there was no denying the clawing ache that ripped a hole in his chest as he got his first glimpse of the small clearing and the cabin at its center.

Or, rather, what little remained of it.

Timber walls had been reduced to cinders. The river rock chimney stood scorched and blackened, a grim marker for the house that was no more. The metal skeletons of assorted furnishings smoldered among the ashes and ruin.

The annihilation was too complete to be an accident.

The surrounding woods had been left virtually unscathed by the fire, but the cabin had been obliterated with precision. And without mercy.

Razor stepped closer, his boots crunching in the charred rubble.

The bitter odors of fuel and fire choked him, but it was the unmistakable scent of death that set his jaw and made dread coil inside him. His pulse hammered, cold and heavy, as he glimpsed the shape of a petite body that lay burned beyond recognition near the center of the destruction.

A snarl rumbled low in his chest.

The woman he'd come to retrieve and bring to safety was dead.

Damn it. He was too fucking late.

He'd failed his old friend.

He'd failed this innocent woman too.

Razor literally owed his life to Theo Collier, so when the human had asked him a few months ago to keep a protective eye on Laurel Townsend, Theo's former lover, Razor had accepted without hesitation.

He could still hear Theo's fearful tone when he'd called yesterday to say that he needed something more than surveillance from Razor. He wanted him to bring Laurel under Razor's personal protection as quickly as possible. He'd claimed it was too urgent—too dangerous—for him to say anything more over the phone, and he'd begged for Razor's trust.

Anytime you need my help, you have it. No questions asked.

That had been Razor's pledge to the human after Theo had saved his life some twenty years ago. That promise tasted like ash as he approached the scene.

The fact that Laurel's vehicle wasn't at the firebombed cabin had given Razor a small shred of hope. He'd thought maybe she had managed to escape the inferno.

That hope was nothing but cinders now too.

Her face bloomed to life in Razor's head. He had hours of video surveillance feed of the quiet cabin, but only scant few frames of the beautiful, but reclusive, brunette who lived there.

A picture reel played through his mind's eye in an instant—her lovely face with its peachy freckles and bright green eyes, her long dark hair bouncing at her back as she drove up to the cabin in a black open-air Jeep then began to carry in bags of groceries.

She had been all soft, generous curves and wholesome sweetness in her gauzy white peasant top and faded jeans, and the sight of her had ignited an unbidden desire in Razor that he didn't want to acknowledge, even now.

Especially now.

"Fuck."

It wasn't bad enough that he'd been covertly watching an old friend's woman without her knowledge. He'd been secretly lusting after her too.

That was a sin he'd have to deal with in his own time.

Sooner than later, he'd have to contact Theo Collier and tell him the awful news. Whatever danger Theo felt Laurel was in—danger dire enough that he'd called Razor and practically begged him to get to her as soon as possible—the worst had occurred.

Now, Razor wanted answers.

Once he knew who had killed Laurel Townsend—and why—he was going to find the bastards and make them pay for what they'd done.

He ground his teeth and fangs together as he stared at the charred remains. Her skull bore a large, jagged hole from a bullet that had been fired into her head at close range. Someone had wanted to make sure she was dead. The fire would have killed her surely enough, but the mortal head wound had made certain of it.

"Son of a bitch," Razor hissed quietly. The woman wasn't his to mourn, but a cold grief carved deep into his chest to imagine the terror she must have suffered. She didn't deserve to die like this.

He couldn't save her now, but he damned well intended to avenge her.

Not only for his friend, but because his own blood demanded it.

As for the body, he refused to leave it for the elements or the forest scavengers.

It was too much to hope that he could find something to dig with in the rubble. Then again, he was uniquely suited to handle the situation without. Every Breed vampire was born with his own individual ability that set him apart from others, and Razor's had helped give him his name.

On a mental command, sharp black talons erupted from the tips of his fingers.

He walked a few yards from the smoldering ruins to find a suitable place to bury the woman. A shaded area of grass near a small patch of wildflowers was the best he could do. Razor began digging. His Breed strength and speed made short work of the task. The shallow grave dug, he walked back over and carefully extricated Laurel Townsend's remains from the ashes.

As he placed her in the grave, he noticed the delicate gold necklace she was wearing. Its chain and small pendant were blackened with soot and warped from the heat of the blaze. One of the links broke loose in his fingers as he touched it for a closer look.

Using his thumb, he rubbed the soot from the misshapen little half-heart pendant.

It would make a grim remembrance for his friend, but Razor would let Theo decide on that. Either way, Laurel didn't need it anymore.

Razor slipped the necklace into his pocket as he knelt beside the open grave. He didn't have any pretty words to speak for her. All he had was a festering sense of anger and regret . . . and bloody minded determination to deliver a cold payback to whoever was responsible for this heinous attack.

He took one last look at what remained of the vibrant beauty who'd lived in his head for the past few months like some untouchable dream.

"I'm sorry," he ground out through his teeth and fangs. "I'm sorry I got here too late."

He would carry that guilt the rest of his life. Just like he'd spend the rest of his days haunted by the memory of a fresh-faced, lovely ghost he had no right to crave the way he had, and no right to mourn now.

On a hard curse, he began covering her up with the dirt he'd dug, raking the cool soil back into the grave. When it was done, he retracted his talons and stood to dust himself off.

The sun was beginning to set. He preferred to ride at night, but any thought of heading directly back to the Darkhaven in Florida had gone up in smoke right along with Laurel's cabin. Instead, he'd use the advantage of nightfall to prowl the small town at the base of the mountain and hunt for information.

Someone down there had to know something. Not only had the fire been deliberately set, but it had also been expertly extinguished before it could spread to the surrounding mountainside.

But who would have done something like this? And why?

It wasn't only the locals in town who had some explaining to do. Theo Collier was keeping something from Razor too. He hadn't pressed him when they last spoke, but he damn well intended to now.

He wasn't going anywhere until he had answers to all the questions churning in his mind.

He headed back down the mountain, retrieving his bike and riding it to the bottom of the serpentine pass that let out at the edge of town.

Twilight cloaked the main street, which was lined with a handful of shops and cafes. Razor waited at the stop sign for the mountain pass, watching the pickup trucks and smattering of cars making their way in and out of the small downtown area.

He was just about to turn onto the main drag when a black Jeep approached the entrance to the pass.

An open-air black Jeep with a pretty brunette behind the wheel.

What the fuck?

Her long hair blew in the breeze coming in from all sides of her vehicle, and her lips were moving to the lyrics of an old pop song playing from the speakers.

He couldn't believe what he was seeing.

He had to be hallucinating, because there was not a shred of doubt in his mind that this woman was the same one he'd been watching for months.

With no one behind him at the stop sign, he dropped the kickstand on his bike and swung off it as she started to turn onto the pass.

He had questions in need of answers?

He was going to start right here and now, with Laurel Townsend herself.

CHAPTER 2

She had no sooner made the turn onto the pass when a lunatic on a motorcycle hopped off his bike and walked right into her lane.

The Jeep's tires shrieked as she stomped on the brakes—not two seconds from ramming into the man. At least, she assumed the giant standing in her way was a man. Either that or a yeti garbed in head-to-toe black riding gear and a matching helmet with a dark face shield that totally obscured his features from view.

She threw up her hands in disbelief. "Are you crazy? I almost hit you."

He stepped around the hood of the idling vehicle and approached the driver's side. God, why hadn't she taken the time to put the doors back on her Jeep today? Normally, she loved driving in the open air, but as the dark stranger came to a halt outside her vehicle she'd never felt more exposed and vulnerable. Although she couldn't see his eyes behind the gleaming dark shield that hid them, she felt the heat of his silent stare like a blowtorch.

She barely resisted the urge to tug the loose neckline of her white peasant top a little higher, or to attempt to tame some of her windblown dark hair. She was wearing baggy denim cutoff shorts and beat-up cowboy boots, but the way his shielded eyes burned she might have been sitting there with nothing on at all.

The upbeat song she'd been singing to as she drove through town was an irritating distraction now. Without daring to look away from the huge, menacing presence standing not two feet away from her, she reached out and muted the radio.

"Are you lost?" She asked the question if only to fill the awkward silence and to pretend he wasn't rattling her down to her bones. "Do you speak English?"

"Laurel Townsend." Two words, spoken from behind the black helmet in a deep, smoky voice.

Holy. Fuck.

All she could do was swallow while her brain began to clang with alarm bells.

Who was this man?

How the hell did he know her twin sister's name?

Willow's heart hammered so hard she wondered if he could hear it. Her tongue felt cleaved to the roof of her mouth.

Think, dammit!

Her sister had told her when she'd arrived in Colorado six months ago that she was in some kind of trouble. Laurel refused to explain more, worried that if Willow knew too much she would be in danger as well.

Willow had guessed Laurel's fear had something to do with her life in Montreal. Now she could only wonder if this man was the danger Laurel had been running from. Either way, she wasn't about to tell him anything.

If she could do nothing else, she had to try to lead him away from the mountain before he got close to her sister. Even if she had to be the bait.

Without answering him, Willow threw the Jeep into reverse and hit the gas.

The wheels screamed in response, but the vehicle wasn't moving. She pushed the accelerator to the floor, wincing at the stench of rubber burning on the asphalt while she continued to go nowhere.

Then she glanced to her right and saw the reason why. Except the reason made no logical sense whatsoever.

The stranger was physically holding onto her vehicle. His booted feet stood braced on the pavement, his strong hands gripping the Jeep with inhuman strength.

Otherworldly strength.

Oh, shit. No.

Was he—?

The terrifying thought didn't have a chance to settle in her mind before a rusted-out pickup truck rambled in behind her from the main road. The old man behind the wheel honked, impatient to get onto the pass.

"Go around," ordered the low voice from beside her.

The old man honked some more, middle finger extended as he thrust his arm out the window. Willow stared at him in her rearview mirror, torn between warning him away from the lunatic he was challenging and jumping out of the Jeep to scream for the old man's help. Yet as desperate as she was to save her sister as well as herself, she couldn't put anyone else in jeopardy in the process.

Instead, she sat there, shocked further when her vehicle stopped straining in reverse and slipped into neutral all on its own.

No, not on its own.

The man garbed in black had done it. Because he wasn't just a man . . . he was Breed.

The pickup truck's horn blared again, a long, ear-splitting peal. Its gray-bearded driver leaned halfway out the driver's side window. "Get outta the fucking way, you idiots!"

The big vampire took one hand away from the Jeep. As it moved, Willow nearly swore she saw sharp, black talons on the tips of his fingers. He reached up and tore off his helmet, uncovering his face and the long, gleaming white fangs behind the savage curl of his lips.

He unleashed the full force of his menacing expression on the geezer in the pickup.

The horn went silent. Then the old truck shot into reverse and peeled away in the opposite direction.

Willow wanted to do the same thing.

If she thought for a second she'd be able to get away, she would've tried.

The Breed male swiveled toward her now. "I'm not going to hurt you, Laurel."

Scorching golden-brown eyes stared at her from under a tousled mane of caramel-colored hair. His fangs glinted like diamonds behind the lush shape of his lips. His face was hard angles and a squared jaw line, which somehow all worked in harmony. She might have considered him handsome if he wasn't a blood-drinking monster.

One that was apparently determined to find her sister.

"My name is Razor."

Fitting, she thought, glancing once more to his hands. There were no talons at the ends of his fingers now, though. They were just big, strong hands—ones that sported a tangle of intriguing Breed *dermaglyphs* on the backs of them.

"What do you want?" Willow demanded, almost afraid to ask.

"Theo Collier sent me."

She lifted her gaze to his face. "Theo?"

She knew the name of Laurel's former boyfriend and colleague. He was a good man, from what Willow understood. According to her sister, Theo was one of the few people Laurel trusted. But anyone could be aware of their connection—especially someone like the lethal menace standing outside Willow's Jeep.

"Where is Theo now?"

"I don't know. That's not important."

"It is to me," she said, wrangling her courage. "How do you know him? Can you prove it?"

He frowned. "You ask too many questions."

Willow scoffed in spite of her fear. "Spoken like someone who doesn't have any believable answers."

"I'm telling you the truth." He scowled some more, growing visibly impatient. "There isn't time for this, Laurel."

It jarred her, hearing him call her by her twin's name. And what did he mean, there wasn't time? What the hell was going on here?

Another car tried to turn onto the mountain pass, but quickly retreated when Razor flashed his dark glare and long fangs at the driver. They were starting to draw attention from other passing vehicles now. Maybe that was a good thing. Maybe stalling the Breed male long enough to alert half the town to his presence was the best way to keep him off the mountain and away from Laurel's cabin.

"I need you to come with me now, Laurel. It's not safe for you here anymore."

His hand came to rest on Willow's forearm and her heart leapt into her throat. His touch seemed electric, the contact zinging through her bloodstream hot and unsettlingly intimate.

She yanked out of his reach. "Keep your hands off me. I'm not going anywhere with you."

Okay, so attempting to stall him was not such a good idea. Escape seemed her best option.

Willow tried frantically to put the Jeep into gear again, but the damn thing wouldn't budge out of neutral. Razor was still holding her there with his impossible strength and the power of his Breed mind.

She knew all too well that he could do much worse if he wanted to.

So . . . why wasn't he?

Was he waiting to take her to a second location before he killed her? Or was he a bounty hunter who'd come to do someone else's dirty work? Did Laurel have some kind of price on her head?

Either way, this vampire had to be lying about knowing Theo Collier. According to Laurel, Theo was a bookish, soft-spoken man from a tiny farm community in Quebec. He'd been a shy, serious student all through college where he and Laurel had met. After graduation, they both had gone straight to work for the same research institute in Montreal. How would an introverted human like Theo ever have come into contact with a dangerous looking Breed male like Razor?

Willow's confusion deepened, along with her suspicions.

"If what you're saying is true, then get Theo on the phone right now. Let me speak to him."

A growled curse slipped past those deadly fangs and far-too-supple lips. "You can talk to him after I get you somewhere safe. The longer we delay, the more danger you're in, Laurel. I can't let them see that you're unharmed."

Something about the way he said that made her blood freeze in her veins. The way his cryptic warning seemed to imply something awful had already happened made the fine hairs at her nape stand on end.

"What are you talking about? Who's *them*?"

"I don't know, but I mean to find out."

Was he really telling her the truth? As much as she wanted to doubt him, the raw sincerity in his bleak gaze took her breath away. She didn't like the feeling of dread that was swamping her now. The feeling that the earth was about to open up and swallow her.

"Do you really know Theo?"

A grave nod. "We met when we were boys."

Willow swallowed. "And he sent you here . . . why?"

"Because he fears for your life, and he knows I'm uniquely suited to this job. And because I made him a promise a long time ago."

"What kind of promise?"

"It doesn't matter right now. All that does matter is that I bring you somewhere safe."

"Safe from what?" Willow nearly whispered. "Safe from who?"

Razor stared at her, a tendon working in his brutal jaw. "From whoever burned down your cabin a few hours ago."

CHAPTER 3

If Razor had his doubts that the woman he'd been watching for the past few months could have somehow escaped the attack on her cabin, those doubts vanished as he stood outside her Jeep in the twilight.

He would know her face anywhere. Her wide green eyes, the soft cut of her cheeks and jaw, those pale freckles that splashed over the bridge of her slightly upturned nose. Her pouty lips that made everything male in him clench with desire every time he saw her on his surveillance feed.

Fuck.

It really was her. Every nuance of her face had been seared into his mind from his first glimpse of her. Now, here she was, sitting right in front of him like some kind of miracle. Healthy and unharmed, beautiful as ever.

And apparently totally unaware of just how narrowly she'd managed to elude death today.

She stared at him in a mix of confusion and disbelief after he'd blurted out the news of the attack on her home.

"What are you talking about?" Her brows knit, and a look of bone-deep dread began to fill her gaze. "The cabin is . . ." Her lips parted on a quiet inhalation. "No, you're lying."

He wanted to be gentle for her, but soft emotions weren't in his nature. Nor did he have time for that even if they were. "I was just there, Laurel. All that's left are cinders and rubble. And a body. Who was the woman left in the cabin while you've been out today?"

Her face drained of color. She swallowed hard but didn't answer him.

"Did you know her?" Razor pressed. "Is it possible that whoever attacked your home might've assumed she was you?"

"No, this can't be true." She sagged back against the driver's seat. A small, pained noise worked its way up her throat now. "Nothing you're saying can be true. It can't!"

She shook her head, but it seemed more like a reflexive tremor than conscious movement. Her shell-shocked gaze turned bleak, as if she herself were suddenly standing with one foot in the grave.

"Get out of my way," she murmured, her voice breaking. "Let me go. I have to see for myself."

"Bad idea," Razor grimly cautioned her. "There's nothing left for you there anymore."

She sucked in a jagged breath. "I need to go. I need to see her right now!"

Damn it. He was getting nowhere trying to explain the situation to her. He had more efficient ways to deal with this problem. Trance her. Commandeer her vehicle.

Then he could drop her somewhere safe, call Theo with the location and be done with the twenty-year promise he'd made.

Not to mention the unwanted attraction he felt toward her, even when she was staring at him like he was the one holding a can of gasoline and a match.

"I realize you're scared, but you have to trust me."

"No, I don't," she shot back. "I don't believe a word you're saying, vampire."

Great. She was only getting more agitated. There was a wild look in her eyes that said she was on the verge of panic and desperate to do anything to get away from him and drive up that mountain.

"Laurel, I'm only going to say this once. Move to the other seat now so I can get behind the wheel and get you out of here."

"Fuck you." She stomped on the accelerator, groaning as the engine revved but the wheels stayed locked in place. She beat her palms against the steering wheel in frustration. "Let me go, damn you! She can't be dead!" A sob tore out of her. "You have to let me see her. You have to let me try to save her!"

Try to save her? What was she talking about?

And now his brain snagged on something else she just said.

Holy hell.

He'd been wrong. The truth hadn't seemed so obvious until she said it. Now, the realization hit him like a hammer on glass.

"You're not Laurel Townsend. The dead woman I found in the cabin . . . that was her."

Those bleak green eyes looked up at him in misery. "She's my sister. Laurel is my twin sister."

Razor reeled back, running a hand over his face. "Ah, fuck."

And just because his luck couldn't possibly get any worse, at that same moment a local police cruiser with lights flashing moved into position directly behind the Jeep.

Razor bit off a curse under his breath. "Stay put," he growled to Laurel's twin. "I'll handle this."

The pair of cops inside the darkened vehicle peered out the windshield into the gathering darkness outside. The driver, the larger of the two, said something to his partner who then lit up a spotlight mounted to his side of the car. The beam nearly blinded Razor's inhuman retinas, but he was more concerned about anyone ID'ing the woman next to him.

"Don't look back at—"

Too late. She swiveled around in her seat and the hard white light illuminated every feature of her face to the officers. Both men seemed to be looking more closely at her than they were the threatening-looking male standing outside her vehicle.

This wasn't going to be good.

Razor focused his preternatural hearing on the two men inside the car.

". . . thought you took care of things," said the driver.

"I did take care of it, Hank."

"Yeah?" The big guy, Hank, scowled from behind the windshield. "Then how the hell do you explain her?"

His partner stared at her, dumbstruck for a second, before his gaze collided with Razor's smoldering glare. He let out a curse. "Holy shit. That motherfucker with her is Breed."

Razor had heard enough. These two cops were dirty,

and now they were about to be dead.

Right after they told him everything he needed to know about Laurel Townsend's murder.

"Don't go anywhere," he said, then stalked forward to confront the officers.

The big guy got on the squad car's bullhorn. "Stay right where you are, vampire. Put your hands up where we can see them. Now."

Razor ignored the command. He kept walking toward them, even as Hank climbed out from behind the wheel with his weapon drawn.

Hank's partner scrambled out of the passenger seat now, too.

Behind Razor, the Jeep's engine revved hard, followed by the scream of its tires on the pavement as it rocketed out of his mental hold. He had to release it. Not only so he could focus on the bigger issue at hand, but because he didn't want Laurel's twin caught in any crossfire.

Because one way or another, things were about to get messy.

His fangs came out as Hank's partner began firing on the Jeep. Razor leapt across the distance, too fast for either human to track him. He brought the cop down to the ground, twisting the man's skull in his hands. He left the corpse on the ground and swung to face the other cop.

Gunfire blasted, one round after another until Hank had emptied his service weapon. Razor had eluded most of the shots, but he looked down at his arm and noticed one round had clipped him in the bicep.

He sneered, baring his enormous fangs at the human. "Now, all you've done is piss me off even more."

Hank's face drained of all color. He scrabbled for a second gun on his other hip, but there wasn't any time for that. Razor was on him in less than a heartbeat, his fangs ripping into the man's fleshy throat.

Part of him wanted to make these deaths protracted and painful—small payback for what had been done to Laurel Townsend—but he'd already risked too much. Attacking them in the open, even under the slim cover of twilight, had been a reckless move. He wasn't worried about himself, but for what two dead local cops would mean for Laurel's sister.

He had to get to her.

Although she hadn't been the intended target of the fire on the mountain, he may have put her life in jeopardy now just through association with him. Any one of the people who saw them stopped together at the bottom of the pass could possibly ID them as persons of interest in the deaths of Hank and his partner.

Which meant Razor had to get the hell out of town fast—and he was taking Laurel's sister with him.

Stepping past the dead human, Razor summoned his Breed genetics and sped into the wooded terrain on foot. He could hear the Jeep's engine a few miles ahead of him on the pass as Laurel's sister continued her climb up toward the cabin.

The red glow of her taillights cut through the tree trunks as Razor veered up a jagged incline, hoping to head her off before she reached the site of the carnage.

She got there only a moment sooner than him. With barely enough time to put the vehicle into park, she jumped out from behind the wheel of the idling vehicle and started racing toward the cabin site.

Razor grabbed her from behind, locking his arms around her and physically holding her back from the carnage. She screamed. Started fighting like hell to break loose.

"It's okay," he growled beside her ear. "I'm not going to hurt you."

"How did you— The cops—"

"They were bad men," he said. "They're not going to hurt anyone else now."

"You killed them?" A panicked noise bubbled out of her. "Oh, my God." Her struggle intensified. "Let me go! I have to see my sister."

"No, you don't." He was never going to purge the sight of it from his memory, and he was only sparing her the same. "She's gone."

"Let me go!" The heel of her cowboy boot came down hard on his foot.

Razor cursed, but the pain hardly registered. "Listen, lady, I'm trying to help you."

"The same way you helped Laurel? Fuck off, vampire!"

She kept bucking against his hold, even though it was useless. Razor wasn't even using his full strength to restrain her. More than anything, he was just trying to be careful to not let her hurt herself. Shifting his grasp on her, he turned her around to face him, holding her by biceps.

She stared at him wild-eyed and shaking with grief. She was a fighter, but she was hurting. From the stark look in her gaze, she was cracking wide open inside.

Inexplicably, Razor wanted to pull her close and wrap his arms around her, if only to erase some of the pain that was etched into her soft features. But that wasn't why he was here.

"Your sister is dead. Those two cops down on the pass had a hand in it. Do you know why they'd want to kill Laurel?"

Mutely, she slowly shook her head. Her throat worked as she swallowed. "Please. I need to see her. I can help her. I have to try to save her!"

That was the second time she'd insisted she might be able to do something to save her sister. Was her shock so deep she wasn't grasping what she was hearing or seeing? She seemed clear-headed enough, so why was she refusing to accept the truth?

"No one can save your sister. I was going to try, but I got here only hours too late. Someone shot her in the head, then burned down the cabin with her inside. She's gone."

Tears welled in her stark gaze. "I want to see her."

"No, you don't. Believe me. After I found her burned body in the rubble, I buried her. I couldn't leave her where she was." He couldn't leave her because he'd thought the woman in the ashes had been the one staring back at him now. The beauty he'd been practically obsessed with like some kind of pathetic, long-distance stalker. "I dug a grave with my bare hands and I put her in it."

Laurel's sister reeled back in his grasp, but at least she wasn't fighting him anymore. Whether from exhaustion or grief, or some of both, she seemed to lean into his grasp as if he were the only thing keeping her standing. "Where is she?"

He gestured with his chin. "Over there, under the shade of the pines."

Her gaze moved past him to the mound of freshly

turned earth he'd left. Razor watched her take in the entire scene of destruction. He didn't have to look to know what she was seeing under the pale moonlight. The blackened remains of the cabin. The ghostly column of the scorched river rock chimney. The rubble and ashes that spoke of the violence that had been done to her sister in her final moments of life.

The prolonged, horrified silence of Laurel's sister was almost too much for Razor to take, but he didn't know what to say or do. He was piss-poor at sympathy and other soft emotions. Just part of the fallout from the way he'd been bred and trained as a Hunter.

All he knew, even now, was killing and cold justice.

He would get back to dealing in both soon enough. Right now, he had a bigger problem to deal with. He was scowling as those big green eyes of hers came back to meet his gaze in the darkness.

There was no fight left in her now. Only confusion and emptiness. Only pain.

"What's your name?" he asked.

She blinked once, then swallowed on a dry-sounding throat. "Willow. Willow Valcourt."

Razor gave a terse nod. "If you want to live, Willow Valcourt, you need to come with me."

CHAPTER 4

She didn't want to believe it.

Her twin sister—her best friend—couldn't be gone. Not like this. Even though thousands of miles had separated them until a few months ago, Laurel had been Willow's beacon all her life. She couldn't be gone for good now. Her heart refused to accept it.

Willow lifted her gaze to Razor's grim face and shook her head. "Why should I believe you? Prove it. Prove to me it was my sister you buried."

His frown deepened. "Are you saying you want me to dig her back up?"

God, no. She recoiled at the thought. She couldn't bear that. The idea of seeing Laurel the way Razor had briefly described her was too much for her to stomach. She didn't think she could handle the horror and pain of seeing what little remained of her sister.

The sober look Razor was giving her now seemed to

say that he didn't think she could handle it either.

"I have something of hers." He reached into the pocket of his black pants and took out a scorched gold chain and pendant. A delicate half-heart dangled from the end of the chain. It was warped from heat, but Willow recognized it instantly.

"She was wearing that when I found her," Razor said, holding the necklace out to her. "It looks like it could've been a gift from Theo. I was going to give it back to him when I see him."

"It's not his." Willow took the damaged pendant from him and carefully held it in her palm. "I gave this to Laurel when we were kids. I have the other half. We never took them off."

In fact, Willow currently wore hers under the flowy fabric of her peasant top.

Razor stared at her, his hawk-like eyes solemn beneath the heavy slashes of his brows. "Do you need any more proof?"

She gave him a faint shake of her head, even though she hadn't totally decided if she could trust him. Though her heart ached with grief, her mind swam with memories and conversations she'd had with Laurel during the past few months. Her sister's seeming paranoia had been justified. Whatever she'd been hiding from had caught up to her in the most horrific way.

And then there was the matter of Lauren's cryptic instructions to Willow. The promise she'd forced her to make in the event that the worst should happen.

Willow never thought this day would come. She'd prayed it wouldn't.

She didn't know what waited at the other end of that vow Laurel had made her swear to keep.

She wasn't even sure what waited at the bottom of the mountain now that Laurel had been murdered in cold blood and Willow was at the mercy of a huge Breed male who'd just admitted to killing a pair of local police officers.

Who was he, anyway? Obviously, he was a lethal menace, but he didn't seem completely psychotic. He almost seemed . . . reasonable. Protective. Trustworthy.

Ridiculous words to describe one of his murderous kind.

Still, he had only tried to help her so far.

Maybe she was the one losing her grip on reality, because there was a part of her that felt thankful Razor was there with her now. Relieved that she wasn't alone to process what was happening. She was grateful that he had been there to look after Laurel's body before she would have been forced to see the horror of her sister's suffering up close and personal.

"We have to get out of here," Razor said, his deep voice cutting through the tangle of her emotions. "I'll drive."

It didn't sound like a request, but Willow wasn't sure what other choice she had at the moment. She followed him back to her Jeep, moving as though in a dark dream. He swung in behind the wheel while she numbly climbed into the passenger seat, moving her purse to the floor.

When she sat there, staring blindly into the darkness at the pile of ash and rubble, Razor pivoted to reach around her. He grabbed the seatbelt above her shoulder and fastened it for her.

"There's blood on your arm," she murmured, roused from her shock-induced stupor by the sight of his injury. She sat up a little straighter. "You're hurt? Is that a bullet wound?"

He grunted. "I'm fine."

Without another word, he put the Jeep into gear and put them back onto the rough trail back down the mountain. The headlights bounced wildly against the bumpy dirt road and the surrounding trees. He flicked the beams off with a low growl and plunged faster into the night.

Willow threw him a startled look. "What are you doing? I can't see a thing."

"I can." His unearthly eyes met hers, sending an arrow of strange heat into her veins. "I know a shortcut. Hold on to something."

She barely had time to brace her hands against the dashboard before he veered off the so-called road and down a steep decline. The Jeep sped through the trees, and how Razor managed to avoid colliding with any of them was nothing short of a miracle.

He navigated the dark, rugged terrain as if he'd lived there all his life, totally in command of the vehicle and the uncharted path beneath them. A few minutes later, they emerged onto the mountain pass several hundred yards from the commotion gathering at the entrance.

Police lights on two parked cruisers flashed blue and red where the fallen officers lay. More emergency vehicles were arriving by the second. Cops and other first responders were positioned all over the road, blocking the only way off the mountain pass if he intended to head back into town.

"Fuck," Razor snarled. "Guess we're taking the long way."

He turned opposite of the ruckus and drove the darkened Jeep onto the pass. Willow braved a glance behind them. They had stirred no notice, the frantic law enforcement teams too busy sealing off the road at the other end to pay them any mind.

The pass began to curve around the soaring wall of the mountain, and then the strobing lights of the crime scene were extinguished completely.

Willow sat forward again and looked at Razor. "What about your bike?"

He kept his eyes on the road, still navigating in total darkness. "It's no good to me now. They won't be able to do anything with it, either. It's untraceable. Unlike this Jeep. We'll have to ditch it."

"Ditch it?" Willow gaped at him. "It's the only car I have."

"Are the plates registered to you or someone else?"

"Me."

"Then it has to go. The sooner the better." He drove faster, pushing the vehicle to its limits on the steep upward climbs of the pass. "Where do you live, Willow?"

She gestured vaguely behind them. "About twenty miles back the way we came, in the next town over."

"So, you weren't living here in town?"

"No. Laurel didn't think it was safe for us to live that close to each other. She didn't want anyone recognizing me when I came and went from the cabin."

"Did anyone in town know her?"

"No, she made sure of that. She never left the cabin, not for any reason. When she needed groceries and supplies, I brought them to her."

Razor made a noise in the back of his throat, but didn't comment. "What about you? Is there someone at home waiting for you to come back?"

Willow shook her head. There hadn't been anyone in

a long time, not even a pet. Laurel was all she had. Now, she was gone too.

"What about a boyfriend?" Razor pressed. "An employer or coworker? Anyone to worry if they can't reach you? Someone who might reach out to law enforcement or be able to tell them anything about you or your sister?"

"No. I make pottery, so I work for myself. As for the rest of it, also no. There's no one waiting for me at home."

"Good," he said. "You can't go back there now. It won't be safe."

"For how long?"

Finally, he glanced at her. She almost wished he hadn't, because the look in his grim stare seemed to say that she wasn't going to like his answer. "Not until it's safe."

She frowned. "I can't just leave my home because you say so."

"You prefer the alternative? How many witnesses do you think there were who saw us talking on the pass? How long do you think it'll take the police before they show up on your doorstep? A couple of hours? A day? For fuck's sake, they could be there waiting for you right now."

"How is that my problem? You're the one who killed two cops back there, not me."

He looked at her again, his dark stare locked on her now. Tiny sparks seemed to smolder in his irises. "I told you, they were dirty. I heard them talking about setting the fire. They killed your sister, Willow. I don't know why, but I mean to find out. Those two cops would have killed you too, if I'd given them the chance."

The starkness of that realization hit her hard, bringing a surge of emotion into her throat, but she pushed it aside. Later, she'd have time to dissolve into a puddle of grief and terror over everything that happened today. First, she needed to make this Breed male understand that she couldn't go anywhere with him. She wouldn't.

Not when she had her promise to Laurel ringing in her ears like an alarm bell.

"So, we'll go to the station and explain what happened down on the pass. We can bring the police to the cabin, show them my sister's grave. They'll surely have to help us get answers, but not if we run."

"I don't know how far the conspiracy goes, Willow. For all I know, there were more people involved in your sister's murder. I'm willing to bet there's something bigger going on here, but I'm not going to risk your life in order to find out. Those two thought you were Laurel. Someone else might think so too. Which means you've got a target on your back now. Until I know for sure who's aiming it, I trust no one. And I'm not letting you out of my sight."

Willow sagged back against the seat. As much as she wanted to refuse to accept everything that was happening—including everything Razor was saying—deep down, she feared he was right. All of Laurel's paranoias and strange behaviors since her arrival several months ago replayed in her mind like a movie she'd only been able to watch in a foreign language until now, when Laurel's vicious murder had suddenly made things clear.

Not everything, though.

Willow had more questions than answers. Apparently, so did Razor.

Like it or not, trust him or not, they were in this together.

She glanced at the charred pendant in her hand, wishing she'd pushed Laurel to explain the full story about why she'd gone into hiding in Colorado. What was she so afraid of? What had been so awful that her sister refused to speak about it? What did any of it have to do with the small key Willow wore on her own necklace?

"Keep this close," Laurel had insisted only days after she'd arrived, her eyes wild with urgency. "Keep it with you always. Promise me."

"Sure," Willow had agreed, despite her confusion. "What's it for?"

"You'll need it if something ever happens to me. But not unless and until then, do you understand? It's important, Wills."

"You're scaring me, Laurel. What kind of lock does this key open?"

"I've rented a storage unit in Breckenridge. It's on a two-year lease. Hopefully, I won't need it, but in case I do..."

"What are you talking about? What's in the storage unit?"

Laurel wouldn't say. The unit had been paid for in cash under a fake name to avoid it being linked to either one of them. Laurel had given her the address and number with strict instructions that Willow not go there unless the worst should happen.

"If the time ever comes, you'll know what to do once you get there," Laurel had insisted. "Just promise me."

"I promise," Willow had vowed. "Anything for you. You know that."

That conversation—and the pledge attached to it—made the key feel like a lump of lead between her breasts now.

Willow touched it absently, uncertain what to do about her promise when Laurel's death had sent her entire life into a tailspin. She never wanted to imagine the day would come that she'd be faced with fulfilling that cryptic obligation, let alone that she might have to do it while being shadowed by a massive Breed male claiming Willow needed his protection.

"How are you doing over there?" Razor's deep voice jolted her back to the here and now. "You haven't spoken for a couple of miles. You hanging in all right?"

She nodded, letting her hand fall back to her lap. "Yeah. I guess so. As much as I can be."

"We've got a lot of road to cover before we get to the other side of this mountain. Plenty of time for you to tell me anything your sister might've said about who or what she was hiding from."

Willow shook her head. "I can't."

"Can't or won't?" he asked, his tone clipped. "You know more than you're telling me. I doubt you'll want me to use my own methods to loosen your tongue."

She gaped at him. "Like what? Tearing open my throat with your claws? Or would you rather do it with your fangs?"

He swore under his breath. "You have such a low opinion of me already?"

"I've seen what your kind can do." She mentally tried to shut down the images that threatened to flood her mind. Old memories from the time when she was a young child, before she and Laurel were orphaned by Rogues that had been unleashed on the public en masse some twenty-two years ago.

Razor was staring at her as if she were the only maniac in the vehicle. "I meant that I could trance you and get you to talk about your sister," he said. "I'd rather you tell me on your own."

"Like I said, I can't. I don't know anything. Laurel didn't want me to know."

"Why not? What was she hiding from up on that mountain? Who was she hiding from?"

Willow shrugged. "I wish I knew. She contacted me out of the blue about six months ago to say she was moving to the area. She asked me not to tell anyone, which was easy since there was no one to tell. After she arrived, she sent me her location in a coded message."

"Code? What kind of code?"

"The kind only she and I understood. It was a twin thing, something we started when we were kids. It doesn't matter now. The point is, she wanted to keep her arrival in Colorado and her location a secret. I knew she was scared, but she wouldn't explain. She said it was for my own protection. I thought she was being paranoid, but now..."

Razor grunted. "Was she ever involved in any kind of criminal activity?"

"Laurel?" A small laugh escaped Willow's lips despite the weight of her emotions. "Never. Not my sister. She was the good twin."

He acknowledged with a wry glance in her direction. "Could she have crossed the wrong person somehow? Done something to someone to turn them into an enemy?"

"No," Willow replied. "Everyone she meets adores her. *Adored*, I mean."

"What did Laurel do for work?"

"Last I knew she was working in the scientific research community, same as Theo. That's what she went to university for—chemistry and science. Laurel loved solving problems and doing things to make the world a better place." Willow sighed. "My sister had a brilliant mind. That's why it shocked me when she said she'd quit her job to move way out here in the middle of nowhere."

A dark look not unlike suspicion crossed Razor's features. "What about Theo? Do you think it's possible she was running away from him?"

"No way," Willow said. "He was the love of her life. I can't imagine how scared she had to be that she'd run and leave him behind." She glanced at Razor in the dim light of the dashboard. "This can't come as news to you, if you and Theo are such good friends that he sent you here to find her. What did he tell you about my sister?"

"We don't talk often. All I know is he wanted me to keep her safe for him."

"He trusts you that much?"

"He does, for all that's worth now." Razor swiveled his head and met her gaze. "I want you to know that you can trust me too, Willow."

She stared at him for a long moment, caught in the intensity of his eyes. "I guess I don't have any other choice, do I?"

"Not if you want to live."

Willow broke his unsettling stare, lowering her eyes to the charred pendant in her hand. "Razor... There is something I need to tell you. Something Laurel said to me." She braved a brief look at him. "There was something she wanted me to do for her."

His keen eyes seared her from across the small quarters of the Jeep. "Go on."

Reaching into her blouse, Willow took out the necklace that matched Laurel's. She held it up for Razor to see and his stare locked onto the small silver key dangling next to the half-heart.

"Laurel made me swear that if anything ever happened to her—if she...didn't make it—that I would use this key to open a storage unit she rented when she first arrived in Colorado."

He cursed under his breath. "What's in the storage unit?"

"I don't know. But I made her a promise and now I need to keep it. I need to unlock the unit and see what she left for me inside."

"Where is it?"

She gave him the location in Breckenridge, which had to be close to six hours away from where they were on the mountain pass.

Razor nodded grimly, then he hit the accelerator and the Jeep sped faster into the night.

CHAPTER 5

They made good time on the pass. Some five hours later, Razor pulled into the storage rental place in Breckenridge.

The small mom-and-pop business on the outskirts of the city didn't look like much at 2AM, but he counted that as a positive. No security gate to deal with as he drove the Jeep onto the quiet lot. No cameras trained on the entrance or on the twenty-odd, one-story rows of concrete-block outdoor storage units either. Weak yellow light shone down from ancient-looking lamps mounted on either ends of the buildings, barely illuminating the rusted steel numbers that hung above the units' garage-style doors.

Not exactly a booming business, and that had probably been the point when Laurel had selected it. This looked like the kind of place to stow something and forget about it for a decade or three. Or hide it where no one would ever think to look.

"Laurel's unit should be somewhere near the middle section," Willow said quietly, as she peered out the windshield.

She'd been silent most of the long drive, hunkered down in the open-air passenger seat in an almost catatonic state. Shock, Razor had reasoned. To say nothing of the grief that had to be pulling her under. She was cold, too. Willow had retrieved an old wool blanket from the back of the Jeep and nestled under it during the drive, but even now she shivered with it draped around her.

This errand in Breckenridge was a delay he'd rather not have risked for many reasons, but he had to admit he was curious to know why Laurel would send Willow here. What had been so important that she'd make Willow swear to it?

Whatever it was, as soon as they had the answer, he needed to put as many miles as possible between Willow and her sister's killers. Every minute they spent in Willow's Jeep was an opportunity for more murderous bastards to close in on them.

She sat up a little straighter now. "That must be the unit over there," she said, pointing at one of the squatty buildings. "Based on the numbers, her unit should be the third one down from the end."

Razor nodded and drove toward the one she indicated. Most of the padlocks on the weather-beaten unit doors looked like relics from a generation ago. The lock on Laurel's unit was the exception. It gleamed under the thin moonlight as the Jeep rolled up with the headlights doused.

Willow slid out of the passenger seat as soon as

Razor put the vehicle in park. He came up behind her as she struggled to move the thick tangle of her hair away from her nape to unfasten her necklace.

"Let me." His hands closed around hers loosely.

He wasn't prepared for the arrow of heat and awareness that shot through him as soon as his fingers made contact with hers. His breath stilled in his lungs, while every other part of him lit up with an electric jolt of desire.

Maybe she sensed the sudden, predatory quickness in his veins too. If not, the low, hungered vibration in the back of his throat was definitely too hard for her to miss. Not to mention the other involuntary reaction his body was having just from being this close to her.

She slipped her hands out from under his without a word as he worked to unfasten the impossibly delicate clasp of her necklace. It took all his focus and a little Breed-influenced mind over matter to get the damned thing open when his fingers felt as useless as sausages.

"Got it," he muttered tightly.

"Thanks." She didn't seem the least bit affected by his touch. She reached up and took the loose necklace from him, then crisply walked the couple of steps away from him to the storage unit door.

"You should let me do that. We don't know what's in there."

She swung a dismissive look over her shoulder at him. "Whatever Laurel left for me in here isn't going to hurt me."

Razor grunted, and gave her a reluctant nod. He stepped beside her as she put her key into the lock and gave it a twist. The metal clicked open.

Willow took off the lock, then Razor reached down

and grabbed the door's handle. He hoisted it up, lifting the door on its rollers. The metallic screech of the pulleys echoed into the quiet all around them.

He stared into the unit and frowned. "What the hell?"

It was empty except for one thing.

Lying in the middle of the dusty concrete floor was an old paperback book.

Its spine was warped, its cover was curled and worn, like most of its dog-eared pages, which fanned up like an accordion. There was a color photograph of some type of yellow bird on the cover. The kind of image found on a field guide or encyclopedia.

At first glance, Razor wondered if someone had gotten to the unit ahead of them and cleaned it out. But then Willow let out a small, strangled gasp and raced inside to pick up the book.

"I know this book," she said, turning to hold it out for him to see. "It's the *Field Guide to North American Birds*. Laurel and I used to have a book like this when we were at the—" Her words halted abruptly, and only for an instant, before she went on. "When we were little, she and I spent hours poring over all the birds in a book just like this."

She fanned through some of the pages, then tilted her head, her brows pinched. "No . . . not a book *like* this one. This *is* our book. The pages have some of our scribbles and annotations on them from all those years ago. She kept it with her all this time?" She looked up at Razor with a mix of wonder and confusion. "Laurel said I would know what to do once I got here and opened the storage unit. Why would she leave this for me now? What am I supposed to do?"

Razor ran his hand through his hair and shook his head. "I don't know. All I do know is that we need to get moving."

"To where?"

"As far from here as we can, for starters."

She clutched the book close, as if it was an extension of her sister that she needed to hold tight. With one last look at the now-empty storage unit, she stepped toward Razor and followed him back out to her Jeep.

"You need to get some rest," he told her, watching as she climbed back into the passenger seat beside him.

"I'm fine," she said, still holding her book like a life line.

Her movements were sluggish and fatigued as she settled in and fastened her seat belt. Her face was pale, her normally bright eyes dull and heavy-lidded. Exhaustion and the weight of the day's events would only continue pressing down on her.

It would only be a few more hours before sunrise. If she didn't get some decent sleep somewhere, she would be dead on her feet before long. He needed her mentally sharp and running on all cylinders—at least until he could decide where to take her that she'd be safe long-term without him.

As a Hunter he had been born and raised to kill, to destroy. He was damned good at those things. Some might say he was the best. One of the coldest, to be sure.

What he had never done before was bodyguard someone, least of all a beautiful woman who was already starting to wreak havoc on his senses.

His only saving grace was the fact that she seemed to dislike his kind as a whole. Her reaction on the road with him a few hours ago replayed in his mind. Christ, had she really thought he might tear out her throat with his talons—or his fangs—if he wanted to extract the truth from her?

He had to admit, it wouldn't have been the first time he'd resorted to such brutal methods, but never on an innocent. Never on her, not for any reason. He was a born-and-bred killer, but he wasn't a complete monster.

Not that she needed to know that. The farther he could keep her from him while still under his protection, the better. For both of them.

He glanced at her again, a mistake that only had him itching to touch her, to smooth some of her windblown hair away from her pale cheek. He could still feel the heat of her small hands caught beneath his larger ones. He could still smell the sweet fragrance of her tousled hair. She was delicate but not frail. Soft but not weak. Vulnerable but not helpless.

Willow Valcourt was everything he'd imagined her to be when he'd watched her through his drone camera's eye during all those months of long-distance torment. She was more than he'd imagined, in fact. But she wasn't his.

She wasn't his to crave back when he'd thought she belonged to another man, and she wasn't his now.

She was still part of his promise to Theo Collier. Where Razor had failed to keep Laurel Townsend safe, he would not fail when it came to Willow.

"I'm going to drive until just before sunrise," he said. "Then we're going to stop somewhere for you to sleep for a few hours. I also need to get a hold of Theo, let him know what's happened."

Willow slid a weary glance at him. "What about your arm? That gunshot wound in your bicep doesn't look like it's healing."

Scowling, he shrugged his good shoulder. She had a point, although he wasn't going to admit it to her. Besides, the wound was nothing that a decent feeding couldn't cure.

He was Gen One, which meant he typically had to feed every few days. When he was healing from an injury, he needed blood more frequently than that, but it wasn't anything he couldn't handle. There would be plenty of opportunity to hunt for a blood Host once they stopped somewhere.

He put the Jeep into gear without answering her concern. He didn't want Willow giving his wellbeing a second thought when saving her own neck was the only thing that mattered.

The less she thought of him as a flesh-and-blood man—Breed or otherwise—the more smoothly these next several hours would go.

As for the time they would be forced to spend in close proximity once they stopped again to wait out the daylight, he would just have to deal with that torture once he got there.

CHAPTER 6

Willow awoke to a soothing, dark quiet. No bracing chill of night air nipping at her. No endless, vibrating rumble of a vehicle's engine echoing in her ears and all the way down to her bones.

No acrid tang of ash and soot clinging to the back of her throat.

Only stillness now.

Only blessed silence.

Had she dreamt the whole thing?

If so, she'd never had such a vivid, horrifying nightmare in her life—not even in the aftermath of what had happened to her parents on that terrible night in her past, when she and Laurel were little more than babies.

God, Laurel.

Was she really gone now, too?

Willow was reluctant to open her eyes and confirm her fears. Not that lifting her lids would be easy. Her eyes felt glued shut, crusted with salt from the steady flow of tears that had racked her even in her sleep.

She didn't remember getting from the Jeep into bed, but she did recall waking up weeping several times over the past several hours, only to cry herself back into exhaustion.

Now, even though her body was rested she felt utterly drained.

With no small effort, she forced her eyes to slowly open. The room was dark, a little dank. She was lying alone on the saggy bed of a small motel room, fully clothed under the thin covers except for her cowboy boots.

The heavy curtains were pulled closed, but a sliver of daylight through the crack between them was enough for her to take a quick inventory of her surroundings. There wasn't much to see. A nicked-up chest of drawers served as a TV stand against the wall opposite the bed. An open metal hanger rack mounted to the dingy wall served as a closet.

And in the shadowed corner an upholstered chair was currently occupied by the hulking Breed male who'd also figured prominently in her disturbed dreams of the past several hours.

He spoke, his deep voice low and rough. "Good. You're awake."

Razor wasn't the friendliest individual in general, but he sounded particularly impatient now. His tawny hair was still damp from a recent shower, and he now sat there in the shadowy corner wearing only his jeans, studying her.

It was hard not to stare back at him. Breed *dermaglyphs* tracked all over his powerful chest and body, complicated tangles and swirling patterns only a shade or two darker than his warm skin color. She'd never seen Breed *glyphs* in person before, and the fact that they covered nearly every inch of Razor's muscular chest, torso, and arms only made them more arresting.

Willow cleared her throat and sat up. "Where are we?" Her voice came out rusty, still raw from her last round of tears. Did he know she'd been crying in her sleep? Or, even worse, had he been sitting there coldly watching the whole time?

She didn't need to ask. His aggravated-looking scowl was answer enough.

"I stopped driving around daybreak," he said. "We got as far as Cheyenne."

"Wyoming?"

He gave an affirmative shrug. "Since you don't have anywhere to go, I figure the safest place for you is anywhere that's not Colorado, at least for the time being."

"How long have I been sleeping?"

"It's going on one, so about six hours. Off and on," he added, leaving no doubt that he'd been watching over her nearly all of that time.

Willow exhaled a sigh and ran a hand through her hair, which felt windblown and matted from her restless sleep. It still smelled like woodsmoke from the fire on the mountain, a horrid reminder of the reason she was in this motel room in the first place.

A painful lump began to build in the center of her chest, bringing fresh tears to the backs of her eyes.

Razor's scowl deepened. "You should eat something."

He indicated an assortment of vending machine

snacks that lay on the nightstand next to the bed. Small bags of chips, packs of crackers and candy bars were heaped in a neat pile next to a bottle of water.

She should be starving, but all she felt was hollow and scared.

"Have you been able to get in touch with Theo?"

Razor grunted and shook his head. "Not yet. The private number he gave me goes straight to voicemail. I don't like it. Something's not right."

Willow's stomach clenched. "Do you think there are bad men looking for him too?"

"I don't know. I can't rule it out."

Willow's heart began to hammer with worry. "We need to warn him, Razor. Do you have any other way to reach him?"

"You let me deal with Theo. As soon as I find someplace safe to leave you, I'm heading to Montreal to find him."

He gestured dismissively in the direction of the snacks he brought her. "Eat, build up some strength. Take a shower if you want. We're only staying here to wait out the worst of the daylight. As soon as the sun sets we leave."

Apparently, he was operating in one of two modes today: barking orders at her, or ignoring her. She supposed she should be grateful for that. One of them needed to be thinking clearly and logically, and it didn't seem to be her. She forced herself to resist looking at him while he was sitting there half-undressed and brooding. Whatever current of unwanted awareness had arced between them back at the storage unit a few hours ago had certainly passed now.

At least it had for him, obviously.

Willow was still fighting to make sense of how she could be feeling anything but shock and bereavement. Inside, her heart was cracked wide open from the loss of her sister. But not even that had been enough to overshadow the unexpected heat she'd felt when Razor's hands had covered hers when he'd helped her remove the storage unit key from her necklace.

She could still feel that uninvited heat now, just thinking about it.

What was wrong with her?

He was Breed, for fuck's sake.

After what had happened to her parents, she'd spent most of her life avoiding his kind. Not that it was hard to do, first at the orphanage in Quebec City, then, later, living in the rural Colorado mountain town that had been her home since she'd stumbled into it after years of living and wandering on her own.

Until yesterday, it was unimaginable to her that she'd be in the same room with one of Razor's kind, let alone reliant on him for her survival. He'd already saved her life once since they met. He even had the bullet wound to show for it.

He got up from the chair and started to pace the tiny room. His movements were fluid and full of power, like a big cat agitated to be trapped inside a cage. If he was the cat, she didn't want to think about what that made her.

Willow watched him surreptitiously as she nibbled at a dry cracker then unscrewed the cap on the water bottle and took a sip. *Glyphs* covered his back just as densely as they did his front. If what she'd heard was true, the more *dermaglyphs* on a Breed, the purer their bloodline. Which meant Razor was almost certainly Gen One. The strongest, deadliest of their kind.

He swung back to begin another track on the threadbare carpet and his eyes clashed with hers. She couldn't look away fast enough to pretend she wasn't staring. Instead, she blurted out the only thing that came to her mind.

"Your arm looks better. The bullet wound is almost healed now."

He glanced at his bicep and shrugged. "All I needed was a few red cells." When he met her gaze again, a flicker of dark amusement crossed his harsh face. "Relax. It wasn't your carotid I tapped. I fed from the desk clerk when we got here."

Willow stared at him. "You make it sound like you went out for a burger."

He gave her a nonchalant tilt of his head. "Everyone's got to eat. Including you. I suggest you get to it."

He went back to pacing and Willow went back to picking at the crackers and chips. Everything tasted like sawdust in her mouth. She knew she needed to put something in her stomach before she fainted from hunger and thirst, but all she could think about was Laurel and the fact that her twin was lost forever.

Grief had her in a stranglehold, but she refused to give in to it while Razor was in the room with her. God knew, he'd likely seen and heard enough already. She hated looking weak to anyone, and always had from the time she was a little girl. That went double when it came to him. Right now, she needed to be strong. For herself, and for Laurel. Her sister was counting on her, even now that she was gone.

Willow thought about the book Laurel had left for

her to find.

Why had it been so important to her sister? What was Laurel trying to tell her?

Willow noticed the book lying on the edge of the chest of drawers across the room. She got up and brought it back to the bed, flipping through the pages while she chewed another dry cracker. Seeing the childish handwriting on the margins next to the birds she and Laurel once studied to pass the time was almost like traveling back in time.

All the little notes, the smiley faces and tally marks she and her sister had recorded whenever they'd spied their favorite birds on the orphanage grounds made Willow long for her twin even more. She could almost hear the echo of Laurel's little girl voice in her ear, excited and happy after what had been such a tragic beginning to their lives.

Was this all that Laurel meant for the book to be? Some small comfort to Willow after her twin was gone?

There had to be more.

How she wished she could ask her. How she wished she would have demanded Laurel tell her everything that had been troubling her and had her so afraid when she'd first arrived in Colorado.

Now, all Willow could do was turn the pages of the worn old book in regret.

And pain. Emotion gathered in her breast, making her vision swim and her breath shallow in her lungs. Against all her effort to contain it, a tear splashed down onto the page. Willow wiped it away, frowning to see one of Laurel's scribbled notations blur under the wetness.

The ink on that one wasn't as aged as most of the

other margin notes and annotations. No, it was relatively fresh by comparison, and written with a different pen. The black smudge on the page drew Willow's eye to the Latin bird name that had been underlined.

Toxostoma rufum. A common Brown Thrasher.

Willow flipped through more pages, curious to see if Laurel had made any other recent annotations. She found another similarly underlined entry on a different page.

Nucifraga columbiana. Clark's Nutcracker.

Like the first, there were no margin notes, nothing to indicate why Laurel might have been recently interested in the entry. There wasn't anything remarkable about either bird, so why had Laurel noted them?

Willow began to flip the pages more urgently, unsure what she was looking for or why. Admittedly, she was desperate for any connection to her twin, no matter how thin or random. And these two underlined bird names certainly seemed random at best.

So did the third notation she found.

Spinus tristis. American Goldfinch.

Willow couldn't think of any reason for her sister to have an interest in those particular birds, never mind why Laurel would go to such lengths to leave the book with Willow. Or was she grasping at straws here? Maybe the book had continued to be a hobby to Laurel and it truly was just intended to be a memento for Willow after Laurel was gone.

As confused as she was, she couldn't convince herself that her twin wasn't trying to tell her something important.

Keep this close, Laurel had said of the key to the storage unit. *You'll know what to do once you get there.*

No, I don't know, Willow thought, miserable with her inability to understand her sister's message and the gnawing sense of loss that pulled her into its grasp all over again. *I have no idea what you need me to do, Laurel.*

Unless . . .

Willow searched the pages for more entries, a hunch niggling at the back of her mind. She found another. Then another. Was Laurel trying to communicate some kind of message through these more recent annotations?

"Find anything useful?" Razor's low growl drew Willow's head up with a start.

"No." Swiping hastily at the wetness that lingered on her cheeks, she closed the book and glanced his way. "Just a bunch of scribbles that don't seem to make any sense to me yet."

He was already scowling, but he let out a hissed curse when he saw her tear-streaked face. His golden eyes seared her from beneath the slashes of his brows. It took him a moment before he spoke. "You going to be all right?"

"Yeah." She sniffled, setting the book aside and trying to pretend she had a strength she didn't quite feel. "I'm fine."

"You didn't eat much."

She shook her head noncommittally. "I'm not very hungry, I guess."

That much was true. The sorrow clogging her throat made eating virtually impossible, even if she could have mustered any kind of appetite. Right now, all she wanted was to spend more time with Laurel's book, but not as long as Razor was watching her like a hawk.

It wasn't that she wanted to deceive him so much as she was loyal first and foremost to her sister. If there was a message hidden inside the book, Willow wanted to understand it before she entrusted it with anyone else.

She made another attempt to dash away the wetness on her cheeks. "Is there soap and shampoo in the bathroom?"

He gave her a grim nod, still piercing her with those unsettling, penetrating golden eyes. He looked as though he wanted to say something more, but he only watched her in silence as she got up from the bed and padded barefoot into the bathroom.

CHAPTER 7

Razor stared after her, but he didn't let go of the growl building in his chest until the door had closed behind her and the lock engaged with a soft click from the other side.

Fuck.

What had he gotten himself into?

The tears she tried to hide from him just now nearly killed him. He stood and started pacing again, not that it helped. He was edgy from the hours of idle time cooped up in the small motel room—most of it spent in torment listening to Willow grieve for her sister in between brief rounds of restless sleep on the bed. He'd never felt more useless, hearing her weep into her pillow and knowing he was to blame for not reaching her sister in time to save her.

If he'd been born with an ability for healing like some of the Breed, he would have done whatever he could to take away Willow's pain. If he'd thought for a minute that he could offer her any kind of comfort, he might have tried. But she'd been alternating between suspicion and fear from the moment she first saw him.

Whether it was her general distrust of the Breed in general or him specifically, Razor wasn't sure. Either way, they'd both be better off if he kept his distance.

He wanted to think that keeping his distance would also prevent him from caring more than he should about her wellbeing, about her future. But she was already under his skin. She just had no idea how deeply or for how long.

It felt like a lie that he hadn't told her about his months-long surveillance of the cabin yet. Granted, he'd been tasked with watching Laurel as a favor to Theo, but it had been Willow who'd captivated him from the instant he saw her. He knew that now.

It had been Willow, not Laurel, who'd become Razor's private obsession. Willow, with her luminous brown hair, her angel's smile, and sinfully lush curves that had instantly erased all other women from his memory and his interest.

It had been Willow's face he pictured when he woke up hard and seething with lust after dreaming she was in his arms, or beneath him in the soft, moonlit grass of the mountainside.

It had been Willow, not her twin sister, who had made him almost lethally envious of Theo to think his old friend had the privilege of calling her his.

Now, here he was with no more than a couple-hundred square feet and one flimsy bathroom door to separate them and he couldn't wait for the first opportunity to get away from her.

For good, if he had anything to say about it.

He wasn't cut out for bodyguarding when he'd been born and raised a killer. He was especially unsuited for the job when the body he was supposed to be guarding was as tempting as Willow's.

Damn, how long had it been since he'd gotten laid?

He knew the answer, and it correlated closely with the amount of time he'd been watching the cabin on the mountainside.

The sound of the shower running on the other side of the bathroom door only added to his aggravation. An image of Willow standing naked and wet under the steamy spray leapt to vivid life in his mind's eye. His blood pounded in response, sending licks of fire through his veins and straight to his cock. His gums ached with the throbbing of his fangs.

Razor groaned. It was going to be a long fucking wait until they were back on the road.

Scrubbing his palm over his tense jaw, he glanced at the book she'd left laying on the bed.

He'd flipped through it once while she'd slept, but hadn't seen anything of value in the text or the childish notations scribbled here and there in the margins. He'd watched Willow page through the book a moment ago, and something in the way she'd hesitated on several of the pages—the way she had seemed to study them—had piqued his interest.

He found the page where her tears had splashed down and smudged some of the ink. Recent ink, given the way it had run under the wetness. Razor smoothed his fingertip over the underlined entry that was still damp and rippled from Willow's tears.

He found more bird names that had been underlined

more recently than any of the other notations in the book too. Seven of them in total. Seven random scientific bird names, each underlined with the same pen, by the same hand. Laurel Townsend's hand.

Razor glanced up from the book, suspicion gnawing at him.

Willow may not have all the answers about the book's possible significance to her sister, but she knew more than she was telling him.

The sound of an approaching vehicle in the parking lot outside pricked his attention. His combat instincts snapped to full alert even before he had crossed the small room and peered out from between the drawn curtains.

The motel had been quiet since they'd arrived early that morning, nothing but a handful of vehicles parked in the spaces outside the one-story building. Which made it all the more unusual to see the unmarked police sedan roll into the sunlit parking lot and head for the motel's front office. Colorado plates. The pair of officers seated inside scanned the smattering of vehicles parked in the spaces on the lot.

"Fuck." Razor cast a glance over his shoulder, still hearing the shower running in the bathroom.

He'd been careful on the drive out of Colorado, and knew they hadn't been tailed. As an added precaution, he'd parked Willow's Jeep around the back of the building rather than in the space right outside the room. Yet as much as he wanted to dismiss the cops' arrival as nothing more than coincidence, he was certain to his marrow it was anything but chance that law enforcement had caught up to them.

Damn it.

His call to Theo after they'd arrived. It was the only feasible way they could have been traced to this location so quickly.

How long would it take for the dirty cop to follow his lead right to their motel room door?

Not nearly long enough.

Razor had to get Willow out of there—and fast.

He crossed the room in a flash and paused only long enough to knock once in warning before opening the bathroom door. Willow sucked in a gasp behind the shower's glass door.

"Hey!" She slid the door open a crack and peered around it, her bright green eyes wide. "What the hell are you—"

"No time," he snarled. "Cops are here."

Behind the steamed glass, her arms came up to shield her from his view, but not quick enough to keep him from drinking in every wet, naked inch of her. Not even the semi-obscured glass could hide her body from his keen Breed gaze.

Her luscious curves and creamy skin lit fire to all his senses—but it was the tiny crimson mark riding a couple inches above her navel that brought his brain to a screeching halt.

"You're a Breedmate." It came out like an accusation. The curse he let fly was ripe and harsh. "You didn't tell me."

"You didn't ask." Still shielding herself, she gave him an equally offended look. "Does it matter?"

All he could do was bite off another dark curse in reply. He didn't have time to process this unwanted new wrinkle, let alone decide how to deal with it.

"Get dressed," he muttered, grabbing a towel off the

rack and tossing it at her. "We've got to go. Now."

She caught the towel in one hand and quickly wrapped herself in it before sliding the glass open all the way and stepping out of the shower.

"Are you sure the cops are after us? How did they find us?"

"I fucked up. Nothing to do about it now. They've gone to the front office, but it won't be long before they're at our door. So, put your clothes on and let's go."

He turned and strode out of the bathroom to collect their things in the other room. She came out fully dressed a few moments later, her long brown hair hanging in damp waves around her shoulders.

She grabbed her boots and stepped into them. "Razor, it's broad daylight out there. You can't go anywhere right now."

"I'll manage. Give me your phone."

"What for?"

"It's staying here, along with mine." He thrust his hand out and she put her phone in it. He crushed the device in his fist, then did the same to his own phone.

Willow gaped at the mangled clumps of electronics now littering the floor. He gestured to the vending machine snacks and bottled water on the nightstand. "Better take that food with you. I don't know when it'll be safe for us to stop again so you can eat."

She swept the whole lot of it into her purse, along with the book from her sister. As he shrugged into his motorcycle jacket, she eyed him dubiously. When she spoke, her voice was grim. "The Jeep doesn't have a top or doors on it. You're going to fry out there."

"We're not taking your Jeep. Should've ditched it before we left Colorado."

"Then what else are we going to drive?"

"I'll figure it out." He gave her a hard look over his shoulder. "Time to go."

Opening the door a crack, he peered out toward the direction of the front office. The unmarked police car was standing outside, one cop waiting in the passenger seat for his partner who had gone inside.

Razor swiveled his head in the opposite direction, his gaze landing on a piece of shit minivan parked four doors down. He'd seen the van's owner at the vending machine when he'd picked up Willow's snacks. The guy looked like he'd been on a serious bender, reeking of alcohol and cigarettes as he staggered back to his room with an armful of chips and candy.

While Razor wasn't in the habit of stealing, he figured he was doing the general public a service by keeping the drunk from getting back on the road anytime soon.

"Come on," he said to Willow behind him. "This way."

They hurried along under the shade of the motel's roof overhang. When they reached the van, it took Razor all of two seconds to mentally unlock the doors and fire up the engine.

"Get in," he ordered Willow. She didn't look enthused to be his partner in crime, but she was also smart enough to realize she had no other choice.

They climbed into the van and Razor drove it out of the parking lot, keeping one eye trained on the rearview mirror to make sure the police didn't decide to follow. They weren't going to get far in a stolen vehicle, and Willow was right about the fact that he couldn't stay behind the wheel for long with the midday sun shining into the windshield.

As if she were tapped into his thoughts, Willow glanced at him. "You should get in back and let me drive until the sun goes down."

He gave a gruff shake of his head. "We don't have that kind of time. Besides, I've seen how you drive your Jeep. I'll take my chances in the sun."

Her brows rose. "Is that supposed to be a joke? From you?"

He smirked despite the torrent of humorless emotions churning inside him. "We're not going to be in this van for long."

"Good," she said, glancing behind her into the dark cavern of the interior where the van's owner had apparently been living on and off. She wrinkled her nose. "What is that awful smell back there?"

"We probably don't want to know."

Razor drove toward downtown Cheyenne, a plan beginning to hatch in his mind as they crossed a railroad track. The tracks appeared to originate in the direction of an industrial compound that was belching out gray smoke in the distance.

He took the next turn that would take them closer to the railyard.

"We need to talk about your mark," he said, swiveling his head to look at her.

She shrugged. "What's there to talk about?"

"Let's start with the fact that you're a fucking Breedmate."

"You think I need a reminder?"

Something in her tone gave him pause. As annoyed as he was to learn this disturbing fact about her, she seemed equally upset to admit it to him. "How long did you plan on keeping it from me, Willow?"

"I assumed you knew. Didn't Theo tell you my sister is—was—a Breedmate?"

Razor scoffed. "No, he fucking did not tell me that. If he had, I wouldn't have—"

"You wouldn't have . . . what?" Her brows knit as she stared at him. "You wouldn't have agreed to help Laurel? You wouldn't be helping me now?"

Razor swore under his breath. "Never mind. It doesn't matter now. We're here, whether either of us wants to be or not."

Her chin rose a fraction. "Well, we don't have to be. Stop the van right here and let me out. I can take care of myself. Believe me, I've been doing just fine on my own since the time I was a kid. I don't need anyone's charity."

"That's not what this is."

"Really? It's starting to feel like it. That is, when you're not glaring or growling orders at me."

He let out a slow breath. "I'm trying to keep you safe, Willow. In order to do that, I need to know who killed your sister, and why. Even if you want me to walk away—even if that's what I want too—that damn mark on your body won't allow me to until I'm sure you're somewhere safe where you'll be protected."

She sat back against the passenger seat, her arms folded in front of her as the van bounced over another railroad crossing. Up ahead of them was the secured gate entrance of a freight yard.

Trucks and tractor trailers rolled in and out of the compound, most of them hauling steel shipping containers that were heading on or off the trains.

"What are we doing?" Willow asked. "Are you planning to hide out here until dark?"

Razor shook his head. "No need to waste time waiting. I've got a better idea."

CHAPTER 8

The steel shipping container was dark as pitch inside and cramped with large crates. Pallets of cardboard boxes wrapped in thick plastic and filled with building supplies packed its long rectangular space nearly to capacity, leaving only a narrow wedge of sitting space for her and Razor.

Willow supposed their traveling arrangements could have been worse. As if the stench in the stolen van hadn't been unpleasant enough, the first container Razor had opened at the railyard carried pallets of various produce being carted across the country. The smell of spoiled, rotting fruit had almost knocked her over. Razor found another container for them to ride in, and so here they were hours later, jostling along on the tracks that had carried them what had to be hundreds of miles away from Cheyenne.

She sat on the hard, dusty floor of the container with

him in near darkness. The only hint of light was a sliver that struggled to come in through the slim gap between the heavy metal doors. She couldn't see the Breed male who vibrated with silent menace next to her, yet she was acutely aware of him.

His big body threw off heat like a furnace. The tight space they occupied together meant there were not even inches between them, so each time the train rocked particularly hard or took an unexpected curve, Willow's shoulder and thigh bumped into his. The contact shouldn't have felt so electric, especially when it was obvious he was furious with her.

She was getting used to his growly nature, but this new stillness from him was even more unsettling than his glowering and grumbling. He'd barely grunted a handful of words at her since they'd left the motel.

Or, rather, since he'd barged in on her shower and saw her Breedmate mark.

His angry words flew back at her again in recollection.

We're here, whether either of us wants to be or not.

Even if you want me to walk away—even if that's what I want too—that damn mark on your body won't allow me to.

She hated that he felt some kind of obligation to keep her safe because of her Breedmate mark. It hadn't been easy for her to accept his protection when he'd been doing it out of some apparent sense of duty to Theo, but now it was even worse.

What she'd told him was true: She had survived just fine on her own for a very long time. She didn't need anyone looking after her, least of all one of the Breed. She had to be out of her mind to be willingly locked inside the same space with a lethal predator.

as if yours is as insignificant to you as a blemish."

She didn't need to justify her feelings; she knew that. But he sounded so incredulous and offended she felt she owed him some kind of explanation. Besides, they had hours of travel ahead of them by his estimation. She'd go mad if she had to spend the time with only her thoughts.

"I grew up wishing that's all it was," she admitted softly. "Laurel and I both did. We'd have given anything if we could've changed what we were. No one asked us if we wanted to be part of that other world—the Breed world. We were born into it, and then that same world ripped our parents from us when were barely old enough to crawl."

He was quiet beside her for a moment. "What happened?"

Willow closed her eyes in the darkness, but it didn't keep the old memories from flooding her mind. The cold, late December night. Christmas lights twinkling on the big tree in the family's Darkhaven living room. Willow and Laurel playing on carpeted floor with some of their new toys as their parents sat nearby.

"Twenty-two years ago, my parents were killed by Rogues that broke into our home."

"Twenty-two years," Razor repeated grimly. "You're talking about the night of Dragos's global attack. The Rogues he turned loose around the world."

"Yes. Laurel and I were too young to understand what was happening. All we knew was the terror. The screams outside . . . the sirens . . . the gunfire. I can still hear it ringing in my ears. What's even worse is the sounds of my parents struggling, fighting for their lives—for our lives." Willow shook her head, trying to push the terror down even now. "My father rushed Laurel, me, and our mother into a closet upstairs. They told us to be quiet, no matter what. We tried not to cry, but we were just babies—barely two years old."

Razor made a low sound as he exhaled, an acknowledgment of what Willow struggled to say. "The Rogues found you."

"They found us," she whispered. "One of them came upstairs. He tore the closet door off its hinges and grabbed for our mother. She fought him. She fought with everything she had, but it wasn't enough. The Rogue slaughtered her."

Razor's voice was deep with sincerity. "I'm sorry, Willow."

"Me too." She took a breath and rallied herself to keep going. "My father was Atlantean."

"Of course," Razor said. "That explains how you and your sister were born Breedmates."

"Right. He was stronger than our mother, who was human. We later learned that he had killed three Rogues singlehandedly that night before coming upstairs to try to save us. He was bleeding everywhere and badly injured. We had no idea how severely until it was all over. He killed the last Rogue and ran with Laurel and me in his arms to find shelter. He must've run with us for miles before he stopped. A small church outside the city took us in."

Willow had been young, but the memories were seared into her consciousness as clearly as if it had only happened yesterday. She shuddered with the weight of those awful recollections.

"After he made sure my sister and I were safe, he went back for our mother."

Razor grunted. "He couldn't leave her there. I would've done the same."

"More Rogues had come by the time he got there. He was found the next day, bled out and holding my mother's savaged body in his arms. One of his Atlantean gifts was the ability to heal others, but he was too weakened from his own injuries and my mother was too far gone to be saved even if he'd had the strength."

"Jesus Christ."

Razor's response hung in the quiet of the container. For the longest time, he said nothing more. Then, he let out a slow exhalation.

"That's why you wanted me to take you to Laurel's body. You were born with your father's gift. You hoped you could bring your sister back."

Willow held back the knot of emotion gathering in her throat. She was thankful for the darkness of their surroundings now, glad that Razor couldn't see the pain written on her face. "I knew it was pointless even to try. I can't reverse death. I just didn't want to believe she was really gone. My sister was all the family I had left." Her voice caught on the words, but she fought it and kept going. "I've been alone most of my life, but I always knew Laurel was out there. Even though we had been apart for years, we kept in contact when we could. No matter how much distance separated us, I could still feel her and know my twin was still connected to me."

"What happened to you and your sister after the Rogue attack?"

"The church my father brought us to that night found a place for us at an orphanage in Quebec City. It was an orphanage exclusively for girls like us."

"A Breedmate shelter," Razor confirmed.

She nodded. "Laurel and I lived at St. Anne's until we were twelve years old. It wasn't always a happy place to be, but we had each other. Until the day came when we were told Laurel was being adopted."

"Just Laurel?"

Willow had asked that same confused question when St. Anne's strict director had brought both girls into her office to share the so-called good news. "A Darkhaven couple from Montreal had arranged to adopt her. They'd come around St. Anne's a few times to window shop. Apparently, they were impressed with Laurel's academic performance and her flawless behavior record."

"What about you?" Razor pressed.

Willow let out a humorless laugh. "My grades were never a problem, but I was always getting on the wrong side of the director, Sister Agathe. Laurel was the good girl, the rule follower. Where she was reserved and quiet, I was stubborn and wild. Sister Agathe used to say the only way Laurel and I were even remotely similar was when we were looking in a mirror."

"Didn't it matter to this couple that the child they wanted to adopt had an identical twin she'd be leaving behind?" Razor sounded defensive, even angry. "They couldn't make room for both of you?"

"The Townsends only wanted one child, according to Sister Agathe. Maybe if I'd been more like Laurel, they might've reconsidered, but . . . it doesn't matter. I couldn't be like her in anything even if I tried. Besides, she was just a better person than me."

Razor made a dubious sound. "I don't believe that."

"You never knew my sister. You don't know me either."

"I know enough. You're a good person, Willow."

She shook her head in the darkness. "If I was, I would've given Laurel my blessing and told her to live a happy life with the Townsends, to not worry about me. Instead, I begged her not to go. I convinced her that we needed to run away together before it was too late."

"Did she agree?"

"Yes, eventually, she did. I knew she didn't want us to be pulled apart any more than I did. But I also knew she wanted a home, a real home. She wanted parents that would love her, and to have a normal life—as normal as we could expect after the way we'd lost our own parents. I wanted that too, but not if it didn't include her. So, I hatched a plan for us to escape St. Anne's and leave Quebec City."

"That doesn't make you a bad person. You were a twelve-year-old child who didn't want to lose your sister."

"I was selfish, Razor. I knew Laurel desperately wanted what the Townsends could give her, but I was willing to sabotage that just so I wouldn't be left alone."

"What did you plan to do?"

"I had saved enough money for two train tickets back to New Brunswick. From there, I planned for us to sneak over the border into Maine and never look back."

"That wouldn't have been an easy thing for two young girls. Deadly dangerous, in fact."

"I know that now. Even then, Laurel understood the risks better than I wanted to. The night of our big escape, she lost her nerve. We had sneaked out of a seldom used maintenance entrance and were two seconds away from freedom when Laurel stopped. She told me she couldn't do it—she was too afraid to run. She begged me to come back inside with her before we got caught."

"What did you do?"

"I couldn't go back in there, Razor. I couldn't sit inside that place and watch her leave the next day knowing she would be gone forever. My plans were in motion. My mind was made up."

"But hers wasn't."

"No," Willow said softly. "Or maybe it was. I think Laurel believed that if she didn't run away with me, I'd stay at St. Anne's. But maybe she just wanted a life with the Townsends. Maybe she wanted that more than she wanted to stay with me, and she didn't know how to tell me."

"So, you kept going by yourself that night?"

"Yeah. Because while she must have believed I'd never run without her, I knew it would be a lot easier for her to go and live her own life if I was already gone. We hugged each other for the longest time. I didn't want to let her go, but I did. Then I ran. I took the train as planned, and I just . . . left. For years I kept running farther and farther away from St. Anne's, until I finally ended up in Colorado."

Willow hadn't expected to tell him the long sob story of her past, or to admit her shame over her attempt to hold her twin back from having the happiness she deserved. Yet to her surprise it felt good to tell someone what she'd been through.

Maybe it was the darkness of their surroundings that gave her courage. Or maybe it was simply the fact that she was so emotionally and physically exhausted she had no more strength to hold anything else inside.

"Laurel and I reconnected a few years later. I tried to give her space to live her life with the Townsends. I didn't want her to know that I struggled, or that I missed her every moment of every day we were apart. I couldn't have been happier when she showed up in Colorado. Even though I was worried for whatever had made her run, the brief time we had as sisters again was like a dream for me. Now, it's all turned into a nightmare."

She lifted her hand to swipe at a tear that spilled onto her cheek, but Razor was there first. His fingertips brushed feather-light against her face, a caress that lingered for only a fraction of a second.

Willow went utterly still at the feel of his touch on her cheek. Her lungs seemed to stop functioning altogether, and all she could hear was the quickening beat of her heart as a flood of heat bloomed in the wake of his unexpected caress.

"Why did you do that?" She blurted the question before she could stop herself. "You don't have to be nice just because you know what I am now."

He scoffed quietly. "That's not why I touched you."

"Then, why?"

"Because I can't sit this close to you and not want to touch you, Willow."

A jolt of shock went through her. She didn't know what to say, or what to do. Part of her wanted him to touch her again, but another part of her—the part of her that still recalled the horror of what Razor's kind was capable of—sat frozen in confusion and conflicting emotions.

At that same moment, the train rocked on its tracks as it approached a crossing. The movement sent Willow off-balance, tossing her against the heated wall of Razor's body. He caught her in his arms, holding her steady as bells clanged outside the container and the train roared through the crossing.

"Sorry," Willow murmured lamely. "It's so dark in here, I can't see a thing."

He made a low, amused sound. "I can see you perfectly. My vision is even better in the dark."

Oh, great. She winced, then abruptly cursed under her breath at the realization that he saw that too. He was still holding onto her. Against the inky blackness of the container, twin embers began to glow like smoldering fire about to erupt into flames.

This wasn't anger lighting up his Breed eyes. It was something far more dangerous . . . and too damn tempting for her peace of mind.

Desire.

Holy shit, he really did want her.

As the amber glow of his irises flared hotter, she saw the quicksilver flash of his fangs. The points were so sharp, like white daggers glinting in the gloom. She should have been afraid, but it was something other than fear that made her breath catch. The temptation to move closer to him instead of away was nearly overwhelming.

She swallowed hard, staring up at him in a mute state of shock. On reflex, one of her hands inched up toward her throat.

With a low curse, Razor let her go at once.

"Relax," he said, his voice clipped and dark. "Your carotid is the last one I'll be biting into anytime soon, Breedmate."

Willow opened her mouth to mumble an apology, an excuse, an explanation—*anything.*

She couldn't find the words. And Razor didn't give her the chance to try. The amber light of his eyes went out like doused candles as he moved farther away from her—as far as their cramped quarters would allow.

"I'm going to rest while I can," he muttered. "I suggest you do the same."

CHAPTER 9

Razor settled back against one of the cardboard crates and closed his eyes—more to conceal the bright amber glow of his transformed irises than out of any true need for sleep.

If only it were as easy to pretend he wasn't still vibrating with desire for Willow.

Unwanted desire, especially now that he knew she was a Breedmate.

The urge to kiss her, to touch her, had coursed through his veins like a lick of fire. The impulse had been to comfort her, but burning underneath that instinct was hot, demanding need. If she had allowed him to do anything more than simply brush the tear from her cheek, there would have been no saving him from the arousal she ignited inside him.

Even now, he burned with the need to feel her lips against his.

He wanted to feel more than just her sweet mouth against him, and that desire had its hooks in him from the moment he first set eyes on her for the very first time all those months ago on his computer monitors.

It was disturbing enough how badly he had wanted her when he assumed she was human. Now, she was completely off-limits.

One slip of his fangs against her tender skin would be a mistake he could never undo. A blood bond was forever, and given his background and the life that waited for him back in Florida with his Hunter brothers, he and Willow Valcourt were a hard no-go.

Which is why he had decided to bring her to Chicago and put her into the far more capable hands of the Order's district commander of that city. On more than one occasion in recent years, Razor had lent his covert, specialized skills to Lucan Thorne and his warrior brethren. While Razor didn't take for granted that he had any personal leverage with the Order, the teardrop-and-crescent-moon symbol on Willow's body was all the persuasion the warriors would need to bring her under their protection.

At least until Razor made dead certain everyone involved in her twin's murder had paid the ultimate price and were no longer a threat to Willow.

His first step on that journey would be tracking down Theo Collier.

As much as he didn't want to think it, he had a sinking feeling he was already too late to get any intel out of his old friend. Whatever he and Laurel had been involved in together had apparently attracted some very dangerous attention.

Trying to unravel the facts without either of them

around to shed any light would be a challenge to say the least. One way or another, he'd get those answers. But first, he needed to get rid of his unwanted and far-too-tempting traveling companion.

He heard her rummaging around in her purse in the dark. Cracking one eye open to the narrowest slit, he watched as she pulled out her keychain. The ring was full of keys, fobs, and charms, all of them jangling softly in her hands. She clicked one of the many items on the loop and a thin beam of light pierced the gloom.

Grabbing the bird book from her bag, she opened it in her lap and aimed the little penlight at the pages. Razor watched her for a while, noting once again how intently she studied the book.

He could imagine Willow as a young girl in the Breedmate shelter, passing the time poring over the illustrations and descriptions with her sister. Just as vividly, he could imagine the horror Willow and her twin had endured the night that Dragos's army of blood-addicted Rogues were unleashed on an unsuspecting world at large.

As young as they had been, it was clear that Willow had been irrevocably scarred by the attack. Little wonder she looked at him in fear, and, understandably, no small amount of revulsion.

The pang he felt at that surprised him. He had never been one to care what others thought of him, but with her it was different. The months he'd spent watching her from afar—wanting her—had given him the illusion of an emotional bond he had no right to feel.

Even when he had believed, incorrectly, that Willow was Theo Collier's lover, Razor had known an undeniable sense of possessiveness for her. He'd felt not only responsible for her but connected to her in a way he'd never felt for anyone before.

He'd watched Willow and felt to his marrow that she belonged with him.

That she was already his.

Seeing her reaction to him a short time ago made that illusion come crashing down like a hammer on glass.

And just in the nick of time, too.

Everything male in him still demanded that she was meant for him alone, from the throbbing of his fangs in his gums to the hard, thickened length of his cock.

He shifted on the hard floor of the container, his body tight and uncomfortably hot with frustrated arousal.

"How long are you going to pretend to sleep?" Willow asked casually, as she flipped the pages in the book.

Damn the female, she was too observant for her own good. A growl curled in the back of his throat. "Who says I was pretending?"

She swung the beam of her little flashlight into his face. "I doubt you ever sleep. Besides, we're stuck in such close quarters, I can practically hear your mind at work from where I'm sitting."

Razor scowled, his arm raised to shield his eyes. If she truly could hear his mind, she'd be on the other side of the container by now. "The light, Willow."

She redirected the slim beam down to the opened book. "Sorry."

"What have you found in there?" he asked. "Before you try to deny it, I can practically hear your mind working too. You're getting close to figuring out why Laurel left that book for you, aren't you?"

She hesitated, biting her lip before exhaling a slow breath. "I'm not sure yet. But there is . . . something."

"Show me."

He moved closer and she angled the open book so they could look at it together. "You see this underlined entry? It's newer than any of the other notations Laurel and I made in the book."

Razor nodded. "I counted seven of them."

She swiveled a frown at him. "You've been looking at this?"

"I glanced at it while you were in the motel bathroom earlier today."

"This book belongs to me, Razor. It's all I have left of my sister."

He grunted in semi-acknowledgment. "If there's something in it that'll help me track down the people who killed her, I need to know. If anything in that book will explain what may have happened to Theo, I need to know that too."

Her face softened, her eyes sobering with concern. "You think something happened to him, don't you? You think whoever went after Laurel has gotten to your friend too."

Razor nodded. "If Theo Collier isn't dead yet, I think he will be soon. Or wishing he was."

Willow swallowed. "I'm sorry, Razor. I mean that."

He wasn't good with emotion, a hazard of his upbringing in the Hunter program. Willow's tenderness only made him yearn for something he'd never had and never missed until he was staring into her soft gaze in the thin illumination of her little flashlight.

He forced a shrug. "Bad things happen to good people sometimes. You know that well enough."

"Knowing it doesn't mean it makes any more sense." She studied him for a long moment, her eyes filled with compassion and gentle curiosity. "How did you and Theo meet, anyway?"

"It was a long time ago."

"How long?"

"Twenty-two years," he said, meeting and holding her questioning gaze.

He could have kept the details about his past vague where she was concerned. He never talked about his years in the Hunter program, or the ones that followed his escape from the ultraviolet light collar that had kept him—and the rest of his Hunter half-brothers—shackled to Dragos's sadistic whims.

He didn't particularly want to revisit that time again now, but Willow's imploring gaze and patient inquisitiveness helped loosen his tongue. Besides, by this time tomorrow she would be safely ensconced in the Order's protection and he would soon be just an unpleasant memory she'd eventually put out of her mind for good.

"Twenty-two years," she murmured. "That's around the same time my family was attacked by Rogues."

He nodded. "It was a dark time for everyone. For many, including me and my brothers, Dragos's evil didn't end on that First Dawn after his Rogues were set loose on the world. I was nine years old then. His laboratory was the only home I ever knew."

"His laboratory?" Willow hesitantly asked.

"I was born into Dragos's Hunter program."

Her eyes widened slightly. "I've heard of it. He bred assassins in that program and kept them obedient to him by fitting them with UV collars."

"Yes, he did. I was one of them. As were my four brothers who managed to escape with me during the chaos of that time. We were lucky, getting away before the Order ultimately destroyed Dragos and his entire operation."

"You were a child," Willow remarked. "Younger than I was when I ran from St. Anne's."

Razor grunted wryly. "Hunters were never children."

"What did you do?" she asked. "Where did you and your brothers go after you escaped?"

"Once we helped each other break loose of our collars, we split up and ran. We didn't know what was happening or where to go. I ran north. I stopped only to wait out the daylight in any form of shelter I could find. When night fell, I ran some more."

"Were you afraid?"

"As a Hunter, I didn't know what fear was. I felt . . . nothing. Only the need to survive." He exhaled. "Eventually, I fell asleep in a barn on a small farm somewhere in Canada. I wasn't sure where. I was awakened by a beam of sunlight slicing in from the opened barn door. A boy walked in—a human boy, about my age. He'd come to feed the horses and found me hiding there."

"Theo," Willow guessed, a small smile playing at the edge of her lips.

"He could've raised an alarm. Anyone else would have. By then, I was gaunt with hunger. I'd been running on bare feet for hundreds of miles every night, wearing just the thin clothing from the lab. I'd hardly seen a human for days, let alone had the chance to feed. My first thought when I saw Theo was my blood thirst. If he had opened his mouth to scream or to call for help, I would've been on him like the predator I am. There's no doubt in my mind that I would've killed him."

"What did he do?"

"He asked me if I needed help." Razor chuckled under his breath at the memory. "No one had ever asked me that in my life. I didn't know how to answer. While I stared at him in mute confusion, someone shouted Theo's name from a distance outside the barn. He told me his father was coming, and that I needed to hide quickly."

"Were you found out?"

"No. I hid at the back of the hay loft while Theo left the barn to keep his father from coming inside to look for him. Later that afternoon, Theo came back with spare clothing and a pair of his father's old boots for me. His acts of kindness that day saved my life."

"How long did you stay in his barn?"

Razor shrugged. "Only a couple more days. The warmth and time to rest gave me strength enough to hunt for a blood Host in the nearest town. Afterward, I pushed on, eventually reconnecting with my Hunter brothers again."

"What about Theo?" Willow prompted.

"Before I left, I told him I owed him a debt. I meant it. I never forgot what he'd done for me. I kept tabs on him after I'd joined up with my brothers in the States. Years later, I contacted Theo and reminded him of my promise—if he ever needed my help with anything at all, he would have it, no questions asked. So much time had passed since that conversation, I'd gotten to the point that I never expected I'd hear from him again."

Willow nodded. "Until he called you a few days ago and asked you to come to Colorado and find my sister."

She hadn't phrased it as a question, and for reasons Razor didn't want to examine, he didn't offer to correct her. What would Willow think if she knew he'd been covertly watching her sister's cabin for months? Or that in so doing, he'd become so familiar with Willow's face and luscious curves that being next to her now was like seeing all his carnal fantasies come to life, yet being unable—or unwilling—to touch?

Part of him wanted to explain the whole situation to her now.

Another part of him was shocked by his own cowardice to admit that he'd been willfully invading the sisters' privacy for months, and then failing both of them in the end when he arrived too late to save Laurel.

In a few more hours his lie of omission wouldn't matter, anyway. Once they reached Chicago, they would go their separate ways and the odds were good he'd never set eyes on Willow Valcourt again.

In the silence that lingered between them, she solemnly gazed up at him. "I'm glad Theo helped you that day, Razor."

His jaw tensed as he looked at her, so beautiful, so compassionate toward him even after the gruff way he'd been treating her for most of their time together. He still wasn't comfortable with emotion or tender caring, despite that his brutal Hunter upbringing was decades behind him.

That it was coming from her was a torment all its own.

"For all the good his helping me did," Razor muttered.

He stood up, feeling caged and twitchy in the close confines. If there had been room to pace he would have already worn a track on the floor. Instead, he moved to the closed doors of the container to peer through the small wedge between the metal panels. It was closing in on sundown, judging by the amount of light and shadows outside the moving train.

"How much longer until we reach Chicago, do you think?" Willow asked from behind him.

"Five or six hours, give or take." Not soon enough for him, that was for damn sure.

He didn't invite any further conversation, feigning full attention on the sliver of visibility outside and the endless rattle and hum of the train as the miles continued to spool away beneath the wheels.

When he finally turned around to look at her again, he found her holding the little penlight between her teeth as she flipped the pages of the opened book in her lap. She paused on one page in particular now, a frown creasing her brow.

"Ohm-uh-gah." Her words were garbled around the obstruction in her mouth. She let the flashlight fall and glanced up at Razor in plain disbelief. "It's a code."

"What kind of code?" He crossed the short distance and dropped down to his haunches beside her.

"These underlined scientific names of the birds. Laurel left me a code." She pointed to one of the notations on the page in front of her. The Latin name read *Epidonax trailli*. "Read the common name for this bird."

"Willow flycatcher," Razor replied. He looked at her and frowned. "What am I missing?"

"She's telling me to pay attention to each of these underlined entries. I wasn't sure until I saw this, but now I know. It's as if she's saying, 'Willow, this is what I need you to do.'"

Razor wasn't nearly as certain as she seemed to be, but he watched as Willow rummaged in her purse for a scrap of paper and something to write with. Retrieving a pen and a crumpled receipt, she started writing down each of the seven underlined scientific bird names.

Epidonax trailli.

Toxostoma rufum.

Nucifraga columbiana.

Spinus tristis.

Agelaius phoeniceus.

Sitta carolinensis.

Nyctidromus albicollis.

"When we were little, Laurel and I used to love creating codes so we could communicate in secret, away from Sister Agathe's prying eyes and ears. One way we did was to create messages using riddles. We'd solve the riddles and use the first letter of each solution to spell out our secret messages."

"Are these bird names some kind of riddle?"

"No. I think it's simpler than that." She glanced at him, excitement shining in her eyes. "Much simpler, but only for someone who knows what to look for."

She studied the list of bird names scribbled on the back of the receipt, arranging and rearranging the first letters like an anagram. It only took her a few seconds before a gasp slipped past her lips.

"I have it," she murmured. Her gaze swung back to him. "*St. Anne's.* Laurel wants me to go back to the orphanage in Quebec City."

Razor scowled, feeling a cold kind of dread begin to form in his gut. "What the hell is waiting for you back there?"

"I don't know, but I need to find out."

"I don't like it."

She raised her brows. "You don't have to like it. It's what my sister wants me to do. This message couldn't be any clearer. Laurel told me once I found this book, I'd know what I needed to do. This is it, Razor. I need to go to St. Anne's."

"And then what?" he practically growled.

"I suppose I'll have to figure that out when I get there."

He cursed, raking a hand over his tense jaw. "Like hell you will. Not without me."

If Willow intended to go to St. Anne's or anywhere else her sister's riddles and codes might send her next, he'd be damned if he was letting her go without him.

He wanted to believe his determination stemmed mainly from his own personal need for answers—and lethal justice—but the quickening of his blood belied all his other motivations. His resolve to protect Willow Valcourt overrode even the duty he had toward her simply because she was a Breedmate.

If she meant to chase the clue her sister left for her, then he would too.

He'd learned enough about the female to know she was stubborn enough to find a way, with or without him.

So, for now, his plans to take her to the Order in Chicago and leave her in the warriors' protection were on hold until he uncovered whatever was waiting for Willow in that Breedmate shelter in Quebec City.

CHAPTER 10

In Chicago, they traded the cramped, dark container for a couple of seats on an all but empty passenger train that took them the rest of the way to Quebec City.

Willow didn't ask how Razor had managed to get them across the Canadian border without the need to show passports. As far as she could tell, he hadn't even been asked to pay for the tickets. Obeying his order to keep her head low and try not to be seen, she'd stood in a quiet corner of the Chicago station and had watched him murmur something to the gate clerk, his deep voice accompanied by that penetrating stare of his. The next thing she knew they were boarding the first-class car and smoothly on their way to Canada.

Somehow, she had managed to fall asleep for most of the hours-long trek that took them well into the next day. As the train rolled into the Gare du Palais station in the heart of Quebec City, dusk was starting to fall.

Willow blinked away her grogginess and sat up. “We’re here?”

Razor only grunted in reply, his gaze fixed on her. She felt suddenly self-conscious, reaching up to try to tame the tangles of her long hair. The dark brown waves felt like a messy rat’s nest, and she didn’t even want to consider how bad her dragon’s breath must be. Hardly the image she wanted to present to Sister Agathe Moreau at St. Anne’s—much less to Razor.

He, on the other hand, looked as alert and easy on the eyes as ever. Not a single tawny wave of his thick, silky hair was out of place. His jaw was shadowed with the hint of a beard that only made his face all the more handsome. As for his mouth . . . well, she didn’t want to let her gaze linger too long there. His full lips were held in a grim line as he studied her, and even though she knew his closed mouth concealed the threat of sharp white fangs, it didn’t make her any less fascinated by him.

She groaned at her unwanted attraction to him, then tried to mask it with nonchalance as she stretched her aching back. “I’d do anything for a toothbrush and a long, hot bath.”

His brows furrowed. “What you need even more is a decent meal. You haven’t eaten for two days.”

“Neither have you,” she pointed out.

“Don’t remind me.” His scowl darkened with annoyance. “Come on, let’s go.”

He gestured for her to follow him off the train. They hung back from the crowd, letting the other passengers disembark ahead of them and move into the station.

“There should be someplace where you can get something to eat,” he said, taking her by the elbow as he cut a determined path through the disbursing knots of people.

Willow knew the warmly lit, vaulted interior of the historic Gare du Palais well. With St. Anne's only a few blocks away, it was this very station she'd run to the night she fled without her sister. Now, she felt like a ghost moving beneath the high-ceilinged, Gothic-style, two-story brick building after so many years had passed . . . and after so much had happened in the last few days.

She didn't realize she'd stopped walking until Razor paused and looked at her in concern. "What's wrong?"

She slowly shook her head. "I never thought I'd come back here again. To this city. To the place I lost my sister for the first time." She stared up into his stern, yet steadying gaze. "I'm scared."

"Don't be," he said, and although he didn't touch her, she felt his eyes move over every inch of her face like a caress. "There's nothing to be afraid of. I'll be right beside you. No one's getting near you without going through me first, and they won't get far, I promise you."

"What if we've come all this way for nothing, Razor? I solved the code Laurel left for me in the book, but I have no idea what she wants me to do once I'm at St. Anne's. What if I can't figure it out? What if Sister Agathe won't even let me into the house?"

An almost gentle smile tugged at the corners of his sensual mouth. "You let me worry about getting in, if that becomes a problem. As for you not being able to figure something out, not gonna happen, beautiful. I've seen your mind work. I've seen your tenacity. If there's something your sister wanted you to do at that place, nothing's going to keep you from figuring it out."

Hearing the way he described her was a surprise. A warming one that touched her deeper than he could possibly know. She had always depended on herself as the woman he seemed to think she was, but after everything she'd been through, starting with Laurel's horrific murder, it was hard to feel she was in control of anything.

Still, she forced a smile in spite of her self-doubt. She hated letting anyone see her weaknesses, and part of her desperately wanted to think she could have the strength and tenacity that Razor believed she had.

"You're right," she said, trying to sound confident and certain. "I'm sure I will feel better once I've had something to eat."

He grunted, his usual response, while his eyes seemed to see right through her. "There's a café over there, unless you want to find something better."

She shook her head. "No, it's fine. Anything will do. Let's go."

With a grim nod, his strong hand was at her elbow again and they headed for the little sandwich and coffee place across the station.

He led her to a small table in back, taking the seat that afforded him a clear line of sight to the café's entrance. Willow took the chair across from him, so that her face was shielded from view to everyone with the exception of Razor. When the waitress came around to take their order Willow asked for water and the sandwich special.

"Black coffee," Razor said when the young woman turned to him. After she was gone, Willow tilted her head at him in question.

"No sense broadcasting what I am," he explained. "The more we can blend in, the less attention we draw to either one of us. Until I know who our enemies are, every time you're out in public is a risk I'd rather not take."

"Right." She nodded, fiddling with the edge of the paper placemat on the table in front of her. "Thank you, Razor . . . for getting me this far."

He studied her for a long moment, his gaze unreadable under the harsh slashes of his brows. "There's no need to thank me. I'm doing this for myself because—"

"Yes, I know," she cut in quietly. "You're here because you feel you have a duty to protect me."

He frowned and began to open his mouth, but at that same moment the waitress returned with his coffee. "You sure I can't get you something more than this?"

He flicked his golden eyes up at her. Something in his gaze made the air tremble with a current of dark energy that Willow felt on the other side of the table.

"Just the coffee," he said. "And the water and sandwich for the lady. Be quick about it. Bring the check with you when you come back."

The waitress bobbed her head in eager compliance, then hurried away to obey him.

Willow stared, dropping her voice to barely a whisper. "You did something to her."

He scoffed under his breath and gave her a bored look. "Just a small mental command. She's none the wiser, but I'll scrub her memory of any recollection of us before we leave just to be safe."

"That's a handy trick. Is that what you did back at the train station in Chicago too? What other cool things can you do?"

His mouth curved in acknowledgment, and the slow, sensual arc of his lips made her pulse beat a little faster.

"You don't really want to know about my methods. Even the harmless ones. Besides, this isn't the time or place for questions."

"That's too bad, because I have hundreds of them."

The admission slipped off her tongue before she could stop it. She stared at him, still transfixed by his wry smile and all the hard, far-too-handsome angles of his face. He wasn't looking away from her, either.

His arresting eyes seemed to reach inside her from across the small table, making her feel both excited and afraid. Not afraid of him, but of the feelings he stirred in her.

The yearning . . . the undeniable physical need.

"Okay, turkey melt special and fries," announced the waitress as she arrived at their table. "And a glass of water. Oh, and I brought the bill in case you two are in a hurry. Can I get you anything else?"

Razor took out some cash—more than necessary for the tab and a tip—and pushed it to the edge of the table along with the handwritten check. "That'll be all."

With a nod and a cheerful smile, the young woman turned and headed off to continue her work.

Willow didn't realize just how hungry she was until the aromas of warm, roasted turkey and melted cheese wafted up from her plate. Her stomach growled eagerly, and she glanced sheepishly at Razor.

He gave a low chuckle. "Go ahead and eat."

She attacked her food with little regard for the fact that he watched her the whole time. She could hardly hold back her pleasured moan at the first taste of crunchy sourdough bread and all the goodness packed between the buttery slices. Even the water was bliss, cold and refreshing as she gulped it down her parched throat.

It took her all of ten minutes to wolf down the sandwich and eat the last French fry. All with Razor watching the entire time. She couldn't decide if his expression was one of amusement or shock, and she was too satisfied to care.

"Feel better?" he asked, not even trying to hide his smirk.

She shrugged, smiling back at him. "I feel like I could take on the world right now. Or, at a minimum Sister Agathe."

"Then we should go."

She nodded. "I want to stop in the ladies' room first and freshen up, as best I can, that is."

"All right. Don't be long. I'll take care of the waitress, then I'll wait for you just outside the café."

They got up from the table, Willow heading to the restrooms in back while Razor strode in the opposite direction where their waitress was busy wiping down an empty table.

Willow paused outside the swinging door to the ladies' room only long enough to see Razor lean in to the young woman and say something to her while his hand moved surreptitiously to touch her forehead.

Stepping into the restroom, Willow made quick use of the facilities then did her best to smooth down her hair and wash up at the sink. A gargle of cold water and breath mint from a nearly empty tin of them in her purse were the best she could do without a toothbrush.

Unfortunately, there was nothing to be done about the dark circles under her eyes, or the stress and grief she could see plainly written all over her face.

But her eyes told a different story. Steely determination filled the bright green gaze that stared back at her in the mirror. Her face, so like Laurel's it startled her sometimes.

"I'm not going to let you down," she promised her twin's memory. "Whoever hurt you is not going to get away with it. I promise you."

With that vow singing through her veins, Willow straightened her shoulders and strode out of the ladies' room with renewed purpose. As he'd indicated, Razor was standing just outside the café entrance waiting for her.

As Willow passed the waitress on her way out to meet him, the young woman gave her a disapproving look. "The restrooms are for paying customers only, miss."

"Oh." Willow feigned embarrassment. "I didn't realize. Sorry about that."

She kept walking, making a beeline for where Razor stood. He was scowling as she approached him. Willow took a steadying breath. "I hope I didn't take too long. Let's get out of here before—"

Her words dried up at the feel of his hands gently cupping her face. His golden eyes seared her. "You were wrong about something."

"W-what?" She had no idea what he was talking about or what to think. All she knew was the shock, the electric excitement, of his touch and the heat of his piercing gaze. Her entire body was short-circuiting as he held her in his tender grasp.

He moved in closer, until scant inches stood between their bodies. "I'm not here with you now because of my duty to keep you safe. Fuck . . . keeping you safe from me is the best thing I could do for you, Willow."

Before she knew what to think or what to say or do, Razor bent his head and kissed her.

Their lips met only briefly, but the jolt of awareness that ignited from just that fleeting brush of their mouths against each other nearly melted her where she stood.

Desire swamped her. Her pulse jumped and sped off at a gallop, until all she could hear was the thrumming beat of her heart in her ears.

In her veins.

In every fiber of her being.

He set her away from him on a low growl. Amber light smoldered in the depths of his irises.

When he spoke, his voice was rough and dark. "Let's go. Before I do anything stupider than that."

CHAPTER 11

Giving in to impulse had never been one of Razor's weaknesses.

Temptation had been equally foreign to him, yet as he gruffly exited the Gare du Palais station with Willow, arousal licked through him like a wildfire—along with the powerful want to take her into his arms again and give in to far more than just the impulse to kiss her.

His body vibrated with dangerous need, making his pace hard and clipped as they strode out into the twilight.

Willow paused beside him, her light green eyes dusky as she glanced up at him from under her impossibly thick lashes. "St. Anne's is only a few blocks away. We can walk from here."

He gave her a curt nod. "Let's go."

They crossed the pavement in front of the train station and headed toward the wide boulevard and bustling network of old streets and narrow alleyways that sprawled on the other side. Willow navigated the twists and turns of the labyrinthine neighborhood with the easy familiarity of a local.

Razor couldn't help but see her as the strong-willed twelve-year-old girl who had run away from the safe haven of the shelter armed only with her wits and stubborn determination. That girl was still present in Willow now, in her courage and her resolve.

She'd confided in him earlier that she was afraid, but he knew she would have made this pilgrimage despite those fears. There was a warrior beneath all her soft curves and winsome beauty. Unfortunately for him, that only made her all the more appealing.

"It's not too much farther," she said, her pace brisk beside him.

They walked another block, Willow finally working her way onto a quiet, upward-sloping street hemmed in on either side by three- and four-story townhomes.

Slender, uneven sidewalks with barely enough room for one tracked up the incline on both sides. Willow walked ahead of him on the tightly settled street, eventually pausing in front of an unmarked, heavy wooden door.

"We're here. This is it."

Razor studied the pale brick building sandwiched unassumingly between its neighbors. There was no signage, no number on the door. If he hadn't known the historic townhome served as a safe house for orphaned Breedmate girls, he never would have guessed. Which had been, no doubt, the whole point of establishing the shelter in this spot when it was founded.

He heard Willow's soft intake of breath before she lifted her hand and used the old iron knocker to announce them. He stood close, all of his Hunter instincts at the ready as the sound of shuffling footsteps approached on the other side of the door.

A pleasant looking human woman who appeared to be in her mid-forties pulled open the door. Her blonde hair was gathered into a conservative bun that complemented the plain black skirt and high-necked sweater she wore. She smiled warmly when she saw Willow.

"Well, hello," she said, her English marked with a French accent. "What a lovely surprise to see you again, Laurel."

Willow didn't show her reaction, but Razor could feel her internal flinch at the revelation that her twin had apparently been to St. Anne's as well.

"My name is Willow," she said, giving the older woman a guarded smile. "I'm Laurel's twin sister."

"Oh, forgive me. The resemblance is so striking, I just assumed—"

"And you are?" Razor interjected. The woman's gaze flicked to him, registering easily enough that he was Breed.

"Madame Claudine Gauthier," she said, still giving him the once-over. "I'm the director of this shelter."

Her demeanor seemed more protective than defensive, and while her tone was cool in dealing with him, she seemed to have nothing but warmth for Willow.

"Please, would you like to come in? We have a policy to be discreet, so I prefer to talk inside rather than on the front stoop."

"Thank you," Willow said, giving Razor a subtle look of warning as they entered the foyer behind Madame

Gauthier.

"It isn't often we see former residents, but visits are always welcome."

She led them into a small sitting room decked out in cushioned furniture, soft rugs, and warm lighting. Bookcases lined the walls, their shelves crowded nearly to overflowing with many hundreds of books.

On the wall facing the room's arched entryway a large, framed portrait of a dour-faced, gray-haired woman stared out from the canvas. Her faint smile seemed intent on projecting mild benevolence, but her eyes told a different story. Beneath her steel-colored brows, her gaze glinted with sternness and what Razor guessed was chronic disapproval.

He stepped forward to have a closer look. A small brass plaque affixed to the lower portion of the ornate black frame declared the portrait a gift to St. Anne's from a Mr. and Mrs. Simon Scrully, in appreciation for the shelter's many years of compassionate, good work.

He didn't have to ask who the subject of the portrait was. Glancing at Willow, he found her transfixed by the old woman's silent glower.

"That's quite an accurate portrait of Sister Agathe," she said. "When did she sit for it?"

"Oh, it must have been about three years ago, I suppose." Madame Gauthier offered a sympathetic smile. "Just a few months before Sister Agathe passed away, bless her soul."

"She's dead?" Willow sounded both shocked and somewhat relieved. "I'm sorry. I didn't know."

Madame Gauthier shook her head. "She went peacefully in her sleep from what I hear. She'd retired from St. Anne's when I was brought in to manage things, so I'm afraid I didn't know her well. I have heard of the Sister's somewhat . . . harsh reputation." She turned a gentle look on Willow. "There have been a lot of changes since you and your sister lived here. Changes for the better, I hope. Please, sit and make yourselves comfortable."

They did as asked, Willow taking a seat on the opposite end of the sofa from where Madame Gauthier had delicately perched. Razor opted for the chair to Willow's left, which gave him a visual line to the room's entrance and the hall outside while also putting him in easy reach of Willow should the need arise.

His Hunter senses had been heightened from the moment they entered the townhome, though he wasn't yet certain if it was because of his indecision about Madame Gauthier or the way Willow's entire being seemed coiled with anxiety and remembered pain.

He hated the circumstances that had sent her to this place as an infant. Now that he'd seen the cold, unkind face of the woman who'd been in charge of St. Anne's during those early years of Willow's life, he almost wished the old hag were still alive so he could personally terrify her into her grave.

"What other kind of changes have there been?" Willow asked Madame Gauthier.

"Well, we have fewer girls here, for one thing. The need has lessened. Twenty-odd years ago when you and Laurel came to live at St. Anne's, sadly, it wasn't uncommon for Breedmate girls to be orphaned during all of the violence of that time. Fortunately, those dark days are behind us now."

Razor grunted. "Don't be so sure. There will always be someone eager to profit off the suffering of others."

She tilted her head at him. "I don't believe I caught your name."

"His name is Razor," Willow replied. "He's my . . . friend."

"Hm." Madame Gauthier scrutinized him for a long moment, and Willow casually leaned forward as though to block her view.

"How many girls live here at St. Anne's now?"

"We're down to four long-term residents," she answered, pride in her voice. "My hope is that shelters like this one will become permanently obsolete before too long. The Order's been instrumental in helping to place our girls with loving, suitable families."

The news took Razor by surprise. "The Order?"

"Yes. St. Anne's used to be dependent on private donors, but now this home and the rest of the remaining Breedmate shelters are funded wholly by the Order."

Just then, a thin, middle-aged woman appeared in the entryway to the sitting room. She wore a gray housekeeping uniform that was almost the same color as the tightly contained bun that sat atop her head, not a single hair escaping. Upon seeing there were guests seated inside, she quietly cleared her throat.

"Oh! Madame Dupont," replied their host. "Look who's come for a visit."

The other woman's eyes lit first on Willow, then swung immediately to Razor. He couldn't decide which of them had stirred the shock that briefly registered in her gaze. Her mouth sagged open for a moment but no sound came out.

Madame Gauthier turned to Willow. "I'm sure you remember Sister Agathe's dear friend, Madame Estelle Dupont? She was one of the young ladies on the housekeeping staff at St. Anne's during the time you and your sister lived here."

"Yes, I remember," Willow murmured.

"Madame Dupont is in charge of all our household staff now. Estelle, this is Willow Valcourt. Laurel Townsend's sister."

"Ah. *Oui.* Yes, of course." The gray-haired woman offered a polite smile and bobbed her head in greeting. "*Mademoiselle.*"

The two older women spoke to each other in rapid French before Madame Gauthier asked Willow, "May I offer you some tea and a little something to eat? Madame Dupont tells me she has just taken a tray of almond biscuits out of the oven."

"Tea would be nice, thank you." Once the older woman had trundled off, Willow leaned forward and spoke to Madame Gauthier. "You said my sister was here recently. When was that, do you recall?"

"Yes, perhaps five or six months ago now. She didn't stay long, but we had a lovely visit."

"Did she come here by herself?"

Madame Gauthier nodded. "Yes, she was alone. She arrived at our door out of the blue, much like you did tonight. Are you concerned about her for some reason, Willow?"

"No. No, there's no reason to be concerned." She glanced at Razor as if she needed to reassure herself. "I was just wondering about her, that's all. We're not, um . . . we're no longer in touch like we used to be."

Although Razor hadn't discussed keeping Laurel's death a secret from anyone at St. Anne's he was relieved to hear Willow avoid showing their hand, no matter how kind and welcoming Madame Gauthier seemed to be.

Until he knew the truth about Willow's sister and whoever wanted her dead, Razor was going to assume they were surrounded by enemies.

"Oh, I'm sorry to hear you've fallen out of contact with her," Madame Gauthier replied. "She spoke very fondly of you when she was here."

"She did? What did she say, if you don't mind me asking?"

"No, of course, I don't mind. I remember she told me how close you both were as children when you lived here. And she told me how much she regretted leaving with her adoptive family to Montreal when she knew you couldn't come too."

Razor heard Willow swallow. The urge to reach out to her nearly overwhelmed him, but he sat without moving, waiting as she fought to contain her emotions. "I was the one with regrets. I wanted Laurel to be happy. It's all I ever wanted for my her."

Madame Gauthier gave Willow a warm, tender smile. "Maybe you should be saying all of this to your sister instead of me."

"I wish she was here right now so I could," Willow said. "Can you tell me anything else about her visit, Madame Gauthier? I'm curious to know if she said why she came back to St. Anne's. Or if she spoke about anything that was happening in her life at the time?"

"No, I'm sorry, dear. As I said, she stayed only briefly. We spoke for a short while here on this sofa, then she asked if she could go upstairs and spend a few minutes in the room you two once shared."

"Our old room?" Willow asked.

Madame Gauthier nodded. "Since it wasn't occupied at the time, I didn't see the harm. Laurel went up for a few minutes and then she came back down to say goodbye and she was gone."

Willow seemed to go stock-still beside Razor. "Madame Gauthier, if you don't mind, I would love to see our old room too."

"Of course," she said. "It'll be a few minutes before our tea is ready, anyway. If you'd like to go up now, please feel free. No one's used that room for a couple of years now. The door should be open."

Willow practically vaulted to her feet. Razor wasn't even a second behind her.

"Thank you," Willow said to their smiling hostess.

"I'm sure you can find your way upstairs on your own. I'll call you back down when Madame Dupont has served the tea."

CHAPTER 12

Curiosity sped Willow's feet as she and Razor climbed the stairs to the second-floor room she'd once shared with her twin.

The aged steps still creaked in all the familiar places, and the scent of lemon-polished old wood permeated the air. The layout of the second floor with its collection of bedrooms spoking off the main hallway didn't seem as large and intimidating to her now, as an adult.

Soft female voices filtered out from an open doorway as she and Razor walked toward the end of the long hall. Willow glanced at the two Breedmate girls inside the room as she passed. They couldn't be more than sixteen, both sprawled on the floor with a small collection of opened textbooks scattered around them.

Willow offered them a smile in greeting, but they were too busy gawking at Razor to notice her.

As soon as she and her handsome Breed protector

had stepped past their door, a peal of girlish giggles sounded in their wake.

Hearing laughter at St. Anne's had been a rare thing when she and Laurel had been there. Sister Agathe's rules had been strict and unforgiving. Madame Dupont had been her devoted pet, always willing to rat out Willow and the other girls for the slightest offense.

Evidently, Madame Gauthier's changes truly were making an impact for the better.

Willow grinned, glancing over her shoulder at Razor. "I imagine you're used to that kind of female reaction whenever you're around."

He grunted, the corners of his sensual mouth lifting. "I have no idea what you're talking about."

Willow rolled her eyes. "Uh, huh."

As they reached the last room at the end of the hallway, her heart was racing, her breath quickening in her lungs. Her fingers trembled a bit as she reached for the crystal doorknob and twisted it.

The old door swung inward on whining hinges, opening into a small, vacant room with narrow twin beds situated side by side against one wall and a smattering of well-worn bedroom furnishings. For a moment, as she stood there, time rewound and froze.

Willow looked at her old bed and she was there again in her mind. She could still feel her bereft desperation as a broken-hearted twelve-year-old, sobbing into her pillow over the news that Laurel had been chosen for adoption and soon would be leaving St. Anne's.

"You all right?" Razor asked, his hand coming to rest lightly at the small of her back.

"Yeah." She nodded, finding comfort and strength in the warmth of his touch. She stepped into the room,

Razor following close behind her. He closed the door once they'd entered, no doubt to keep their conversation from the prying ears down the hall.

"Nothing's changed in here." Walking over to one of the beds, she took a seat on the edge of the mattress. "This was where Laurel used to sleep. That one was mine."

Razor gave a grim nod, then he strode to the sole window in the room and moved the curtain to peer outside at the moonlit, old city. The window overlooked the narrow back alley that ran behind the townhouse and its neighbors, a view Willow had gazed out at countless times herself when she lived here.

She got up from the bed and joined him at the window. "Laurel and I used to play a game on nights when bad dreams woke us. We'd sit on this windowsill and look up at the starlight, watching for shooting stars, each of us trying to be first to spot one and write down the date and time. It was a silly game, but it gave us something to hold on to when it didn't seem like we had anything left."

Willow stared out through the glass, looking up at the half-moon and the blanket of darkness that cushioned it. Clouds obscured most of the stars tonight, but there was still a small comfort in the familiar view. Was this what drew Laurel up to their old bedroom when she was here last? The need to revisit the familiar?

Still, it didn't explain why she'd send Willow here too.

"Why did Laurel leave that code for me?" she wondered aloud. "She knew she was in danger six months ago, but what was so important that she'd detour way out here before coming to find me in

Colorado? Why send me here after her death and not give me any clues as to why she wanted me to go or what she wanted me to do once I got here?"

She turned her head to look at Razor. "Did she think I'd find closure here if her fears came true and she was killed?"

"Maybe Laurel thought you'd be safest here," he suggested, his deep voice gentle. "Maybe your sister knew the Order is in control of St. Anne's now, and the book and the code she left for you was her way of lighting a path for you to safety under their protection."

"Safety among the Breed?" Willow shook her head. "Not my sister—and no offense, but she had no love for your kind. After what happened to our parents, she lived in terror of all the Breed. Even more than I."

Razor's face seemed tighter somehow, his square jaw rigid as he listened to Willow describe her sister's bias against his race. "It's understandable. Both of you had every right to feel that way."

"I don't," she said. "Not anymore, I mean. Not since I met you."

He scoffed lightly. "Ironic, considering what I am, what I was raised to be."

"No, Razor." She reached out to him, unable to resist the need to touch him. Her fingers lit tentatively on his tense cheek. "I don't see you that way."

He stared at her for a long moment without speaking. Nor did he move to draw away from her touch. His eyes drank her in, making all the air in the room seem to contract and press in on her.

Willow's heart galloped under the heat of his intense, golden gaze and her lips burned the way they had after his surprising kiss outside the cafe. More than anything, she wanted to feel his kiss again.

She needed him with a yearning that astonished her.

Razor scowled and cleared his throat, taking a step back. "We shouldn't stay here long."

"Right," she agreed, hearing his annoyance in the deep rumble of his voice. "We've come so far to get here, I can't leave without being certain why it was important to Laurel. Not to mention I agreed to stay for tea."

Razor gave a dubious grunt. "A delay we shouldn't risk, but you didn't ask me."

"Don't you ever relax, even for a minute?"

"I will, once I know you're safe."

He sounded so gravely serious she had to smile. "I feel safe with you."

His gaze bore into her, those golden eyes smoldering. It took him too long to speak. When he finally did, a low curse rolled off his tongue. "I shouldn't have kissed you, Willow. I'm supposed to be protecting you, not . . . not letting myself get distracted by how much I want you."

She drew in a shallow breath at his admission. "I don't want your apology for that. I liked it. I wanted you to kiss me. Razor, I want you too."

His reply was a wordless snarl. Then his large hands came up to frame her face and his mouth crushed down onto hers.

His kiss outside the café had been gentle and teasing. This kiss scorched her with the intensity of his desire. Willow burned along with him, every cell in her body lighting up delicious fire and overwhelming need.

His lips devoured hers. When she gasped at the blaze erupting within her, Razor's tongue slid past her parted teeth. Arousal surged inside her at the searing invasion. He groaned against her mouth, his strong arms caging her, pulling her into the hard heat of his body.

Her name rasped out of him, while the sharp points of his fangs grazed her lips.

It should have frightened her, the awareness of how vulnerable she was to this man . . . to this lethal Breed male.

Instead, all she felt was desire.

Marrow-deep, consuming desire.

His hands moved down her body, leaving hot trails wherever he touched her. His grasp on her was possessive, demanding. Her body answered with total surrender.

God help her, if he flung her down beneath him on one of the narrow beds she would've been powerless to stop him. Worse, she couldn't think of anything she wanted more.

Their breath mingled, hot and rapid as their kiss deepened.

Her heart hammered so loudly in her breast, it sounded like a drum in her ears.

Thump, thump, thump.

Oh, shit. It wasn't only her heartbeat she heard.

"Willow, are you in there?" Madame Gauthier's voice filtered in from the other side of the closed door.

Razor tore away from Willow's mouth on hissed oath. He looked more annoyed than contrite, with his irises blazing and his fangs gleaming like diamond daggers behind his wet, parted lips.

The doorknob jiggled but didn't give. "Did someone lock this door?"

Willow shot a worried glance up at Razor. "You?"

she whispered.

"Barely in time," he confirmed grimly.

"Is everything okay in there, Willow?" Madame Gauthier asked.

"Yes. Everything's fine. We'll, ah . . . we'll be down in just a minute."

She winced, mortified to hear the guilt in her voice. There was nothing to do about it. Her only saving grace was the fact that Razor had managed to mentally bar the woman from entering the room.

"The tea should be ready any minute now," Madame Gauthier said after an excruciating hesitation. As pleasant as she was when they met, she was still St. Anne's director and her disapproval over this indiscretion was obvious in her voice. "I'll be waiting for you downstairs."

Willow bit her lip. "Thank you, Madame Gauthier."

Her footsteps retreated. Willow let out her breath on a giggle behind her hand. "That was a close call."

Razor glowered. "I'm glad you're amused."

She was more than amused, but unfortunately those other feelings he'd stirred in her would have to wait for another time. "Your fangs are showing."

His eyes flashed hot. "That's not all that's showing." He pulled her against him, where the hard length of his erection jabbed into her abdomen. She moaned at the feel of all his hard strength and her unbearable longing to have him inside her. He chuckled under his breath. "Not so amused now, are you?"

She sent him a narrow look. "You're cruel."

He arched a brow. "Never said I wasn't."

Willow stepped away from him, her thoughts troubled. "I'm not ready to leave this room yet, Razor. I feel like I'm missing something crucial. I feel like the reason Laurel sent me here is in this room somewhere. What am I not seeing?"

"Whatever her reasons, she obviously didn't want anyone else to know she was directing you here. Why else would she obscure the clue like a hidden treasure in that book?"

"Hidden treasure . . ." Willow turned the phrase over in her mind. "Oh, my God."

Was that it? Could that be what Laurel was trying to tell her to look for at St. Anne's?

She walked across the room to the small writing desk that stood against the far wall.

"What is it, Willow?"

She couldn't answer him. Her mind was buzzing with anticipation as she pulled the desk away from the wall, then hunkered down onto her haunches. There was a nearly imperceptible notch in the baseboard, just as she remembered.

Excitedly, she dashed to the bed where she'd tossed her purse and rifled through the handbag until she found what she was looking for. Her keychain full of girly charms and beaded talismans jingled as she rushed back with it to the spot on the floor.

Razor strode over to her and dropped down beside her. "What are you doing?"

Using her house key, she tried to pry off the small section of baseboard but her fingers were trembling too much in her impatience.

"Here," Razor said. "Let me."

A black talon sprouted from his index finger. He wedged it behind the baseboard and popped the piece off the wall.

A hollow just big enough for a child's hand was revealed behind the removed bit of baseboard. "I used this hidey hole to store the train money I saved up for the night Laurel and I were going to run away. She's the only other person who knew about my hiding place."

She picked up her keychain again and flicked on the small flashlight. Leaning down, she aimed the thin beam of light into the hole. She gasped as the light caught on a small metallic object inside.

"There's something in here, Razor." She reached inside and pulled the item out, holding it in her open palm. "Holy shit. This is what Laurel wanted me to find."

Razor stared at it for second, then met her excited gaze. "A flash drive."

Willow nodded. "The question is, what's on it?"

His face was grim. "Something important enough that she didn't want anyone but you to find it."

Willow glanced at the drive with a mix of elation and regret. "Do you think whatever's on this is the reason my sister was killed?"

"That's what we need to find out."

She looked at him. "I don't know anything about technology, Razor."

"Leave that to me," he said, a glint of wry confidence lighting his gaze. "Come on, let's get out of here."

CHAPTER 13

They headed downstairs, Razor carrying the flash drive in his pocket.

If it had been up to him, they would have kept walking right out the front door but Madame Gauthier came out of the sitting room to meet them as soon as they reached the bottom of the stairs. Her gaze was still warm and kind, but now it held an edge of suspicion too.

"We generally don't allow locked doors here at St. Anne's," she said, splitting her disapproval between them before settling on Willow. "Madame Dupont has just gone to fetch our tea, dear. Come, let's sit."

Razor had to work to bite back the low growl that built in his throat as the director pivoted back into the sitting room. He held Willow back with a meaningful look, but she subtly shook her head.

"I don't want to be rude," she whispered. "I'll only stay for a few minutes."

He scowled, impatient to get his hands on the flash drive. Of course, he had no way of cracking into it at the moment, so until he figured out their next move he had no solid plan of action even if they left now.

"A few minutes, no more," he cautioned under his breath. While she drank her tea he'd use the time to decide his next course of action.

They moved into the sitting room, Willow resuming her seat on the sofa while Razor opted to stand. He took up his position next to the portrait of Sister Agathe, feeling like a scowling gargoyle looming over the pleasant scene.

Delicate porcelain cups, saucers, and crisp white linen napkins rested on the coffee table between Willow and Madame Gauthier. The two women began a friendly conversation, Willow listening with apparent enthusiasm as the director told her about some of the additional changes she'd been implementing at St. Anne's since she was put in charge.

Razor wasn't paying much attention to anything being said. He waited with growing impatience for Madame Dupont to deliver the tea so he and Willow could get the hell out of there. His acute Breed hearing picked up the sounds of busyness in the kitchen somewhere on the first floor of the large townhouse, but as the minutes dragged on his annoyance grew.

As did his sense that something was wrong.

His hackles prickled with suspicion. He was about to stalk out of the sitting room to look for the old woman when she toddled in carrying a silver service tray.

Issuing hasty apologies and excuses in French, she set the tray on the edge of the coffee table and began to pour the tea. She seemed nervous, casting uneasy glances at Razor as she hurried to deliver the refreshments to the women.

Her hand caught the edge of Willow's filled cup and tipped it, spilling the tea across the table. "Oh, no! Sorry, sorry!"

"It's okay," Willow assured her. "Here, I'll help you."

Razor took a step forward, his muscles tense as the old woman continued uttering apologies in French while she hastened to clean up her mess.

Madame Gauthier let out a sympathetic sigh. "It's all right, Estelle. Just a little spill, although there went most of the pot."

"I make more," the old woman said in broken English. "I will hurry."

"No." Razor's stern interruption made all three female gazes swing toward him. The idea of a further delay made all his battle instincts clang with alarm. "No more tea. Willow, we need to leave. Now."

Something wasn't right. He'd had that feeling even before Madame Dupont dumped half the pot of tea over the table. Now, he was certain.

The serving woman's anxious glance at her wristwatch only confirmed his suspicions. As did the beads of perspiration gathering above her lips.

He lunged for her. "What the fuck are you up to?"

"What is the meaning of this?" Madame Gauthier gasped, aghast as Razor bore down on her employee. "Take your hands off her at once!"

"Razor," Willow said, her eyes wide with shock. "What's going on?"

"She's done something." He glowered at the gray-haired woman in his grasp. "You're trying to keep us here. Taking forever to bring the tea, then conveniently spilling it so you need to make more."

"Non! Non, sil vous plais!" A string of panicked denials spilled off the old woman's tongue in French. Terror filled her face, but all it did was fortify her guilt.

If Willow hadn't been sitting there to witness his fury, he would've let his talons convince the woman to tell him what he wanted to know—right before he tore her head off her shoulders.

"You called someone," he guessed, zero room for doubt in his mind. "Tell me who you're working with."

Madame Gauthier looked thoroughly confused. "What are you talking about? Estelle, what is the meaning of this?"

Her colleague continued blubbering excuses and lies, vigorously shaking her head. At the same moment, the muffled sounds of someone infiltrating the townhouse from the back brought Razor's head up sharply. Multiple someones.

"Fuck."

He knew the rear alley access point was a vulnerability as he'd looked down at it from the window upstairs. Now, his dread was confirmed.

With no further use for Madame Dupont, he gave her skull a violent twist in his hands. Madame Gauthier let out a horrified scream as the lifeless body dropped to the floor.

The boots that had been stealthily moving into the house rushed inward at full tilt, accompanied by the sounds of weapons jangling.

Four or five heavily armed men by Razor's guess.

He grabbed Willow's wrist. "Stay behind me. If they want you, they need to come through me first."

He knew more than a hundred different ways to kill

a man with his bare hands but he wished to fuck he had a gun on him too. Feeling Willow at his back and knowing any one of the intruders' rounds could have her name on it made his blood boil with battle rage.

His talons erupted from his fingertips. In his mouth, his fangs punched out of his gums. His gaze burned red even before the first gunman in black fatigues stepped into his line of sight.

The bastard came in shooting. Except he wasn't firing regular bullets.

The man leading the charge was armed with something even worse.

Ultraviolet rounds.

Razor had only a split second to react as soon as he saw the pale glow of light inside the bullet ripping toward him. He dodged out of range, feeling the bullet scorch his bicep as it tore past him and narrowly missed. He went airborne, pouncing on the human gunman in a flash of movement. His talons shredded flesh and bone as the rest of the assailants opened fire with standard rounds.

He took a few hits in the seconds it cost him to twist the UV weapon's muzzle into a pretzel. The fresh bullet wounds were merely an annoyance in the face of his concern for Willow's safety.

The cacophony of more gunfire filled the air. One of the intruders in black shouted to another. "Get the woman!"

He abruptly fell silent. Razor slashed the man to pieces in one swipe of his talons. Then he ran through a third in the next instant, reveling in the blood and gore that painted the walls because it meant there were only two assholes left with a chance to get near Willow.

He would have liked nothing more than to coat the whole damned townhouse with these assailants' lives, but impatience got the better of him. Retracting his talons, he grabbed one of the dead men's semiautos and fired twice—a lethal round for each of them.

The attack was over almost as quickly as it began.

Bloodied corpses littered the sitting room and hallway outside, the carnage cloaked in gun smoke and sudden silence. Razor pivoted, his gaze searching out Willow.

She ran to him on a jagged cry, wrapping her arms around his torso. She looked him over in a frantic rush, choking on a sob. "Razor . . . oh, fuck. You're bleeding. How many times were you hit?"

"I'm okay." Better that he was sporting several gunshot wounds than reduced to ash by a single UV round. He hated to think how close he'd come to that. One lucky shot would have ended him and sent Willow into enemy hands. He smoothed her mussed hair, one arm looped around her. "Don't worry about me. I'll heal. Are you all right?"

"Yes." She gave him a wobbly nod, then turned her head and sucked in a breath. "Oh, no. Madame Gauthier . . ."

Razor hadn't been the only one struck in the attack.

An ugly, growing bloom of blood covered the shelter director's chest. Her face was slack and pale, her lips turning bluer by the second. She was mortally wounded, fading fast.

Willow pulled away from Razor's loose embrace to go to the woman.

"Willow, we should go," he cautioned her. "There's no time to waste."

"No." She swung a hard look at him. "She had nothing to do with this. You heard her confusion, Razor. She's innocent. I can't let her die in front of my eyes."

On the stairwell leading to the second floor, the pair of Breedmate girls crept down from their room. They screamed and burst into tears as soon as they saw the carnage, and their beloved director lying lifeless on the sitting room floor.

Razor cursed, moving to corral them before they came all the way down. "It's all right. It's over now. You're safe."

They broke into hysterics, both of them inconsolable. Given little choice, he tranced the girls with a light touch of his palm to their foreheads then sent them back upstairs to bed. By the time he returned to Willow's side in the other room she was already at work trying to heal the fallen director.

Razor watched, amazed at Willow's calmness and care. Her hands rested on the gaping gunshot wound, a warm glow building beneath her palms. Being near so much human blood was a torment to his Breed senses, but he couldn't tear himself away from Willow's side if he tried.

Gradually, the stain that had been growing on Madame Gauthier's torso slowed, then stopped spreading. Her face, which had been going from pale blue to ashen white, began to regain a little color. Her breathing increased, lifting her chest as she started taking in more air. Her eyes flickered beneath her closed lids, then blinked open.

Sucking in a sharp breath, she attempted to sit up. She saw the blood covering her body and the large hole in her blood-soaked clothing. Her eyes went wide. "I've been shot. Those men with guns—"

"They can't hurt anyone now," Willow gently assured her. "You're safe. We all are, thanks to Razor."

"My girls." Madame Gauthier levered herself up from the floor. A jagged cry tore from her mouth as she quickly scanned the aftermath of the attack. "I have two residents upstairs. I need to make sure nothing happened to them."

"The girls are fine," Razor interjected. "They're back in their beds, sleeping peacefully. I tranced them just a minute ago. They won't wake up until morning."

Willow glanced at him, sympathy shining in her tender gaze. "This is going to haunt them for the rest of their lives. They'll never be the same after what happened here."

Razor could hear the regret in her voice, and he knew she spoke from experience. He wished he could erase her memories of the violence she'd endured at an even younger age. Too much time had passed for him to help Willow, but he could offer some small mercy to the Breedmate girls upstairs.

He reached out and caressed her cheek. "I'll see to it they don't recall any of what happened here tonight."

"Thank you," she murmured, leaning into his touch for a brief moment before returning her attention to Madame Gauthier. "Are you in any pain?"

"N-no." The woman glanced at her healed wound in disbelief. "I don't understand. I was sure I felt my life slipping away."

"Willow brought you back," Razor said. "I hope you won't make us regret it. Who were those men?"

"I don't know. I swear it." Her gaze strayed to the very dead Madame Dupont. "You accused Estelle of calling them here. Why? What could she have to do with any of this?"

Willow glanced at Razor before deciding to answer. "Someone had my sister killed. Now, they're after me."

"Oh, no." The older woman grasped Willow's bloodstained hand. "I am so very sorry. And you think Estelle was involved in something as terrible as that? But why? What could she possibly have to gain?"

Razor grunted. "We'll never know now. Could've been money. Could've been coercion. Whatever her reasons, she called those bastards here."

Madame Gauthier closed her eyes and silently spoke a prayer before looking at Willow and Razor with firm resolve. "I don't know how to apologize for Estelle's betrayal. Or for what happened to your sister, Willow. If there is anything I can do to help make some of this right . . ."

"There is," Razor said. "First, I'm going to get Willow out of here. You said the Order funds the shelter now?"

"That's right. For the past several years now."

"Good. Then I want you to call your contacts with them and tell them what happened. They'll send someone out to handle everything from there. Tell them I'll be in touch to explain when I can, and nothing more. Do you understand?"

She nodded agreeably. "I understand."

While he had his own back channels to the Order, after what happened here tonight he didn't want anyone else calling the shots when it came to Willow and her wellbeing. No one was getting near that flash drive she'd found in her old room, either. It wasn't that he didn't trust the warriors of the Order—in fact, aside from his own brothers, the Order members were the only other individuals he knew who couldn't be swayed by promises of money or power.

But he wasn't ready to go there yet.

Someone had just tried to light him up with an industrial-sized dose of UV so they could get their hands on Willow. This shit was beyond personal now.

Until he uncovered whatever was on Laurel's flash drive, this fight belonged to him.

As he moved to retrieve a few weapons off the corpses littering the floor, Willow helped Madame Gauthier get to her feet.

"What about my poor girls upstairs?" the director asked. "What'll I do about them?"

"They're fine," Razor said, stowing a semiautomatic pistol in the back waistband of his pants. "They'll be asleep until noon tomorrow. That should give the Order plenty of time to come in and clean up. Before we go, I'm going to scrub their memories of tonight. They won't remember a thing that happened here."

"Thank you—both of you." She looked at Willow once more. "Are you sure you'll be safe if you leave? Where will you go, dear?"

"Never mind where she's going." Despite the woman's apparent innocence, Razor practically growled at her well-meaning question. "If more men like these follow us before we're out of the city I'll be coming back to look for you—and you won't see me coming until it's too late."

Madame Gauthier swallowed hard, her eyes wide. "I only meant—"

"I don't care what you meant. Just do what I told you." He glanced at Willow. "I'm going to deal with the girls upstairs. I only need a couple minutes. Then we're out of here."

She nodded. "Okay."

He stared at her, feeling something break loose inside him at the sight of all the blood that covered her hands and clothing. Not her blood, thank fuck. But all it did was remind him of how damned close he'd just come to losing her forever.

Before he could think better of the idea, he crossed the body-strewn floor in two strides and pulled her into his arms. She crushed against him, making his gunshot wounds scream in protest.

He didn't care. Right now, she was the only thing that mattered.

Willow had survived the attack unharmed. She was still breathing, still warm and soft against him. Feeling her in his embrace made him feel the strangest sense of profound relief . . . and bone-deep terror.

She was safe for now.

She was alive.

He was grateful as hell for that particular miracle. But coming this close to losing her had made him certain of one thing he didn't fully understand until now: If anything ever happened to this precious woman, he would burn down the whole fucking world in his fury.

CHAPTER 14

They left out the back of St. Anne's after Razor took care of mind-scrubbing the two Breedmate girls.

Willow could still feel his strong arms wrapped around her as they stepped out into the cool night. He had been gruff with Madame Gauthier and utterly merciless with Estelle Dupont. To say nothing of the five heavily armed men he'd slain with his bare hands. And those monstrous talons.

If Willow had wondered about the breadth of his lethal abilities as a former Hunter, tonight all her questions had been answered in vivid, brutal detail.

Yet she felt no fear for him as she exited the townhouse at his side.

What she felt was a profound sense of gratitude. She felt connected to him in a way she hadn't allowed herself to until she'd stepped into his embrace in the aftermath of the attack and realized he was holding her just as tightly. More so, even.

It was overwhelming, all the things she was feeling for Razor—feelings that had been building and deepening into an emotional bond she couldn't deny.

She watched him make a quick check of their assailants' SUV, which was parked in the alley. Even in the thin moonlight she could see the blood leaking from his wounds. Not that it stopped him or even slowed him down a little.

"You need to let me heal you, Razor."

"I told you, I'm good." It was the same thing he'd said when she voiced her concern inside the shelter moments ago. She knew him well enough to understand he'd probably power through even a near-mortal injury, but that didn't make her worry any less.

He finished rummaging through the vehicle, closing the door with a low curse. "It's clean. No IDs, no registration. Nothing to indicate who they were or who they might've worked for. They're fucking ghosts."

He'd searched the bodies inside and had found more of the same.

Raking a hand over his jaw, he turned to face her. "I didn't see any tracking devices, but it's too much to risk taking their vehicle."

Willow took the flash drive out of her pocket. "What do we do with this?"

He held out his hand. "I'll keep it safe for you." When she hesitated, his gaze held hers. "Do you trust me?"

She nodded, realizing she trusted him more than anyone now. She gave him the drive and he put it in his front pocket. "We can't use the train or any other public transit when we don't know if there are more men like them lurking around the city. We're going to have to hoof it for a while."

"It's okay. I can walk." She frowned, looking at his alarming collection of gunshot wounds. "Are you sure you can?"

He stepped forward and tenderly cupped her cheek in his palm. Rather than answer, he leaned down and kissed her. It was only a momentary brush of his lips against hers, but the contact left her smoldering with desire.

When he drew back, his eyes were glittering with amber sparks. "Let's get moving. I want to get as far out of the city as possible before we draw any more unwanted attention. Won't be easy to do that when we're both covered in blood."

Willow's hands were clean, but her white peasant top and faded jean shorts were stained dark red and sticky from her work on Madame Gauthier. "There's a second-hand clothing shop not far from here, but it's probably closed for the night by now."

"Show me."

They kept to the smaller streets, bypassing the main thoroughfare which was alive with traffic and pedestrians at close to 8PM. After a few minutes of weaving through the thickly settled city neighborhoods, Willow spotted the small resale shop nestled between a dry cleaner and another space with a *For Lease* sign in the front window.

As she suspected, the second-hand store had closed a couple hours earlier. Razor didn't seem fazed by that fact at all. He led her around to the service door on the rear alley of the small retail block, where he proceeded to open the locked steel door with the power of his mind.

Willow smiled. "That's a handy trick."

He shot her a wry, meaningful look. "I have many hidden talents."

Silently opening the door, he motioned for her to hang back as he stepped across the threshold and peered into the darkened shop. Then he glanced back at her with a nod. "No one's here, but stay close to me anyway."

She did as he said, following him inside. The place smelled faintly of incense and the acrid smell of the dry cleaner next door. They passed a tiny washroom, then a pair of curtained fitting rooms and the payment counter on the opposite side, the floorboard creaking under their footsteps as she and Razor walked farther into the shop. Circular racks of hanging garments took up most of the floor space allowing only a tangle of tight walkways between them.

Willow gravitated toward a collection of flowy blouses but Razor shook his head. "Pick something boring and dark. All the better if it's warm. We could be outside for a while, and it'll be cold this far north."

She nodded, drifting to a different rack while he studied her from where he stood near a table of folded men's flannel shirts. "You need to try to blend in, Willow—although that's not going to be easy."

"Why not?"

"Because you're a woman who stands out." He frowned, his gaze drinking her in like a caress. "Do you even realize how beautiful you are?"

Although his compliment made her heart stutter, she scoffed quietly and glanced away from him. "Laurel was the beautiful one," she admitted, busying herself with the rack of oversized sweatshirts in front of her. "Yes, I know, we were identical twins but if you looked close enough there were differences. Her eyes were a brighter green than mine. She didn't have as many freckles. She was always smarter than me, prettier, thinner . . ."

Willow was so accustomed to cataloguing her flaws compared to her sister, she was still reciting the long list when she realized Razor had crossed the small shop and was standing right beside her.

"Don't do that," he said, his voice low and solemn. "Not with me. I see you, Willow. *You,* with your gorgeous eyes and those fucking adorable freckles."

He reached out, smoothing his thumb over the ones on her cheek as he tilted her face up toward his. "You," he murmured, "with that resourceful, clever, stubborn brain of yours, and your angelic face that's had me twisted into knots from the moment I saw you for the first time."

Willow swallowed, caught completely off-guard by the sincerity in his tone. In the raw honesty she saw in his brutal, handsome face.

His hand left her chin to trail down the side of her arm, then onto her hip. "And these curves?" He exhaled a sound that seemed to be half-moan, half-sigh. "Don't even get me started on what your soft, sexy curves do to me."

"Razor . . ."

One small step brought her body right up against his. He didn't move. He didn't pull back from her, didn't remove his hand from where it still rested on her hip. He didn't even seem to be breathing from what she could tell.

But his eyes lit with amber sparks, crackling hot as

he stared into her gaze.

Willow reached up, sliding her hands around the back of his neck and rising onto her toes until her mouth met his. She kissed him, unable to stop herself.

The things he'd just said, the way he'd looked at her, the yearning he ignited inside her every time she was near him . . . it was all too much. Compounded with the relief she felt to be able to touch him now and feel his warm, strong body against her, she could have kissed him forever.

Except she didn't miss the slight flinch of his muscles as he brought his arms around her and kissed her back.

He'd been denying the gravity of his wounds, but she knew. He was in agony. His Breed genetics may be working to heal him on their own, but she couldn't allow him to suffer another minute when she had the ability to help him.

He leaned into their kiss with a moan, his mouth moving hungrily over hers. The sharp points of his fangs grazed her lip as his tongue slid between her parted teeth. She wasn't sure how she expected to keep her concentration focused on healing him when every cell in her body was lighting up with arousal, but she gently moved her hands from around his neck and brought her palms down onto the solid planes of his chest.

He kissed her harder, more feverishly, as she opened her mouth to him and mentally called upon her Breedmate talent to heal. A small vibration built beneath her fingers as the mending power awoke and began to flow into him.

Razor drew in a breath, his big body stilling against her. "Willow."

"Shh," she soothed him. "Shut up and let me do this for you."

He slowly drew away from her. Although his brows were harsh, furrowed slashes over the blazing amber of his eyes, the look on his face was pure wonder. He stared at her as she worked on each wound, his gaze boring into her with unspoken awe.

Willow watched with satisfaction as each of his injuries knit together with fresh, healthy skin. "How does that feel?"

"Better," he admitted, his voice gruff and low. "Almost as good as your mouth felt on me."

Heat suffused her cheeks. "I liked the feel of your mouth on me too."

The sound he made in the back of his throat was almost animal, a deep purr that sent shivers of electricity through her. He reached for her hands, and instead of drawing her back into his arms, he gently pulled her touch away from him.

"I think you'd better stop touching me now. I'm healed enough, and we need to keep moving before they send more men after us. Next time, they're going to know to show up armed with more than just one UV weapon if they want to take me down."

"UV?" Willow gaped at him.

He gave her a grim nod. "They didn't come to play. Those first few shots they took at me were with ultraviolet rounds. Bullets I can handle. All it would've taken was one lucky shot of UV to ash me."

"Oh, my God." Her heart clenched at the thought. She'd been so relieved they had both survived, but she hadn't even known the worst of it. "Who would make such an awful weapon to use against you?"

"There are plenty of people who'd prefer the Breed no longer existed. Most of them have been dealt with in recent years by the Order, but hatred for our kind runs deep. It probably always will."

"I'm sorry, Razor." She slowly shook her head, realizing it hadn't been so long ago that she might have counted herself among that number. Her sister Laurel too.

In the space of a couple days, she'd come to view Razor as not only her ally and protector, but as the sole person she could trust.

She was coming to view him as something much more than any of those things.

Judging from the solemn look on his handsome face as he gazed at her now, she felt she was coming to mean something more to him as well.

His hand came to rest tenderly on the side of her face. "Thank you for healing me."

"Anytime," she whispered, still grappling with the thought of just how close to death he'd been tonight.

He leaned forward, but instead of claiming her mouth in another scorching kiss, he pressed his lips to her forehead. "Think you can find something ugly to wear in here?"

After changing clothes and using the washroom to clean up, they grabbed a couple of jackets off the racks and prepared to leave. Razor had traded his black leather for a pair of jeans and a thick plaid shirt over a black T-shirt. At his direction, Willow donned loose denim, a thermal long-sleeve and an oversized olive hoodie sweatshirt that hung halfway down her thighs and made her look like a drab dumpling.

"Perfect," he said, smirking at her.

He, on the other hand, looked like a big, sexy Breed lumberjack who was about to go chop down a forest with his bare hands.

"I'll take your old clothes," he said, stowing them under his arm along with his own.

As she slung her purse onto her shoulder, Razor transferred the flash drive to the pocket of his jeans. Then he pulled several bills out of his pocket and left the money on the counter as they walked out of the shop.

Stone-cold killer and a Breed male to boot, yet he was courteous enough to pay for the second-hand clothes rather than steal them. She smiled and shook her head, watching him ditch their ruined garments in a dumpster out back.

He frowned. "Why are you looking at me like that?"

"I'm just trying to figure you out," she said, not even trying to conceal her fascination over all the intriguing contradictions he posed. "You're not what I expected. Who does all this for someone they'd never even seen until two days ago? You're a good man, Razor."

"No, I'm not." He gave her a look that seemed more conflicted than flattered. "And you shouldn't try to figure me out. You'll only be disappointed."

With that, he closed the dumpster lid and turned away from her. "We'd better get moving."

His abrupt change of mood troubled her, but even that mercurial side of him was becoming familiar to her. Comfortable, in fact. She fell in beside him, walking swiftly to keep up with his long-legged pace. "Where can we go now?"

"This far north? Not a lot of options. Fewer now that we know we've likely got eyes on us here." He gave her a brief sidelong glance. "There'll be more where they came from, so we need to stay ahead of them while we can."

She nodded, trying not to relive the carnage back at St. Anne's. At least Madame Gauthier and the two residents at the shelter tonight were safe. Willow had never felt much affection toward Estelle Dupont even as a girl, yet the woman's betrayal cut deep.

What on earth had Laurel been mixed up in to warrant so much bloodshed and death?

As glad as Willow was to have recovered the hidden flash drive her sister left for her to find, part of her was terrified to know what it contained.

Her thoughts were a tumbling mess of doubt and dread as she hurried through the city alongside Razor. Up ahead the bright lights of a corner gas station and convenience store glowed a milky white against the darkness. Razor headed that way, his gaze trained on the large semi-truck refueling at one of the pumps.

"Maine license plates," he murmured as they neared the station. He paused in the shadows of the convenience store building and glanced at Willow. "Stay put for a minute while I go talk to the driver."

He didn't give her a chance to question him. Setting off at a determined pace, he walked up to the rumpled, sixty-something old man at the fuel pump. Willow saw the edge of uncertainty on the driver's face when he first saw the huge male approaching him. He soon relaxed, giving a consenting nod as Razor took out a sizable amount of cash and handed it to him.

The money disappeared into the old man's jacket pocket as Razor jogged across the concrete to Willow. "We've got a ride out of Quebec City. He's agreed to take us across the border into Maine."

"What are we going to do once we get there?"

"Find somewhere safe to lie low for awhile." Razor took her hand in his. "Come on. Let's get out of here."

CHAPTER 15

The trucker did as agreed, letting Razor and Willow ride along for the roughly two hours from Quebec City to the small border crossing into the U.S. at St. Zacharie, Maine.

Razor's two hundred dollars cash bought the transport and another two hundred to the rural station attendant on duty at the border purchased entry back into the States with no questions asked.

It was closing in on 10PM as the truck rolled along the forested stretch of an unpaved, narrow two-lane highway through the North Maine Woods. Razor sat in the passenger seat of the spacious sleeper cab, while Willow perched silently on the edge of the bunk in back.

Although she projected an air of calm, he knew she was anxious and uncertain. Little wonder, considering everything that had happened to her over the past few days. That kiss back in the second-hand shop probably wasn't helping the situation for her. It sure as fuck wasn't helping Razor to keep his head screwed on straight.

Damn, how he wanted her.

His body was still pulsing with need, his blood still running hot and electric with the memory of her lips on his. It was all he could do to stay focused on the endless ribbon of roadway when everything male in him was laser-trained on the woman seated just barely out of reach behind him.

"Can't say we see a lot of your kind up this way," the trucker said, one of few attempts at smalltalk he'd made since they got into the cab. "You got somewhere in particular you're headed?"

"No." Razor grunted the reply without elaborating.

As innocuous as the old man seemed, the less anyone knew about their movements, the better. Either way, the trucker would be getting a quick mind-scrub as a bonus as soon as he dropped them off.

Razor did have someplace particular in mind, in fact. He wasn't sure he'd be welcomed with open arms, especially considering he'd be arriving with a Breedmate female in tow and an apparent target on both their backs. Hell, he shouldn't even consider dragging his problems to someone else's door, but it wasn't as if he had a lot of other options.

If was only his neck on the line he'd take his chances elsewhere, but not when it came to Willow.

Hopefully, his brother would understand.

Razor stared out the windshield with his jaw set. If Knox wouldn't give them shelter, there might not be any other choice than to reach out to the Order for help he wasn't sure he'd get after the mess he left for them at St. Anne's.

Up ahead about a half mile a wooden sign came into view, its hand painted lettering illuminated by the truck's headlights: *Welcome to Parrish Falls.*

"You can drop us at the corner up there," Razor instructed the old man.

The trucker nodded, slowing his rig on the empty road as they neared the center of what purported itself to be a town but seemed like little more than a quiet crossroad and a tiny diner.

Despite the late hour, the lights were on inside the small eatery. The golden glow pierced the darkness like a cheery little beacon amid the vastness of the wooded landscape that crowded in from all directions.

Razor glanced behind him at Willow. "You hungry?"

Although she looked wary of the abrupt pit stop in the middle of nowhere, she nodded without asking all the questions that lurked in her eyes. She trusted him completely; that much was clear. He just hoped to hell her faith wasn't misplaced.

The trucker braked to a smooth stop and put the vehicle in park. "You're not gonna find another ride out of here until tomorrow," the old man advised while Razor helped Willow climb out of the passenger side of the cab. "For the right price, I'd be willing to take you folks clear on to Millinocket where you can catch the Interstate."

"Here is good enough," Razor said. Once Willow was outside, he stepped back up into the truck. "Almost forgot something."

The trucker frowned. "What's tha—?"

Razor placed his hand on the human's furrowed brow, trancing him. "You never saw us. In a minute you're going to drive on to wherever you're heading and forget tonight ever happened."

He would have preferred to mind scrub the border station attendant too, but at least that loose end didn't know where he and Willow had ended up. He jumped back down to the road beside Willow.

"Come on," he said. "Let's cross the road before he comes out of his trance. He'll assume he just pulled over for a quick doze before continuing on his way."

Taking her hand in his, he led her across the gravel two-lane. "What are we doing here, Razor?"

"With any luck, getting you a warm meal."

The sign on the entrance had been flipped to *Closed* but the door was still unlocked. Razor pushed it open, the bell overhead jingling as he and Willow stepped inside.

"We closed ten minutes ago," an amicable female voice called out from somewhere inside. "If you want coffee for the road, go ahead and have a seat. I'll brew a fresh pot."

Razor motioned Willow to sit down at the counter but he remained standing as the woman who invited them in came back through the swinging doors from the kitchen.

She held an empty ceramic coffee cup in one hand and a glass coffee carafe in the other. Her pretty face and warm hazel eyes matched the welcoming tone of her voice. Her dark hair was swept up into a messy bun at her nape and she wore a loose, thick-knit sweater over a girly floral skirt that fell just shy of her shearling-lined ankle boots.

Most notably, her belly was round and very heavy with child.

"You must be Leni," Razor said, offering her a fond

smile.

He'd never met his brother's Breedmate in person, but they'd spoken on the phone once, more than six months ago now when Knox and Leni had run into trouble of their own. Razor had been in touch on and off with Knox in the time since, but nothing recent.

Lenora Calhoun stared at him for a moment. "Um . . . Razor? Where did you—"

At that same moment, the kitchen door swung open again and a big Breed male stepped out, scowling as he dried his hands on a red-gingham dish towel.

Razor locked eyes with his Hunter brother. "Hey, Knox."

He looked different from the last time Razor had seen him, and not only because the former assassin and general badass was currently wearing a white kitchen apron over his dark jeans and untucked flannel shirt.

Knox's dark brown hair, which he'd always shorn close to his skull now fell tousled and loose around his face and neck. His cheeks and square jaw were covered in a thick, short beard that gave him a wolfish quality, made all the more pronounced by the dark slashes of his lowered brows and the laser-bright hue of his grayish blue eyes.

"Sorry for the unannounced arrival," Razor offered.

Without replying, Knox tore off the apron and tossed it onto the counter between them. Then he glanced at Willow and his expression took on a grimmer look.

Razor's brother had been aware of the fact that he'd been keeping an eye on a certain mountain cabin in Colorado for the past several months. Knox had even busted his ass a time or ten about Razor's increasing long-distance obsession with the gorgeous brunette subject of his observation.

What he didn't know—much like Razor himself—was that the woman he was supposed to be watching for Theo Collier and the one Razor had actually been seeing during his months of drone surveillance was her twin sister.

He felt a sudden jolt of dread that Knox might say something stupid about that covert assignment before Razor had a chance to explain himself to Willow on his own time.

Awkwardly, he cleared his throat. "This is Willow Valcourt. Willow, meet my brother, Knox, and his mate, Leni."

"Hello," she murmured to the couple.

"Hi, Willow." Leni smiled, sliding easily under the shelter of her mate's muscled arm.

Knox gave Willow a curt nod of greeting, but his gaze immediately swung back to Razor. "I'm going to guess this isn't a social call."

As always, his brother cut right to the chase. "I didn't have anywhere else to go, or I would have."

Another tight nod, then Knox shot a glance toward the diner's front door and the lock clicked into place on his mental command. "We shouldn't talk here in the open. The house is around back. Follow me."

Razor helped Willow off the counter stool, then they stepped into the kitchen behind Knox and Leni. The diner lights went dark along the way, Knox using the power of his mind to lock the back door once they'd all exited to the rear of the place.

The white, two-story hip-roofed farmhouse stood a short walk behind the diner. The house was likely close to a couple centuries old but had been lovingly cared for, judging by the tidy exterior and the well-tended landscaping that framed the wraparound, covered porch. Hanging flower baskets were overflowing with cheery blooms on either side of the front door.

Razor never would have guessed Knox for the white picket fence type, but the home he and his mate shared was the epitome of cozy, small-town charm. He wouldn't have figured Knox to be helping out in the diner's kitchen either, yet somehow the life he'd made with Leni seemed to fit the big male now.

They entered the house, walking behind Knox and Leni down a short central hallway and into a cozy little kitchen in back. His brother turned on a large pendant light that hung over the center of a small breakfast table, then indicated the chairs situated around it.

They all sat down, Knox taking the chair directly across from Razor and eyeing him with suspicion under the spotlight overhead. Fitting, since this brotherly reunion was likely to turn into an interrogation.

"Never expected to see you this far north, Raze. What kind of trouble are you in?"

"It's serious," Razor admitted. "Bunch of assholes tried to ash me with ultraviolet bullets earlier tonight in Quebec City. I figured it was a good idea to get the hell out of there."

Knox's grim expression went even darker. "UV? Fuck. I know you can be a prick, but what'd you do to piss someone off that bad?"

Razor chuckled at the brotherly jab. He understood his brother wasn't pleased with the situation, but hearing him defuse the gravity of it with dark humor went a long way toward reassuring him that his brother would be on his side no matter what. At least, he hoped so.

"Razor didn't do anything to these people," Willow interjected. "They tried to kill him because they're after me now."

Knox's scrutinizing stare slid to her. "After you for what?"

"Willow's sister was murdered a few days ago," Razor said. "Her twin sister . . . in Colorado."

He'd been hoping to pull that laser-focused wolf's gaze back onto him and it worked. Knox frowned. "Her twin sister."

Knox didn't frame it as a question, but there were a hundred of them firing off in the male's shrewd stare.

"Yeah," Razor said. "Willow and Laurel were identical twins. Breedmates."

Leni's voice was tender with sympathy. "Oh, Willow. I'm very sorry for your loss."

Willow's head bobbed in response. Her green eyes shone with pain under the lamplight, but she kept herself together. "Laurel had gotten into some kind of danger in Montreal, evidently. That's where she was living and working until about a year ago. She ran to Colorado to get away from whatever it was and to be close to me, but she didn't run far enough. Somehow they found the cabin she was living in outside town and they . . . they killed her, then burned it down with her inside." Her voice caught on the words. "She was all the family I had."

Leni reached out to her, covering Willow's hand with hers. "I don't know what to say. There are no words for that kind of pain."

"Thank you," she murmured quietly, visibly struggling not to break down.

Razor moved his hand to her back, lightly stroking her and wishing he were better equipped to offer the kind of emotional comfort and support she deserved.

All the while, he felt Knox's gaze boring into him from across the table. "Obviously, there's more to this story," he said. "I think you'd better explain it to me, Raze. Particularly since you've just brought it to my doorstep."

"I will," he said, meeting his brother's eyes. "I'll tell you everything. First, I just need to know if Willow and I can stay for a day or two, until some of the heat on us has a chance to cool down."

"You gonna at least tell me what kind of heat we're talking about? Who's after you two?"

"I don't know. But I do know what they're after." He glanced at Willow, wanting her agreement to share what they'd found at St. Anne's. She gave him a faint nod, then he took the flash drive out of his pocket and placed it in the center of the table. "They're after whatever's on this."

Knox picked up the device and stared at it for a long moment before leaning back on an exhaled curse. "These bastards were willing to ash you for this? What the fuck do you think it contains?"

"No idea, but get me access to a computer and I'm going to do my damnedest to find out."

Willow nodded at the flash drive in Knox's hand. "My sister hid that for me to find in case anything happened to her. I need to know what's on it, and why it cost Laurel her life. If not for Razor coming to Colorado when he did, I'm sure I'd be dead by now too."

She glanced at him, and the warmth of her tender regard cut through him under the weight of his guilt for the truth he still hadn't told her.

Knox grunted, setting the flash drive back on the table. "If it's all right with my mate, our home is yours for as long as you need it."

"Of course, it's all right with me," Leni said. "I'm sorry, I'm being a terrible host. Willow, can I get you anything to eat or drink? I have some cold chicken and potato salad left over from my sister and nephew's visit yesterday afternoon, or I'd be happy to make something else for you instead."

"No, thank you," Willow replied. "I'm fine."

Razor slipped the drive into his pocket and looked at her. "You said you were hungry when we stopped here."

She started to shake her head, but Leni abruptly stood up. "Well, I could have a little something. I'm going to get the food, and maybe you'll join me. Besides, I have a feeling the guys have some catching up to do."

"Yeah, we do." Knox lifted his chin at Razor as he got up from the table. "Come on out to the garage with me. You can finish explaining what's going on out there."

CHAPTER 16

Although Willow had been reluctant to impose on Leni any more than she already was, she found herself relaxing easily into the other woman's company as the two of them nibbled on cold fried chicken and creamy potato salad at the small breakfast table.

"This is delicious, Leni. Thank you."

"My pleasure." She gave Willow a warm smile. "No one has to twist my arm to eat lately. Seems like I'm hungry twenty-four-seven now that this little guy's arrival is getting close."

"When are you due?"

"Four and a half weeks." She beamed as she spoke, resting her palm atop the large swell of her belly. "I don't know who's more excited to meet our son, Knox or me."

Willow smiled, struggling to picture the immense, scary-looking Breed male who'd practically stared holes through Razor across the table in the role of doting father. Then again, if Knox's obvious adoration of his pretty mate were any indication, their child was going to be welcomed into a home filled with warmth and love.

"How did you and Knox meet?" Willow asked, taking another bite of chicken.

"Oh, it's a long story. He showed up here in Parrish Falls last winter during a time when I was going through some . . . difficulty with my nephew's father and his family. Knox kept Riley and me safe when no one else could have. He protected us, saved my life more than once."

Willow nodded in acknowledgment. "Razor's already done the same for me."

"I can't say I'm surprised. He and Knox are both good men, despite what they may tell you—or what they've been taught to believe about themselves."

"You're talking about the Hunter program? Razor told me he was born into that awful laboratory and that he'd escaped with some of his brothers when he was very young. He hasn't said much more than that, though."

"These aren't men who easily talk about their feelings or what they've endured. There are still things that Knox won't talk about with me," Leni said, a shared understanding in her voice. Her gaze lingered on Willow, studying her with quiet intensity. "You care about him very much, don't you?"

Willow hesitated to answer, even though the truth of how she felt about Razor sat at the tip of her tongue. "We hardly know each other. It's only been a few days."

Leni's expression softened. "Still, when you know, you know. Time is irrelevant when it comes to the heart."

"It sounds like you're speaking from personal experience. Is that how it was with you and Knox?"

She nodded. "I was drawn to him immediately, even though getting involved with a seemingly dangerous man was the last thing I ever thought I'd want. My sister had gotten mixed up with dangerous men and it nearly cost Shannon her life. But Knox was different. As lethal as he is, he's even more honorable and kind. He's protective of the few people he allows into his heart. I'd only known him a matter of minutes before he came to my defense in the diner the first night he arrived. We've been together ever since, and in that time he's shown me his goodness in a thousand different ways."

Willow couldn't help but smile at her new friend's obvious joy. "I'm happy for you, Leni."

An inquisitive light shone in the woman's hazel eyes. "We weren't supposed to be talking about me. I'd asked how you feel about Razor—unless you don't want to tell me. Sorry, I've never been much good at socializing. If I'm prying, just—"

"No, it's okay," Willow said. "It's actually nice being able to sit and chat around a kitchen table like this. It's the first time I've felt something close to normal these past few days."

Leni nodded sympathetically. "Have you and Razor been on the run this whole time?"

"Yes. It was too dangerous to stay in Colorado after . . ." She couldn't finish the thought. Leni reached out and squeezed her hand reassuringly, giving Willow a chance to find her voice again. "My sister secretly rented a storage unit. She gave me the key, saying if anything ever happened to her I should open it, that I'd know what to do once I did."

"She knew she was in danger," Leni replied soberly.

Willow nodded. "She refused to confide in me about it. She said it would be safer for me the less I knew. When Razor and I got to the storage unit the only thing inside it was a book. It was ours when we were kids. She'd left me a code in the pages, something only I would know how to solve. The answer sent us to the orphanage in Quebec City where we found that flash drive. Laurel and I once lived there as kids after we lost our parents. A Breedmate shelter."

"Oh." Leni's eyes went a little wider at that. "I didn't realize."

"Yes. I'm a Breedmate."

There was a time, not so long ago, that Willow would've rather swallowed her tongue than accept the fact that she was a Breedmate. Now, sitting here with Leni, a woman who was also part of that rare number and clearly happy to be mated to her Breed partner, made it easier for Willow to start thinking of herself as who—and what—she truly was.

To be honest, it was being with Razor that had brought her the furthest in accepting she'd been born with the teardrop-and-crescent-moon symbol and all the other extraordinary gifts that came with it. Her ability to heal others. Her half-Atlantean blood that was uniquely suited to accept an eternal bond with one of the Breed and bear his children.

All things she had been trying to run away from for as long as she could remember.

And now?

She wasn't ready to consider how she felt about blood bonds and being mated to someone like Razor.

No, not someone *like* him.

Him, specifically.

Since she was being honest with herself about all of that, she also had to consider Razor with a clear eye. It was becoming so easy to let herself feel close to him, to long for something more from him, especially after they had kissed.

The intensity of her emotions and her genuine care for him was making it harder to remember that her Breedmate mark was the reason he was still with her at all, still doing everything in his power to protect her and keep her safe. Without it, she was all but certain he would have left her back at the motel in Cheyenne or somewhere else along the long road they'd traveled together so far.

Still, regardless, he hadn't known about her mark when he helped her escape Colorado. All he'd known then was that she was Laurel Townsend's twin sister and she was in danger. That had been enough for Razor to act.

As for the two of them and where they'd be once Razor had the truth about who had killed Laurel and what had happened to his friend, Willow couldn't guess. Nor did she want to.

She had to mentally shake herself back to the here and now as her silence stretched and her thoughts swirled around all the questions that were in need of answers.

She lifted her gaze to Leni's and gave a mild shrug. "Razor and I are both committed to the same thing—finding out who killed my sister and why. I don't know where we'll go from there."

"Hm." Leni's smile said she suspected otherwise, but

she didn't press.

They ate for a few minutes more, then Willow helped clear the table and load the empty plates into the dishwasher. She couldn't stifle the yawn that overtook her once everything was put away and tidy once more.

"I'm sorry, you must be exhausted," Leni said, drying her hands on a towel and leaning back against the counter. "The guys could be out there for a while yet. Why don't you let me show you to our guest room upstairs? It's not much, just a little attic studio."

"It sounds wonderful to me." After the places she'd slept the past couple of days, or tried to, just being invited into Leni and Knox's home felt like heaven already.

"This way." Leni indicated a back stairwell that opened into the rear of the small kitchen.

Willow followed her up to the cozy apartment located at the top of the stairs. It was tiny but welcoming, its single room containing a bed with a handmade quilt and crisp white linens, a tall antique bureau, and a small writing desk situated beneath a curtained window in back.

"There's a connected bathroom with a shower tub," Leni pointed out. "Knox has made lots of repairs and improvements to the place."

"It's lovely," Willow said.

"I'm glad you like it," Leni said. "Make yourself comfortable for a minute. I'll be right back."

Willow drifted over to the window, which overlooked the backyard lawn and the forest beyond. Moonlight bathed the landscape in soft, milky shades.

Closer to the house, tucked at the end of the unpaved driveway stood the one-car garage where Razor and Knox had gone. A dim light glowed from inside, but the men were nowhere to be seen.

A few moments later, Leni came back holding a small laundry basket containing several items of folded clothing. She placed everything on the end of the bed. "Take what you like and leave what you don't. I won't be offended. Most of this won't fit me for months anyway, so consider it yours to keep. I brought a few things of Knox's for Razor too."

"That's so kind of you, Leni. Thank you." Willow gravitated toward a floral midi-skirt and a chunky oatmeal-colored sweater, pulling both pieces out of the pile.

"Those were some of my favorites too. I think we're fairly close in size—or would've been, before Knox knocked me up." She grinned. "I'll leave you alone now so you can get settled and relax. If you have any things you'd like me to toss in the wash for you, just drop them in the basket and bring them down whenever you want."

"Thank you," Willow said, warmed by her generosity. "Um . . . Leni? How long do you think Razor and Knox might be?"

"Judging from the glower on my mate's face earlier, I'd say they've got quite a bit of catching up to do. I'll let Razor know where you are when they come back in. He can bunk down on the sofa in the living room . . . or not." Leni smiled. "I'll leave the sleeping arrangements up to you two."

With that, she strolled out of the room, quietly closing the door behind her. As her footsteps retreated down the stairs, Willow pivoted toward the window and walked up to it to peer outside. The light still glowed in the garage down below. Overhead, the moon had climbed higher into the night sky as the hour crept closer to midnight.

Willow yawned into her hands and glanced at the bed. As tempting as it was to lie down in her resale shop clothes and sleep for a year, she couldn't stand the idea of crawling into the clean cotton sheets in her current state.

The brief shower she'd taken at the motel in Cheyenne seemed like forever ago considering everything she'd faced in the time since. Washing up in the resale shop restroom had only removed the worst of the blood and grime from her skin.

What she needed was twenty minutes under a hot shower—or, better yet, a long soak in the bathtub.

One of the items Leni had left on the bed was a thick chenille bathrobe. Willow picked it up, savoring the normalcy of the soft fabric and the golden warmth of the cozy room around her.

It felt selfish and indulgent to long for a few minutes of calm, but God, how she needed it right now.

She sat down on the end of the mattress to remove her boots and ankle socks, then, clutching the soft robe against her she padded barefoot across the rug and into the small bathroom to start the water.

CHAPTER 17

Knox hadn't said much as Razor filled him in on the highlights of his past few days and nights on the run with Willow. His Hunter brother listened in grim silence, eyeing Razor with typical, dark intensity from his leaning stance against his workbench in the garage.

Razor cleared his throat after describing the ambush at St. Anne's and the multiple dead bodies he'd been forced to leave there for the Order to clean up in his wake.

Knox grunted, his muscled arms folded against his chest. "The warriors are going to want answers from you about that sooner or later. My money's on sooner."

"Yeah, I know. And they're going to get them—but not until I see this thing through on my own terms. These fuckers tried to ash me. It's personal now."

Knox's icy blue eyes narrowed with scrutiny. "Seems like you've been taking this whole thing personally for a lot longer than that. Going on six months now, if I had to guess. Isn't that about how long you've had an eye in the sky on that little Colorado cabin in the mountains?"

Razor cast his brother a flat look. "I figured you'd come around to that eventually."

"Kind of hard to ignore when it looked like you were sitting on hot coals in the kitchen."

Razor started pacing, suddenly feeling twitchy in the confines of the small garage. "I've let things get kind of fucked up where Willow's concerned."

"No shit," Knox said. "For starters, why are you willfully endangering this woman when you know she's a Breedmate? You should've asked the Order to protect her instead of taking matters into your own hands."

Razor gave a wry scoff. "I seem to recall a similar conversation with you not so long ago."

"That was different. Leni didn't want to leave her home. She had reasons that she needed to be here and not with the Order under their protection."

"They would've found a way to make it work," Razor pointed out. "Anyway, in the end Leni was safest with you, right?"

"Yes, but Travis Parrish and his family weren't coming after me with UV bullets."

"No, they just hired a Hunter to take you both out."

Knox's jaw visibly tightened at the reminder. "I handled the situation."

"I'm handling this one too," Razor said.

"Are you?"

"Yes."

"Is that why you're pacing the garage like a caged cat? You might as well tell me what's got your balls in such a knot. I don't have to use my ability to read your guilt to know you're drowning in it."

His brother's unique gift for uncovering a person's sins with a single touch had to be a burden to him, but even without the extrasensory talent Knox had a way of cleaving right to the heart of a matter. Razor used to think of himself in a similar way, but whatever his skills and sharp intellect, they all seemed to fail him when it came to Willow.

He paused, facing his brother. "She doesn't know about my surveillance of her sister's cabin."

Knox let out a short breath. "Why the fuck not? Seems like that's something she'd want to know. Hell, doesn't she deserve to know?"

Razor nodded. He could hardly argue the point. "Yes, she does. You think I don't realize that?"

Knox's stare felt like a surgical blade. "How many hours did you spend watching that cabin, brother? I saw you myself. Monitoring that mountainside all hours of the day and night. Glued to your screen every time that pretty brunette who lived inside came into the frame. You were obsessed, Razor. Talk about letting things get fucked up—now you're tangled up with her identical twin sister—"

"It wasn't her." Razor's bitten-off reply sliced through his brother's words. "I wasn't watching Willow's sister. I thought I was, but it wasn't her. It was Willow."

Knox frowned. "What?"

"Laurel never left the cabin, not even for supplies. Willow brought everything up the mountain to her sister. Willow was the woman in the Jeep. She's the one I'd been obsessed with, as you so aptly put it. Willow, not her twin."

"You sure?"

He was certain to his marrow. To the core of his being, he knew it was Willow's face seared into his heart and mind. He would have known it even if Willow hadn't confirmed it for him.

"Willow told me she was the only one coming and going from the cabin. Whatever her sister needed, Willow brought it to her. Laurel didn't want to take the risk of leaving and getting caught."

Knox grunted. "But she didn't mind letting her twin take the risk?"

It was a thought that had occurred to Razor too, though he'd been loathe to say it to Willow. He lifted his shoulder in acknowledgment of Knox's comment. "Laurel wouldn't even have to ask, as far as Willow's concerned. Willow adored her sister. She would've done anything for her. No risk would've been too great. There's still nothing Willow wouldn't do for her, even now that Laurel's dead."

Knox didn't say anything for a long moment, just studied Razor while he spoke. "This woman has really gotten to you. I enjoyed busting your balls about it whenever I caught you watching her back at the Darkhaven in Florida, but this is something else. Whatever's going on between you and Willow, whatever you're feeling for her, it's real, isn't it?"

Razor heaved a sigh. "I'm not equipped for relationships, Knox. You of all people should understand that."

"I do. I also know that equipped or not, you'll figure it out. Telling Willow the truth seems like a good place to start."

"You don't get it," Razor said. "All her life Willow's

lived in her twin's shadow. She's grown up believing Laurel was smarter than her, better than her, more deserving of a good life. How's she going to react when I tell her I've had a drone on her sister's cabin for the past several months? She's going to think the same thing you did—that I was obsessed with her twin, or worse, that I still am. The fact that I didn't tell her right upfront only makes me look guiltier."

"All the more reason to clear the air now, not later."

Razor knew he was right. He'd never been a coward, yet the idea of hurting Willow by telling her the truth made his chest feel caught in a vise. She had already been through more pain than she deserved. He hated that he would be adding to it in any way.

But Knox had a point. If Razor wanted any kind of relationship with Willow beyond the journey they were on to find her sister's killers, he needed to be honest with her.

Knox strode forward, clapping him on the shoulder. "It's getting late, and I've got a mate waiting for me inside."

"Yeah," Razor agreed. "Any chance I could pop that flash drive into a computer tonight yet and see what I can find on it?"

"No chance of that in my house," Knox said with a smirk. "I don't have much use for technology up here, but Leni's sister and nephew should be able to help you out tomorrow. Shannon caved and bought Riley a laptop a couple months ago. The kid's only seven, but he already knows more than I do about computers and software."

"In other words, not much?" Razor quipped.

Knox grinned. "Not all of us are born hackers, Raze.

Let's go inside. I'll ask Leni to call Shannon in the morning. Meanwhile, you've got someone waiting on you back in the house too."

They exited the garage together, Knox switching off the small light on the way out. Heading back into the kitchen, they found the room empty, all the dishes cleaned and put away.

"Willow will be upstairs in the attic guest room," Knox said, gesturing to the back stairwell. "Depending on how your conversation goes, you'll find a pull-out sofa in the living room. Good luck, bro."

Razor gave him a one-finger salute and shook his head. He waited until Knox had walked away to head up the front stairwell before he began the climb up to the attic. The door was closed, nothing but silence on the other side.

He hesitated there, debating whether he should disturb Willow or just head down to the living room for the night. His closed fist hovered an inch from the door, then, with a softly muttered curse, he let his knuckles rap lightly against the thick wood panel.

"Willow? You still awake?"

No reply. He stood there for a moment, telling himself to walk away. Just as he was about to turn and head back downstairs, he heard soft movement from inside as Willow approached the door.

She opened it slightly and peered around the panel. "Razor. Sorry, I was getting ready to take a bath when I heard you knock."

Her mass of long brown hair was gathered in a loose twist at the back of her head and her freckled cheeks were flushed like ripe peaches. The shawl collar of a dove-gray flannel robe plunged dangerously low from what he could see through the narrow opening of the door.

Every male cell in his body fired off with instant awareness.

Big mistake coming up to talk to her this late at night.

He'd already seen her naked once before, and the memory of her lovely curves and soft, flawless skin had been living in vivid detail in his head ever since. Now he had the added torment of picturing her stepping into a tub full of frothy bubbles while he was going to be prowling the house like a wraith downstairs.

Fuck. He was going to kill Knox for sending him up to talk to her now instead of waiting until morning.

"I shouldn't have disturbed you," he muttered irritably. "I'll leave you to it."

He turned around, ready to make a hasty retreat.

"Razor, wait." The door creaked open all the way and his boots halted on the top step. When he pivoted back, Willow was standing just inside the room, barefoot and adorable, looking like a dream wrapped in gray flannel. "You were gone quite a while with Knox. How did it go with him?"

"Good. Fine. No problems." The words came out short and staccato, made worse by the roughness of his voice. Christ, could he sound any more dismissive?

Her expression seemed to say she agreed. "Okay, well . . . I just wondered."

Razor ran a hand over his jaw. He didn't want to leave her feeling like she was a bother to him, but he didn't want to have this conversation on the attic steps either. "You should finish up . . . whatever it is you're doing and get some rest. We can talk tomorrow."

"You're sure? I don't mind if you want to come in,"

she said, giving a mild shrug. "I'm too wired for sleep right now, anyway."

The low sound he made in the back of his throat was somewhere between a growl and a groan. If he had any sense, or honor, he'd tell her goodnight and haul his already uncomfortable hard-on down to the living room sofa rather than accept her invitation to step inside. Especially while there was only a scrap of flannel standing between her luscious body and all his dark desires.

All the things he should do went up in flames as he stared at her in her current state of near-undress. "I guess I could come in for a minute."

She stepped back, allowing him to stalk inside before closing the door behind them. "Leni left some clothes for you if you want them."

He grunted, bypassing the open bathroom door where her bubble bath waited to instead glance at the foot of the bed where what looked to be a few items of Knox's clothing lay folded next to some other items apparently given to Willow. Her hoodie and baggy jeans from the second-hand shop in Quebec City lay there too, along with her lacy bra and bikini panties.

The reminder that she was naked under that robe hit his senses like flash fire.

His gaze flared amber at the sweet, warm scent of her that still lingered on her shed clothing, and on the delectable woman standing right next to him. As if she wasn't tempting enough already, he could hear the speeding pace of her heart. Could almost imagine how hot and fragrant her blood would be on his tongue. Not to mention all the other parts of her that he'd been dying to taste.

His fangs erupted from his gums and it was all he could do to hold his craving in check.

"Your brother and his mate seem very nice," she prompted him. "Are you sure Knox is okay with us being here?"

Razor cleared his throat, if only to give him a chance to tamp down the desire that had him in a stranglehold. "He's my brother. He knows I'd do the same for him if the tables were turned."

"You two seem close."

He pivoted to look at her. "Of all my brothers, Knox and I are the tightest."

She nodded. "Where are the others now?"

"Florida. We built a Darkhaven together in the Everglades. Knox lived there too, before he ventured north and ended up here with Leni."

Willow listened quietly, something unreadable in her schooled expression. "Is that where you'll go next? Back home to Florida?"

He lifted his shoulder. "I suppose. Haven't really had time to consider what's next."

His noncommittal response tasted like a flat-out lie when he'd been doing nothing but thinking about what was going to happen after he got the answers—and the retribution—he was after. Going back to the Everglades Darkhaven was the most logical next step, but nothing about his current state of mind was logical.

Standing this close to Willow, seeing the tenderness in her beautiful face as she was looking at him now short-circuited every reasonable thought he had except the one that was hammering like a war drum in his veins.

Mine.

It was the bone-deep reaction he'd had to Willow

Valcourt from the first moment he saw her. Every minute he'd spent with her in the time since had been a test of his self-control. A test of his honor as a man, and as the self-appointed guardian who was determined to ensure her safety and protection.

She was anything but safe with him, especially when she was gazing up at him with those long-lashed eyes that were as green and entrancing as a forbidden forest.

The memory of their all-too-brief kiss in the resale shop came back to him as he got lost in her unflinching gaze. She had wanted him too. That had been revelation enough, but there had been more to her kiss. She cared about him. He'd tasted it on her lips, and in her tender touch as she'd healed him.

He saw all of that in her beautiful eyes now, and more.

She cared about him.

She believed in him. Trusted him more than anyone now.

Her body moved closer at the same time he did, both of them closing the distance as if neither could resist the pull that drew them together. But when her hand came up toward his face he bit off a tight, hissed curse.

"Willow, we need to talk."

Her hand lowered at once and she abruptly glanced away from him. "I know what you're going to say."

His short exhalation was full of self-loathing. "No, I don't think you do."

When her gaze swung back, that endless green forest had become shuttered. "I'm not looking for promises, Razor. I know you have more important things waiting for you somewhere else."

"Ah, fuck." She couldn't have misunderstood his

intent more. He cursed again, furious at himself for how badly he was fucking this whole thing up with her. "Willow, you don't—"

"Please, let me finish," she said, adamant now. "I'm not fooling myself into thinking I'm ever going to have the kind of life your brother and his mate have made together. And that's fine with me. I've never needed much to be happy."

He scowled. "Willow, you deserve . . . everything."

Her smile wobbled as she shook her head. "I'm not going to ask you for that. But after everything that's happened, I just want you to . . . I just need you to stay with me for a little while, Razor. I need something real to hold on to, even if it's just for one night."

Whatever flimsy resolve he wanted to believe he had when it came to this woman crumbled under the raw honesty of her plea. She looked so tender and vulnerable, even though he knew how strong she truly was. He'd seen her strength and courage every minute they'd been together, yet here she stood, opening herself to him in such a painfully honest way it staggered him.

"Willow." He reached out, gently wrapping his hand around her nape. Her skin was hot to his touch and velvety, her tiny veins pulsing against his palm and fingers. Her blood called to his, adding dangerous fuel to the possessive fire already roaring within him. How could she even think he might want something other than what he held in his hands right now?

When he found his voice to speak again, his voice came out as rough as gravel for the depth of his need. "You deserve so much more than I can ever give you, Willow. Being with you like this, touching you, is all I've been thinking about since I first laid eyes on you."

With that, he closed the short distance between them and leaned down to claim her mouth with his.

His kiss was fierce, full of the self-directed anger he felt over the fact that he had given her any room to doubt her worth in his eyes. If he had promises to give her, he would have pledged them all right then and there. All he had to offer was the current moment. Until he'd seen his personal mission through to the end and knew with total certainty that Willow's life was no longer in danger, he couldn't promise her any kind of future—least of all, with him.

He'd never be worthy of her. He knew that. If he were, he'd have already confronted the lie he continued to let grow between them.

He shoved the damning thought out of his mind as he lost himself in the pleasure of Willow's mouth on his.

With one hand still clamped around the back of her neck, he slid his free hand up beneath the loose fabric of her bathrobe. Her skin felt impossibly soft under his fingertips, her sweet curves making him fevered with possessive need. Still kissing her, he traced a path from her hip to the silky underside of her breast. She trembled as he caressed her, a soft moan spilling into his mouth from her parted lips.

He plunged his tongue past her straight little teeth, deep into her mouth. The impulse to claim her, to brand her as his, beat like a hammer in his veins. He groaned with the depth of his desire, his fingers rolling the swollen bud of her nipple into an even tighter peak.

"You're so damn sexy," he growled against her lips. "Do you have any idea how long I've been wanting to feel you like this?"

She couldn't possibly guess how many months he'd

imagined her naked in his arms, in his bed. All the hours she'd been haunting his dreams, even when he was awake. All the times he got hard just looking at her beautiful face in his drone footage, craving the one woman he was certain he could never touch because he believed she belonged to another.

Now, Willow was his.

For tonight, at least, she was his.

Untying the robe's flannel belt, he drew back so he could look at her. His vision was swamped with amber, his pupils no doubt narrowed to thinnest slits in his heightened state of arousal. His fangs throbbed as he drank in the sight of her nudity.

It wasn't enough just to look. He needed to touch. To taste. To claim.

He pushed the robe off her body, running his greedy hands over every lush inch of her. Willow panted softly as he stroked and kissed her, granting him full access to indulge his fevered exploration. He wanted to go slowly for her, but lust had him on a dangerously thin leash.

A low, animalistic sound rumbled up from the back of his throat as he moved his hand down to the juncture of her thighs. "So fucking beautiful. So wet for me already."

The little whimper she gave when his fingers delved into her folds nearly undid him on the spot. So did the searing silkiness of her cleft.

Razor was burning up with the need to be inside her.

There were no pretenses about where they were heading tonight. No need to pretend he had the patience to dance around the idea of fucking her. She wanted it too.

On a snarl, he tore off his flannel shirt and the black

tee under it. As soon as his chest was bared to her, Willow reached for him. Her touch was feverish and hungered, her gaze meeting his with the same depth of need he felt pounding inside himself.

Their mouths came together once more, tongues clashing, hands grasping at each other.

Willow let out a soft groan as she reached for the zipper of his jeans. "I wish I'd had time for my bath first."

"Later," he growled, helping her free him from the rest of his clothing. He ground his molars together so hard when her fingers wrapped around the shaft of his cock it was a wonder they didn't shatter. "Ah, fuck . . . I need to be inside you."

"Yes, you do," she said, giving him a saucy grin.

They went down to the mattress together, Razor covering her with his body. He was dying to bury his cock in her, but the urge to feast on her sent his mouth on a slow path from her lips to the creamy swells of her breasts. As tempted as he was to run his tongue along the silky column of her throat, he knew better than to trust his self-control that far.

Instead he savored her dusky nipples and the satiny smooth skin of her abdomen. Her Breedmate mark rode just a couple of inches above her navel. The first time he'd seen it, he'd been pissed as hell. Now, he traced the tiny crescent moon and teardrop symbol with the tip of his tongue, struck once more by just how extraordinary Willow Valcourt truly was.

Not just because she was a Breedmate.

Because of the incredible woman she was.

A woman for whom he would move heaven and earth to protect.

Mine, his blood screamed inside his head.

"Mine," he growled softly against her skin as he moved lower down her delectable body.

She sucked in a sharp breath as he closed his mouth over her sex, drawing her clit against his tongue. He suckled her, wringing the sweetest sounds from her as she tensed and writhed on the bed. He didn't let up until she came.

Once she had, he prowled back up the length of her, kissing a hot trail to her parted lips. Her head was turned, her lids closed as she spiraled down from the crest of her climax.

"Eyes on me, beautiful," he ordered her in a voice that was thick for the presence of his fangs. "I want to see your face when I make you come this next time."

Her gaze locked with his as he positioned his cock and slowly, inch by inch, pushed inside her to the hilt.

CHAPTER 18

He felt so good inside her, she nearly wept from the pleasure of it.

Willow wasn't a virgin, but the handful of casual, often awkward, times she'd been with other men had left her somewhat ambivalent about the whole notion of sex. Being with Razor was a revelation, least of all for the fact that he was Breed—although it was impossible to ignore that fact as she held his fiery amber stare while he rocked in and out of her body.

The glow of his irises and the narrowed slits of his pupils was a hypnotic combination, one that would have terrified her only a week ago but now only added to the intensity of her arousal for him. All the harsh, ruggedly handsome angles of Razor's face and square jaw looked wilder in his passion, leaving no room for doubt that he was something other than human, something much more than mortal.

The *dermaglyphs* that covered his shoulders, arms, and torso swirled and churned with deep colors. Darkest indigo, rich wine, and molten gold pulsed along the intricate arcs and tangles of his Breed skin markings. She'd never seen anything so extraordinary. Everywhere she touched his *glyphs* their heat and mesmerizing, changeable colors tingled against her fingertips.

She couldn't stop touching him, drinking in every intoxicating nuance of him. Power radiated from every magnificent inch of Razor's body, all of it concentrated on her, on her pleasure. He was an unstoppable force, a formidable being who was also the sexiest man she'd ever known.

And his fangs . . . those sharp white points had never seemed longer, more lethal than they did now. Yet Willow felt no fear to see them poised only inches from her throat.

Far from it.

Some visceral, unfamiliar part of her stirred awake with hunger inside her as she held on to Razor and watched him move above her. His body was a perfect fit for hers, his otherworldly gaze cleaving into her soul with each consuming stroke of his hips against hers.

"God, you feel good," he uttered through clenched teeth and fangs. "You have no fucking idea how long I've been wanting this . . . wanting you."

Pleasure licked through every fiber of her being as his tempo intensified. Longing for something she couldn't quite name kindled deep in her core as she watched the torment brew and rage in his transformed eyes.

She'd tried to put on a brave front with him moments ago, claiming she didn't want anything more from him than just tonight. Part of it was true. She wasn't going to expect anything permanent or meaningful from him. That didn't mean she didn't want it. It didn't mean she didn't want . . . *him*.

Dare she believe the fierce light in his eyes when he looked at her now? Could she trust the fevered, possessive words he growled as he pushed her toward the steep edge of her release?

It was an intoxicating combination, especially for her, having been born into her twin's shadow. Razor made her feel as if no other woman existed for him, not only now, with their naked bodies entwined and moving together in matched, urgent rhythm on the bed, but every time he looked at her.

She was falling fast, with no net waiting to catch her.

A low groan vibrated through him as he plunged ever deeper, each thrust catapulting her higher and higher.

"Oh, God," she gasped out brokenly. "Don't stop."

His irises flared brighter at her command. "Not a chance."

He lowered his head and took her mouth in a consuming, dizzying kiss as he surged forward with a barrage of relentless strokes that seemed to drive all the way to her soul.

She couldn't hold back her cry as her climax broke. The depth of her bliss shattered her into what felt like a million starlit pieces. Every cell in her body felt electric and weightless.

As much as she wanted to close her eyes at the astonishing intensity, there was no tearing her gaze away from the fire building to a crescendo in Razor's amber irises. He drew back to watch her come, still moving inside her like a storm.

"You're so fucking beautiful like this," he grated out harshly. "Christ, I knew you would be. But you're even more than I imagined."

Willow stared up at him, still trembling from the power of her release. Each hard thrust of his hips stoked the embers of an insatiable hunger within her. She gave in to it, reaching up to grip the back of his neck and drag him down for her kiss.

He moaned into her mouth, meeting her with equal passion.

When her legs came up around his hips to urge him deeper, the sound he made was unearthly and dark, filled with a hunger that seemed to match her own. He drove into her with abandon then, until pleasured tears filled her eyes and another release sent her flying.

He came on a coarse shout, clutching her close and thrusting hard.

They lay there entwined for some time, stroking each other's sweat-sheened bodies. Willow could barely hold back her soft cry of protest when she felt him start to move from atop her.

He moved to the edge of the bed, reaching out to her. "Come with me."

She took his offered hand without questions, then followed him into the adjoining bathroom where her abandoned bubble bath waited, the suds all but gone, the water certainly gone cold by now.

Razor popped the drain to let some of the tepid water out, then ran the faucet to replenish it. He poured some of the fragrant bath soap under the flowing water, then turned his attention back to her.

His hands were tender on her face as he drew her

close for another kiss. Arousal still pulsed in every hard angle of his strong body, but his lips covered hers with a gentleness, a reverence, that staggered her.

"Turn around," he murmured, his voice low and rough with rekindling desire.

She did as he asked, uncertain what he intended. Standing in front of him, she felt his hands come to rest lightly on her shoulders. Then he traced his fingers down the length of her arms, with unhurried tenderness.

Her long hair was a tangled mess that hung haphazardly at her back, having come undone on the bed. Razor carefully gathered the disheveled tresses in his strong hands, lifting them up and away from her neck.

His breath fanned hot against her nape as he leaned in and placed a soft kiss there. Willow shivered, every fiber of her being lit up at the feel of his mouth poised so dangerously at her neck. Her breath seized in her lungs, her veins charged in anticipation of the moment she would feel his bite.

She craved it even more than her next breath.

His tongue brushed lightly over her sensitive skin, followed by the low, strangled-sounding rumble of the curse he bit out as his mouth retreated. His fingers continued to move in her hair with surprising delicacy, extricating the pins that had held her bun in place before it came apart on the bed. When he finished, he turned her back around to face him.

"After you." He indicated the tub full of refreshed water and inviting bubbles.

Willow couldn't contain her smile. Taking his hand for support, she stepped into the tub and slowly dropped into the frothy, warm water. Razor stepped in after her, his big body crowding the small space and sending some of the suds sloshing over the edge.

He sat facing her on the opposite end, his long, *glyph*-covered legs bent, knees sticking out of the thick layer of bubbles. Reaching for her, he pulled her forward until she was on his lap straddling him. "That's better."

His erect cock rubbed against her as he cupped her face and pulled her into another dizzying kiss. She wrapped her arms around his bulky shoulders and neck, giving in to the consuming taste of his mouth on hers. They'd just had each other yet there was no denying the arousal still burning between them.

Willow reached down and positioned him where she wanted him, then sank down onto his shaft.

"This is even better," she said around his pleasured moan.

"Oh, yeah." He caged her in his arms as she began to move on him.

What began as slow, unrushed strokes quickly burned into something uncontrollable. They made love again and again, until the water began to cool once more and the bubbles were nothing but a memory.

Then they took their time caressing and soaping each other's bodies. Willow had never been shown such tender care or affection. That it came on the heels of explosive, insatiable passion only made her all the more aware of the fact that she was falling fast and hard for Razor.

Worse than that, she realized. She had already fallen.

Tonight had only left no room for doubt.

CHAPTER 19

Razor awoke in bed with Willow the next morning, her head nestled into the crook of his shoulder, her soft breaths warm against his neck as she slept.

He couldn't recall the last time he'd slept for hours straight, let alone with a female beside him. Not that Willow could be lumped into the same category as any of his random hookups over the years. She had ruined him for anyone else, and not simply because making love to her had been the most intense experience of his life. It hadn't taken being inside her last night—multiple times—for him to be certain of one thing.

Willow Valcourt was his.

His heart and body knew it. Hell, even his blood knew it, with or without the bond that would lock her destiny with his.

Unfortunately, as incredible as last night had been, he'd let his selfish needs get in the way of the truth he owed her. He couldn't pretend she belonged to him in any way until he'd cleared his conscience about his surveillance work for Theo Collier.

Too bad he hadn't found the self-control—or the honor—to do the right thing before he'd pounced on her like a lust-filled animal.

Guilt pricked him as he savored the feel of her sleeping so peacefully in his arms. She had been as ravenous as him last night. It was damned hard to have any regrets when the memory of her gasping his name as he made her come so many times he'd lost count was still fresh in every overheated cell in his body.

His cock twitched back to eager life as their hours of mind-blowing sex replayed in his mind.

Fuck.

If he stood any chance of having the difficult conversation she was long overdue, he was going to need a cold shower first. Or an Arctic plunge.

He extricated himself from the tangle of her limbs, taking care not to disturb her sleep as he slipped out of bed and moved silently into the bathroom. He ran a quick shower then got dressed and finished cleaning up at the sink, using one of the fresh toothbrushes Leni had brought along with some other toiletries and the changes of clothing she'd given them.

Willow was still asleep when he came out a few minutes later. Razor frowned, loathe to wake her even though what he needed to say shouldn't wait.

He wasn't looking for excuses but the idea of hurting her, especially after last night, made his mouth taste like ashes as he stood next to the bed and watched her resting so contentedly.

As a Hunter, he'd never considered himself a coward

but standing there now he could hardly deny it. The last thing he wanted to do was give Willow any reason to doubt him, yet he knew every minute he delayed was only going to erode her trust even further.

He took a seat on the edge of the mattress and tenderly swept some of her silky dark hair from where it curled against her cheek. She stirred like a kitten at his light touch. The soft moan that escaped her slightly parted lips sent an arrow of heat straight to his cock.

He was just about to wake her when the sound of the farmhouse's back door being thrown open sounded from downstairs. A child's voice followed. "Aunt Leni, we're here!"

Instead of the gentle awakening Razor had intended for Willow, her eyes popped open with a start at the sudden ruckus in the kitchen below.

"It's okay," he told her as she levered up onto her elbow in alarm. "Leni's sister and her son were due to come here this morning with a laptop for me to use for the flash drive. Apparently, they've arrived."

Down in the kitchen, more voices joined Leni's nephew's, his mother hushing him because it was early and people could still be asleep, then still more chatter as Leni welcomed her family inside.

"What time is it?" Willow asked.

Razor stroked her cheek. "Just after nine."

"I should get up." She gave him a sheepish look. "I never sleep this late."

He smirked. "Neither do I. I'm sorry if last night was too much."

"Last night was amazing," she said, her mouth curving in a sexy, unrepentant smile. "Too bad we had to stop for sleep."

He groaned. "Keep looking at me like that and I'll be tempted to start all over again."

Biting her lower lip, she laughed and shook her head. "With everyone right downstairs in the kitchen? Forget it."

"I can be quiet. Stealth is one of my specialties."

She lifted a brow. "I'm not sure I can be quiet if I let you back into this bed with me. Besides, you've got the advantage over me. You're all showered and clean, while I'm—"

He leaned in and silenced her with a kiss that started on her mouth and ended with one of her rosy nipples caught between his teeth. "Delicious," he finished for her. "Every sweet inch of you."

She ran her hands through his damp hair, her gaze searching his. "Last night really happened, didn't it?"

He nodded. He couldn't tear his gaze away from her. She was so beautiful it made his chest ache. The way she looked at him, as if he were the most fascinating thing she'd ever seen, made him yearn to be everything she saw in him. He wanted to be more than that to her. Deep down in his bones, in his marrow, he wanted to be all that she deserved.

Which couldn't happen unless he was completely honest with her.

"Willow, I—"

The sudden, rapid thump of small feet on the steps leading up to the attic yanked his attention back to full alert. Razor vaulted to his feet even as he mentally locked and held the door closed in case the inquisitive seven-year-old coming up the stairs thought to barge in.

Willow let out a small gasp behind him as she pulled the quilt up over her naked body.

"Riley, where are you?" A female voice Razor didn't recognize rang out from the kitchen. "I better not find you going up to the attic."

The footsteps halted at once. "But Uncle Knox said—"

"Downstairs, young man. Now."

"Aw, Mom." Deflated, the boy thumped back down as he was told.

Razor glanced at Willow, who'd gotten off the bed and was wrapping herself in the bathrobe. He thought she might be upset or embarrassed, but instead she was struggling to hold back a giggle.

"You should go join them," she said. "I'll clean up and come down in a few minutes."

All the things he still hadn't said to her lingered on his tongue. He stared at her in a heavy, awkward silence, trying to decide how to reel in the moment again so they could talk.

She tilted her head at him. "Is anything wrong, Razor?"

He abruptly glanced down. "No. Nothing's wrong. I'll see you downstairs."

"Okay." With a smile and a nod, she padded into the bathroom and closed the door.

Scrubbing his hand over his jaw, Razor stood there for another moment, then stalked to the door and headed down to the kitchen.

An attractive blond stood at the sink washing out a travel cup. He might have guessed her to be in her early thirties but her blue eyes had a world-weary quality to them, as if she'd lived and seen more than her share of hardship.

"You must be Razor," she said, drying her hands on

the dish towel. "I'm Shannon, Leni's sister. I hope Riley didn't wake you guys up just now. He's really excited to meet his Uncle Knox's brother."

Razor shook his head. "No. It's all good. Nice to meet you, Shannon."

At the same moment, Leni entered the kitchen followed by Knox and the boy, who held onto the big Breed male's hand as if they were the best of friends. Razor never dreamed he'd see the day his formidable Hunter brother might look so comfortable and relaxed. As strong as the impulse was to bust his balls a bit, deep down he realized he was simply happy for Knox.

If not a little envious.

Knox released Riley's hand and nodded toward Razor. "I told you he'd be down quick enough if you went upstairs to say hello."

Riley grinned.

Razor narrowed a look on his brother. "You sent the kid upstairs? I might've known."

Knox chuckled. "Couldn't let you sleep all day. I take it things went better than you thought they might last night?"

Razor cleared his throat. "I don't want to talk about it."

His curt response made Knox exhale a slow, understanding breath. "I hope you know what you're doing, brother."

He didn't, obviously. Not that he had any intention of discussing the situation now. He glanced at the boy's eager face, which was lit with fascination under his tousled blond hair.

"You must be Riley."

The kid nodded enthusiastically. "Are you really

Breed, like Uncle Knox?"

"Yep."

Even though the human world had been aware of their vampire neighbors for two decades, it still felt strange sometimes to acknowledge his otherness so openly when fear and mistrust from mortals remained an issue that might never go away.

Riley seemed anything but afraid or suspicious. He stared at Razor's forearms where his *dermaglyphs* arced and tangled all the way onto the backs of his hands.

"You've got more *glyphs* than I've ever seen. Even more than Uncle Knox!"

Razor chuckled at his candidness. "I hear you're pretty clever with computers."

Riley nodded. "I brought you one of mine. It's in the other room. If you want, I can show you how to use it."

"I think I can figure it out. Thanks for letting me borrow yours."

"Sure," he said, beaming with pride. "I got two, so you don't have to give it back until you're done."

"I appreciate that, Riley. Thank you."

"Before anyone gets busy doing anything," Leni interjected, "I'm going to make some breakfast. Razor, do you think Willow will want some?"

He nodded. "That'd be great. Thanks, Leni. She's taking a shower now and should be down shortly. Thanks for the fresh clothes and toiletries."

She smiled. "My pleasure."

"I thought that shirt looked familiar," Knox said, frowning at Razor. He glanced archly at his mate. "You gave him my favorite shirt?"

Laughing, she walked up to him and brought her arms around his torso. "We owe Razor more than just a shirt for how he helped us when we needed it most. Wouldn't you agree?"

He growled low under his breath. "I love that shirt."

"And I love you," she murmured, rising up onto her toes to kiss his bearded chin.

Riley let out an exaggerated groan. "All you two do is kiss and hug all the time."

Everyone laughed at the boy's outburst.

"Just wait," Knox advised his nephew. "The day will come when you meet a special girl and that's all you're going to want to do too."

Riley made an appalled face. "Yuck, no way!"

They talked for a few more minutes while Leni and Shannon went about starting breakfast for themselves, Riley, and Willow. Razor and Knox took a seat at the small dining table in the kitchen, catching up on things at the old Darkhaven back in Florida and Knox's new life in the North Maine Woods.

The more they talked, the more Razor wondered about where he truly belonged. Having been born into Dragos's Hunter program, pondering a future had been a concept he'd never considered. He lived for the moment, trained simply to fight one battle and to survive to fight the next.

Once he'd settled in the Everglades Darkhaven with his other escaped brothers, he'd thrived on challenging his mind as much as his body and his physical skills. Pleasure was as basic as feeding, a necessary task to keep his mind and body sharp and functioning at optimum capacity. Love had never factored into anything he did. The future was something others planned for and pined for.

But now?

He watched Knox with Leni and he couldn't help imagining how it might be for Willow and him. A happy life together. A future somewhere safe and quiet. A blood bond and a family of their own.

When he thought about Willow, he wanted it all.

Holy hell.

Was he falling in love with her?

A soft creak on the attic stairwell brought his head around just in time to see her step down into the kitchen. Her freckled cheeks were pink from her shower, her glossy hair hanging in damp waves around her shoulders. She wore a chunky sweater and a flowered skirt that fell almost to her ankles. She looked refreshed and lovely, and the private smile she gave him twisted his insides into a pleasant knot.

"Sorry I slept so late." She glanced at the breakfast feast being prepared on the stove. "Leni, that smells delicious."

"Just bacon, omelets, and biscuits. I hope you're hungry."

"Starving," Willow admitted. She turned her smile on Leni's sister. "Hi, I'm Willow."

"Shannon," the other woman said. "Pleased to meet you."

"Can I help with anything?"

"Sure," Leni said. "You wanna chop some peppers for the omelets?"

Willow nodded. "Sounds great."

She got right to work, joining in as if she'd known Leni and her sister all her life. Razor watched her with silent intensity, unable to tear his eyes away from her as she chatted easily with the other women and Riley, the most relaxed he'd ever seen her.

She looked at peace.

She looked happy.

Razor could hardly tear his gaze away from her. When he finally did, he found Knox watching him intently. His shrewd eyes had seen it all, including the longing Razor couldn't have hidden from him if he tried.

Knox exhaled a long, slow breath and slowly shook his head.

He didn't have to say a word. Razor could read his brother's look plainly enough.

If Razor wanted to deny he was falling in love with Willow, he'd only be lying to himself.

He was already long gone.

CHAPTER 20

Willow was glad to have something to keep her busy as she helped Leni and her sister make breakfast. It was all she could do to hold her silly schoolgirl smile in check whenever her eyes met Razor's penetrating gaze in the small kitchen.

Even though he was seated on the other side of the room with Knox, she felt his presence like a constant caress of her senses. He stirred something deep inside her that had been building even before the night of amazing lovemaking they'd shared. She felt him in the core of her being, in her bones. In her blood.

The idea that he had only been a part of her life for a handful of days and nights seemed impossible to her as she stood at the counter chopping vegetables and listening to Riley's excited chatter as he vied for both hers and Razor's attention.

It felt so normal, so wonderfully mundane, even

though the circumstances that brought her to this place were anything but normal or mundane. It was all too easy to imagine that she and Razor somehow belonged in this place, not as two relative strangers on the run from dangerous men, but as a couple who might one day be making a life together as a family too.

Willow's heart squeezed at the idea.

It had been so long since she'd allowed herself to indulge in the fantasy of having some semblance of family. Growing up orphaned after a horrific tragedy and then being separated from her twin at such a young age had forced Willow to become independent as a means of survival. She held her emotions inside, the only safe place she knew.

And other than Laurel, she didn't let herself get attached to anyone.

At least, not until Razor stormed into her life.

She glanced over her shoulder at him, where he was patiently listening to Riley excitedly recite his recent high scores on a computer game he liked to play.

"Impressive," Razor remarked with a nod. "I've played that game a few times myself. It's a good one."

"What're your high scores?"

Razor pretended to think about it for a moment. "You know, I don't recall exactly. Probably not as good as yours."

"Yeah," Riley agreed with a child's utter certainty. "Prolly not. I'm really good at it."

Razor chuckled at the boy's boast, exchanging a knowing look with Knox and Leni. When his eyes swung to Willow, his mouth curved in a slow, intimate smile that sent a warm vibration through her veins.

Riley tugged his shirt sleeve. "Razor, let's go play it

now. I have it on my laptop."

"How about another time, all right?" Razor's deep voice was grave beneath his gentleness with the boy. "Willow and I have something we need to do on the computer first."

Willow felt her smile catch at the reminder. The morning had started off so nicely, she wasn't ready to think about the circumstances that had brought them to Parrish Falls. As determined as she was to find out what was on Laurel's flash drive, part of her was terrified too. What could be so important to make Laurel go to the lengths she did to protect the drive from being recovered by anyone but Willow? Or what if they had come all this way and were unable to access the device at all?

She didn't know what to hope for. She was only glad she had Razor there along with her.

"What about after?" Riley prompted his new best friend. "Can we play a game then?"

"Riley." Shannon pivoted away from the stove with an apologetic look. "The game will wait however long it has to wait. You've got things you need to do first too, starting with eating some breakfast. Go on and wash your hands now."

The admonishment earned a groan from Riley, but he did as his mother asked. Meanwhile, Knox and Razor made room at the table for everyone else as Willow volunteered to set out the plates and utensils. With the table set and breakfast served family style for all but the two Breed males, Willow took the empty chair next to Razor.

As hungry as she had been when she woke up, the specter of her sister's murder and dread over the potential reasons for it reduced her appetite to almost nothing.

She nibbled on the delicious omelet and barely finished the bacon, washing it down with a little bit of coffee and a sip of water. Razor's hand came to rest on her thigh under the table, his touch warm and comforting as they made smalltalk with the others and waited for the opportunity to slip away to begin working on the flash drive.

"You okay?" Razor asked quietly, his face grim with concern.

She managed a nod, but his solemn expression told her he saw through the calm front she was working so hard to maintain. Maybe everyone could see through her. Once breakfast was finished and Willow got up to help clear the dishes, Leni gave her a sympathetic look.

"We'll take care of all this," she said. "You two can take the laptop into the den for some privacy. Take all the time you need."

"Thank you," Willow replied.

Razor nodded in gratitude to his brother, then let his palm ride gently at Willow's back as they left the kitchen to retrieve the laptop from the living room. The adjacent den had a door, which Razor closed behind them once they were inside.

He went right to the task at hand, taking a seat in a leather armchair and opening the computer on the coffee table in front of him. With the flash drive in his hand, he paused, glancing up at Willow.

"If you're not ready to do this right now—"

"I am," she said, despite the fact that her legs felt wooden beneath her and her hands were trembling so hard she had to fold her arms in front of her just to hold herself together.

Frowning, Razor set the flash drive on the table and went to her. He pulled her into his embrace and simply held her for a long moment. The warmth and strength of his body enveloped her like a balm. The steady beat of his heart pulsing against her cheek as she leaned into him was a reassurance and a comfort she greedily drank in, regardless of how vulnerable it made her feel to need Razor's presence like she did.

He stroked her hair, then pressed a kiss to her brow. "I'm not going anywhere," he murmured, as if he understood her feelings even without her speaking them aloud. "No matter what's on that drive or what's still to come after we open it, we're in this together, Willow."

She nodded, then pulled back to look up into his solemn face. "You really mean that, don't you?"

His answer came in the form of a kiss. Not the heated, hungry kisses they'd shared last night but a tender one. A kiss that brushed over her lips with such care and sincerity it swept her breath away. When he drew away his irises smoldered with crackling amber sparks.

"The flash drive is yours, Willow. You're calling the shots here. What do you want to do?"

She took a fortifying breath. "Let's fire it up."

He nodded once, then led her by the hand to the seat next to his. She leaned forward in her chair, watching as he slipped the drive into the laptop and clicked to open it. A digital folder full of files filled the screen. Razor clicked on the first one.

Willow didn't realize she was holding her breath until Laurel's face appeared on the laptop monitor. All the pent-up air in her lungs leaked out of her on a jagged sigh.

"Hey, Wills." The video had been recorded in what appeared to be a hotel room. Laurel looked tired and fatigued, but still vibrant and beautiful—so heartbreakingly real—as she stared into the camera and offered a sad little smile. "If you're watching this, I guess it means I'm dead. God, what an awful cliché. Just know that I'm sorry to be dragging you into my problems like this. The last thing I wanted was for you to be part of it." She glanced down briefly and slowly shook her head. "Unfortunately, you already are part of it. If they've gotten to me, they're going to be coming for you next."

The coil of dread Willow had been feeling all morning grew a bit colder as she listened to her sister's ominous warning. She glanced at Razor and found him staring at the screen with a deepeningly suspicious scowl.

"I suppose I should start at the beginning, right?" Laurel asked rhetorically. "I'm too ashamed to tell you any of it in person, but at this point—now that you're watching this video—the only chance you have to survive is if you know the whole story. And my role in it."

Willow swallowed. She'd never seen her sister speak with such gravity or remorse. Being her twin, Willow could almost feel the weight of Laurel's regret just by seeing her face and hearing her voice on camera.

"Working at the Unity for Wellness and Safety Institute in Montreal had been a dream for me," Laurel said. "I couldn't believe Theo and I both landed jobs there fresh out of college. The UWSI may be a small research institute, but it's considered one of the best in the world. The most cutting-edge technologies, the most prestigious programs, the most innovative scientists. And, due to all of that, UWSI is also the recipient of the most generous research grants, many of them funded by anonymous, powerful organizations and individuals . . . all with their own private agendas as I later realized. By the time I learned the truth, it was too late."

Onscreen, Laurel reached for something nearby. She held up a small vial filled with clear liquid. "Two years ago, Theo and I were assigned to an experimental project called Serenicure, which was tasked with finding a cure for Bloodlust in the Breed. Its mission was to help put a stop to Breed predation on humans. I know I don't have to tell you how committed I was to that cause, Wills."

A low, menacing sound emanated from Razor. "I don't like where this is heading."

Willow didn't either, but she couldn't find words for all the emotions suddenly churning inside her. She reached over to hold on to Razor's hand as Laurel continued to speak.

"The effort to potentially eliminate Rogue violence once and for all by reversing Bloodlust was more than just an assignment to me. It became my obsession. Other clinics and institutes had attempted their own formulas for treating vampiric behavior, but none had succeeded. The closest anyone had come to suppressing Breed behavior was a clinician from a small, specialized practice in Massachusetts. His name was Dr. Henry Lewis."

"Son of a bitch," Razor muttered.

"You know him?"

He gave a tight shake of his head. "I only know of him—and his work. That sick bastard served Dragos and his breeding lab back in the day. Henry Lewis concocted some kind of chemical mix that held Breed transformation at bay. He used it on some of the Gen

Ones created in Dragos's lab, most notoriously on a Breed female named Tavia Fairchild before she eventually caught on and killed the asshole. Tavia's mated to Sterling Chase now, the chief of the Order's Command Center in Boston."

Willow stared at him, unsure which part of that information surprised her more. "I didn't realize you're that familiar with the Order's warriors and the general workings of their organization."

He shrugged absently, most of his attention still fixed on Laurel. "I've done a few favors for them over the years. I find it pays to have allies in as many places as possible."

Willow nodded, glancing back at the laptop screen as her twin was explaining more about her work for UWSI.

"Using Dr. Lewis's formula as a base for ours, Theo and I and our team began creating new compounds of our own. Some of them failed miserably early on, but there was one formula that showed promise. Or so we thought. Given the unique physiology of the Breed, we were given no choice but to test on live subjects. We conducted numerous trials in the UWSI lab in Montreal. Unfortunately, some subjects could not tolerate the treatment at all. Death was often instant and horrific. We saw nothing but setbacks during those initial months."

Although Razor remained silent, his fury rolled off him in palpable waves. Willow felt sick to her stomach as she listened to Laurel describe the deaths of living individuals—their chemical-induced murders—all in the name of science.

Willow reached out and hit the pause button on the video. "I don't want to hear any more of this." She rose from her chair and began to pace the rug-covered floor.

Her skin felt too tight on her body. Her heart was racing in her rib cage, nausea roiling in her gut. "How could she participate in something like this, Razor? How are these experiments any different from what Dragos did to you and all the rest of his laboratory prisoners?"

Razor got up and went to her, gently pulling her into his embrace. "I'm not going to say I agree with what your sister just described, but there's not a Breed member alive today who'd deny the chance to find a cure for Bloodlust. A true cure."

Willow shook her head. "At what cost, though?"

"I can't answer that. Neither can your sister now. Or Theo, if they've gotten to him as I suspect they have." Razor pulled back, tenderly brushing her cheek. "All I know is I'm not going to stop searching for answers until I'm certain you're safe. And in order to do that, I need to hear everything Laurel has to say."

Willow nodded in agreement. "Okay."

They went back to the laptop and Razor tapped the screen to resume Laurel's message.

"I never wanted my work to be used to harm anyone," she said as the video began playing again. Her voice was emphatic as she stared into the camera. "I was trying to help make the world a better place, including for the Breed individuals we treated in our trials. I wanted to make a difference, Wills. I wanted to do something lasting and good. I really believed that's what UWSI was all about too."

Onscreen, Laurel stared at the vial of clear liquid she still held carefully in her fingers. "Despite our initial failures, I knew our formula could be a success. All it was missing was a reparative property to speed recovery and cellular regeneration. It needed to be able to halt death and accelerate healing." Laurel's gaze returned to the camera. "So, I secretly altered the formula in the only way I knew how."

"Oh, Laurel," Willow gasped, reading the whole truth in her twin's gaze.

"No one knew I'd added some of my own genetic material into the formula, not even Theo at first. I wasn't sure it would work, but I knew I had to try. Using my white cells, I created a new version of the formula, Serenicure-L, and arranged for a new set of trials." She smiled, but there was nothing but sadness in her eyes. "To everyone's astonishment, the new formula exceeded all expectations. Our test subjects not only survived the treatment, but thrived. Their Bloodlust reversed almost instantly with no apparent adverse effects. They were healed. The new formula had put every case of blood addiction into permanent remission."

Willow wanted to feel some relief at this remarkable breakthrough, but Laurel's increasingly grave expression formed a knot of cold in her breast instead.

"It wasn't until a week later that we recorded the first death. Then another followed. And another." Laurel's voice caught. "It turned out, my new formula had one disastrous flaw. It did cure Bloodlust, but at the same time it eliminated blood hunger entirely. One by one, our subjects refused to feed. Then they began to starve and die."

"Shit," Razor uttered low under his breath, his grasp on Willow's hand tightening.

"I was devastated," Laurel said. "I told Theo what I'd done, and he agreed we needed to destroy Serenicure-L and all the previous iterations of the formula. What we didn't know was that wheels were already in motion with UWSI management. We considered the trials to be a complete failure, but they saw opportunity. The early formulas killed too swiftly and obviously to be of any use, but my version was a subtler solution to a problem UWSI and its benefactors ultimately wanted to solve. The complete eradication of the Breed as a species."

"Oh, my God," Willow whispered, horror gathering like acid in the back of her throat.

She glanced at Razor and found his eyes crackling with amber sparks, the tips of his fangs pressing behind his tightly closed mouth and clenched jaw.

"Serenicure-L was being slated for a major rollout," Laurel continued. "It wasn't going to be branded as a cure for Bloodlust after the fact, but as a preventive therapy for all members of the Breed. UWSI and their powerful investors planned to introduce their new vaccine, Serenivax, on an accelerated release. Rumor had it they were seeking the highest bids from firms like Scrully Pharmaceuticals for the distribution rights."

"Scrully," Willow murmured aloud. "Why is that name familiar?"

"Evidently, they were one of St. Anne's sponsors," Razor replied. "I noticed the portrait of Sister Agathe had been donated by Mr. and Mrs. Simon Scrully. But you may also have heard of the company from its dubious reputation. They made headlines a few times in recent years, first when the patriarch, Simon Scrully, began hiking prices on his patented medicines. The company was in the news again not long ago. The heir-apparent, Lars, took over the company following his father's death, then proceeded to get on the wrong side of the Order and wound up dead himself a few months ago."

"That must've been after Laurel recorded this video," Willow guessed, based on the timeline of when her sister arrived in Colorado. "Do you think she could've been running from Scrully Pharmaceuticals as well as UWSI?"

"It's possible," Razor said. "The company's known for having very deep pockets—and the shady associates that usually come along with it. That kind of wealth and power doesn't just evaporate even if the company no longer exists. There's always someone ready to step in and take the reins."

Willow nodded, returning her attention to Laurel as she continued to speak. "I couldn't let this formula be released, Wills. I had to do something. So, I did. With Theo's help, I downloaded all of the project's records onto this flash drive and deleted everything from the UWSI servers. Then I took all the existing test samples and formula specimens from the UWSI lab and I ran." She indicated the vial she held. "This is the last remaining dose of Serenicure-L."

Laurel unfastened the stopper on the vial, then turned the container upside down and poured it out into a trash bin. Using a ceramic coffee cup, she smashed the glass vial into a napkin and tossed that into the bin too.

A conflicted, regretful look haunted her gaze as she lifted her eyes to the camera again. "Destroying the formula doesn't mean I'm safe. Theo stayed behind to help cover my tracks, even though I begged him not to. I'm terrified of what they might do to him. I'm terrified for myself too—and for you. Now that UWSI knows my blood was the key to making Serenicure-L, you can't be safe either, Willow. If they can't have me, make no mistake, they're going to want you. Your blood."

Razor snarled, low and menacing. "Over my dead fucking body."

"I still believe there's a true cure for Bloodlust," Laurel said. "We were so close to finding it. That's why I took the records with me and hid them somewhere only you would know to look for them. So, now that I'm gone, the choice is yours, Wills. These files, my work, it's all that's left of me. You decide what to do with the contents of this drive. Destroy it, or give it to someone you trust. All I ask is that you try to forgive me—not only for this monstrous thing I created, but also for dragging you into it." Laurel swiped at an errant tear that streaked down her cheek. "No matter what, please know that I love you, Willow. I always have, and always will."

With that, Laurel reached toward the camera and the screen went dark.

Willow sat there for a moment, overcome by everything she'd just heard and seen.

Emotion bore down on her, leaving her feeling as though the dam she'd erected to keep all of her grief and anger and confusion at bay since Laurel's murder was suddenly blown to pieces.

A sob wracked her, jagged and raw.

She got up from her seat and hurried to the door of the den, clumsily throwing it open and racing out before the tide of her pain and sorrow drowned her.

CHAPTER 21

"Fuck."

Razor popped the flash drive out of the laptop and jammed it into his pocket as he vaulted off his chair to go after Willow.

Knox and Leni were still in the kitchen with Riley and Shannon. Judging from everyone's concerned looks, Willow had already run through the room on her way upstairs to the attic guest room.

"Why's Willow sad?" Riley asked, frowning at Razor.

Knox's furrowed brows seemed to indicate the same question, although he didn't say a word as Razor rushed past them all. He took the steps two at a time, reaching the closed door at the top of the stairwell in seconds flat. He knocked lightly on the wood panel and it creaked open.

Razor entered, his chest squeezing to find Willow seated on the end of the bed, weeping into her hands.

Closing the door behind him, he went to her, gathering her into his arms.

She gave him no resistance, as if the weight of her emotions were too heavy for her to bear alone. He held her in a loose grasp, stroking her back as her sobs wrenched out of her and hot tears wet his chest through the flannel of his shirt.

He'd never seen her so openly distraught, not even on that first night they spent together in the Cheyenne motel, when she'd cried herself in and out of sleep. He hadn't known what to do for her then, so like a coward he'd simply let her hurt alone.

He didn't know how to lessen her pain now, either, but holding her through it was as much for himself as it was for Willow now. He couldn't bear the thought of her suffering, emotionally or physically. Her pain was his, even though he had always assumed it would take a blood bond for him to connect on such a profound level with a woman.

He didn't need a blood bond to know that how he felt about Willow would be part of him forever. He'd been falling in love with her little by little from the moment they met. Longer than that, because he'd known in his veins that she was his even when he could only watch her on his drone camera from afar.

He held her until her tears dried up and the sobs that had wracked her body subsided. Even after she was all cried out, her breathing resuming a normal tempo, she still clung to him. Razor dropped a kiss onto her soft brown hair.

For a long while he said nothing, giving her time to decide what she needed from him. Finally, she shifted in his arms, then slowly drew back enough to lift her gaze to his.

"Are you all right?" he asked her, his voice rough and quiet. He couldn't resist reaching out to brush away some of the wetness from her reddened cheeks.

She inhaled a shaky, but steadying breath. "I don't know what I am right now. Shocked. Sad. Horrified." She let out a small, bitter sound. "I'm just so damn furious with her, Razor. I hate that Laurel didn't think she could tell me any of this while she was still alive. Maybe we could've done something together to fix this."

Tenderly, he stroked the side of her face. "Your sister was ashamed of her work, even though she believed she was doing it for the right reasons. You were the only safe place she knew to run to, but telling you what she'd done meant risking that she'd lose you if you knew the truth."

Willow shook her head. "Instead, she kept me in the dark. She denied me the truth, which is as good as a lie. She denied me the choice when she should've given me the chance to know what she'd done and let me decide for myself."

Razor struggled to keep his own guilt in check as he listened to Willow's rightful anger. The lie of omission that had been gnawing at him all this time burned like acid on his conscience as he held Willow in his arms and tried to console her over losing her twin and the secret that had sent Laurel to her grave.

He hadn't known what to expect when they opened the flash drive. Certainly not the explosive revelations that Laurel Townsend had delivered. Not only had she been involved in developing a cure for the Breed's most feared ailment, but she had also inadvertently created a serum that in the wrong hands could be used as a tool for committing a slow-motion genocide on the entire Breed population.

Now, the fate of both those scientific developments lay in Willow's hands.

If Laurel was correct, then now it was Willow's blood that was the key to either saving the future for the Breed or risking its end.

"Laurel left you with another choice to make instead, Willow. What do you want to do with the information on the flash drive?"

She studied his face, those soul-searching green eyes reaching deep inside him. "What do you think we should do?"

He stilled at the question, and the weight it carried. "I can't tell you how to decide that. You have to do what you believe is right."

"Laurel seemed so certain she was close to success with her formula. What if she's right? What if she really was on the verge of creating a true cure for Bloodlust? You said yourself that's something no member of the Breed would turn their back on."

He nodded grimly. "That's right."

"Then don't we have to try? I don't want Laurel's death to be in vain. I don't want all those patients who died in her trials to have been for nothing, either."

"What are you saying?"

"Laurel said to find someone who can be trusted. You're the only one I trust to help me decide what to do, Razor. You're the only person who's never lied to me."

Ah, Christ. He only wished he were the man she seemed to think he was. Some part of him he hardly recognized hoped he could be worthy of the faith she placed in him now.

While it hadn't been a betrayal of her trust that he'd been watching her sister's cabin all these past months, withholding that fact from her was nothing less than a lie. One he could no longer stand to keep inside him.

"Willow, I . . ."

"I know what I want to do with the drive, Razor." She spoke over him, as if she thought he might try to persuade her away from the decision she'd clearly already made. "I know what I need to do with it, but I don't want to do it unless you agree."

He stared at her. "Tell me."

"I want to give the flash drive to the Order. Let them carry out Laurel's work. I assume they have the means."

Razor nodded. "They do. Lucan Thorne and his warriors have endless resources and capital at their disposal."

"And they'll have me too," she said, resolve shining in her gaze. "I want to do whatever I can to contribute to the cure my sister was trying to develop. If the healing properties in my blood might be part of the solution, then I want the Order to have access to it. Whatever they need to get this right. Whatever it takes to vindicate Laurel and help fulfill her mission to do something good and lasting."

Pride filled him as he looked at her, as he listened to the ferocity and commitment in her voice.

"Do you have any idea how incredible you are?" he murmured, marveling at the courage and honor she possessed, even when her heart had just been broken open. He slowly shook his head, nearly at a loss for words. "I was born and bred for destruction, for killing. You have every right to wish my kind extinct for what was done to your parents, instead you want to try to save us."

She made a dismissive noise and started to shake her head. "I'm only doing what any decent person would."

"No. You're doing what only Willow Valcourt would do." He cupped her face in his hands. "I've been sitting here wondering how I'll ever be able to prove myself worthy of a woman like you. Now, I realize I never will be. You are . . . beyond extraordinary. God, you bring me to my knees."

Her eyes began to fill with tears once more, but it wasn't sorrow he saw in her beautiful face. It was affection. It was deep caring, so pure and unbridled it nearly undid him.

On a reverent curse, he pulled her toward him and took her mouth in a passionate kiss.

She was so soft in his arms, melding against him and meeting the strokes of his tongue with equal desire. He should have known that his first taste of her last night would only make him hungry to have her again.

And he was starving for her.

Her lush curves ignited his arousal, rendering him hard as granite as they continued to kiss and caress each other. His fangs surged from his gums, fueled by both his lust for her and his blood thirst, which had already gone unattended dangerously long.

Not that he could blame his craving for Willow's blood on the physical need to feed. She stirred more than just an urge for nourishment.

She made him crave a taste of her vein that would seal her to him forever.

As his mate.

His lover for the rest of eternity.

He wanted it with a depth of obsession that shocked

him.

A growl curled up from the back of his throat, whether in warning to himself or Willow he couldn't be sure. She answered him with a pleasured, greedy-sounding moan that sent an arrow of heat licking through his veins.

Despite the discipline that told him he was perilously close to the edge of something he may not be able to control, Razor pivoted with Willow, moving her beneath him on the bed.

Their clothing came off in a blur of impatient hands and urgent kisses.

The instant they were naked, Razor thrust inside her. The wet, hot feel of her wrenched a curse from him. She was sleek and soft around his cock, her legs wrapping around his waist to take every inch of him. He drove deep, his vision filled with amber, his fangs throbbing as intensely as the rest of his fevered body.

His desire for her was an untamed, possessive thing. All it knew was the need for this woman. *His woman.*

"Fuck, you fit me so perfectly," he uttered against her lips as they continued to kiss and move together on the bed. "I don't think I'll ever get enough of you."

She smiled, scoring his back with her short fingernails as she held onto him, meeting every hard thrust of his body. When she spoke her voice was breathless with pleasure and heat. "Mm, that's good, because I know I'll never get enough of you."

Her words were lost in a moan as he picked up the pace. While his own release was roaring up on him with startling speed, it was her unraveling that spurred him into a driving, powerful rhythm. He thrust deep and hard, then pulled out nearly to the tip, setting a relentless tempo that had her writhing beneath him and making the sexiest sounds as their bodies moved together.

She came on a stifled scream, which he caught with his kiss. His fangs felt enormous as he claimed her mouth with his lips and tongue. Her sex gripped his cock as her orgasm overtook her. He groaned with the incredible feel of her delicate muscles rippling along his shaft, her tight sheath clenched around his length like a velvet fist.

He rocked into her with deeper strokes, an animal in his chase for release.

But another urgent hunger rode closely behind, stirring the more dangerous predator inside him.

Opening his eyes to watch Willow as she continued to come, he couldn't bite back the otherworldly snarl that curled deep in his throat.

His vision radiated amber light and heat against the creamy beauty of her face. His fangs ached with the urge to feed.

To claim her as his.

As another tremor washed over her, Willow arched beneath him, her lips parted on a shivery sigh. She was so damn gorgeous. So fucking sexy it actually hurt to look at her. She was flame to the tinder of his self-control, but he was more than willing to burn.

Her pulse hammered under the force of her orgasm. Razor felt it everywhere their bodies touched. He heard her heartbeat drumming as hard as his own. Against his will, he let his gaze drift to the tender artery throbbing at the side of her delicate throat.

Mine.

The possessive impulse coursed through every cell in his body, until it was all he could feel. All he could hear was the steady pound of her blood racing just under the surface of her silken skin.

There was only one thing that could quench the need that owned him. He licked his lips, his mouth suddenly gone dry as dust.

A low curse tore out of him as he wrestled with his desire to make Willow his forever and the thin shred of honor he wanted to believe he still possessed where she was concerned.

When his fiery eyes lifted to her gaze, he found Willow staring at him. Her lids were heavy over her dusky green eyes, her face flushed with the glow of her climax. He'd never seen her look so breathtakingly lovely. She gazed up at him like an angel . . . his angel.

The miracle he didn't deserve and surely never would.

He could only imagine what she saw as she stared up at him while he continued to thrust into her with savage passion. Him, with his eyes transformed into smoldering coals, the *dermaglyphs* covering his muscled body churning like multi-colored serpents all over his skin. And his fangs, elongated like sharp-tipped daggers behind his peeled-back lips.

He had to look like a monster, like something out of her childhood nightmares. Yet she gazed up at him with open affection and a staggering depth of desire.

"I'm not afraid," she murmured softly, as if she understood the direction of his thoughts, his worst fear. "Nothing about you scares me, Razor."

He could only growl in denial, incapable of words when want for this woman owned every part of him.

She reached up to him, placing her palm against his cheek. A shy smile played over her kiss-swollen lips. "I lied to you last night," she whispered. "I told you I didn't want anything from you, only to be with you for a little while. That's not true. I want everything with you."

He snarled, scowling. When he finally found his voice it came out like gravel. "Don't say that. Not when I—"

She cut off his feeble attempt at a warning with a kiss that incinerated his threadbare claim of honor. Wrapping her hands around his nape she pulled his head down to her, scorching him with the fire of her mouth's demand. Her tongue swept past his teeth and fangs, bold strokes he felt all the way to his cock.

She'd just come a few moments ago but already he could feel her body contracting around his shaft as another orgasm began to build inside her. His own release bore down on him like a freight train, too powerful to stop.

When her tongue began to tease the lethal points of his fangs, he felt himself pitching toward the steep edge of a staggering release.

A curse boiled out of him as he broke away from her kiss and began a fierce, uncontrollable rhythm. Willow watched him with a look of shared hunger on her face.

The pulse at the side of her neck hammered even harder now.

His gaze rooted on it despite his every effort to look away, to resist the temptation of her vein.

Instead of taking pity on him, she slowly turned her head to the side, offering him the gift he had no right to claim. The most sacred piece of her that he could never give back.

It was too much for him to resist.

He wanted her too desperately, for too long.

As his release ratcheted tighter and his tempo grew wilder, the last shred of his control snapped its fragile leash.

He came on sharp roar, and at the same time lunged down and sank his fangs into the tender column of her throat.

Willow's blood hit his tongue like a taste of pure starlight. Sweet and hot, yet infused with an elusive, cosmic power that astonished him. One sip fired his senses as if they'd been dormant all his life and were suddenly awakened and set aglow.

He felt her in every cell of his being. In his heart. In his blood, bones, and marrow.

In his very soul.

A deep self-loathing spiraled in the pit of his conscience for how selfishly he'd taken this extraordinary gift. Too late for regret, although it churned inside him like a black tide beneath the staggering pleasure and power of the blood bond that now linked him to Willow.

And while he hated himself for losing control when there was still the matter of the secret he had yet to tell her, he couldn't stop drinking from her vein.

He couldn't stop savoring the rush of power flowing into him from this woman who had turned his life upside down and ruined him for any other.

He was never going to forgive himself for what he'd just done.

The more damning question was, would she?

CHAPTER 22

She hadn't known what to expect when she invited Razor to take her vein.

She'd expected pain from his bite, so the sharp piercing of her throat hadn't come as a complete surprise. It was the sensations that came swiftly behind the fleeting jolt of discomfort that caught her totally unaware.

Pleasure like she'd never known before exploded inside her, all of it radiating from the point of contact where his mouth had fastened onto her neck. His fangs sank deep, then retreated as her blood began to course into his mouth. Each frantic pulse of her heart, each possessive tug of the suction from his lips and tongue against her tender skin, made her orgasm spiral tighter, higher, until she could hardly contain the enormity of how good he made her feel.

Clutching him against her as he drank, knowing the

significance of what his bite meant—that he had just initiated a bond that would link him to her forever—only added to the depth of her pleasure. He'd just come moments ago, yet if anything it had only made him harder inside her. He rode her relentlessly, until she thought she might die from ecstasy.

She had no hope of holding back the rush of release that detonated within her. She came with his name a broken cry on her lips. He plunged deep at the same time, shuddering with the force of yet another climax of his own.

Willow hung on to him as they shattered together. As powerful as her release had been, so too was the depth of her love for him. The words spilled off her tongue before she could even think to keep them inside.

"I love you, Razor."

She tried to tell herself the sudden stillness that seemed to wash over him was only her imagination. She wanted to believe the low curse that vibrated deep in his chest wasn't a sound of regret.

But he had gone still. The curse she heard was followed by another, this time more vivid. Full of barely couched anger.

Razor's tongue swept over the punctures he'd created in her throat. It was an intimate sensation, yet it sent a cold chill through her.

"Fuck," he hissed, his hot breath fanning the side of her face as he began to push away from her. "Fuck, Willow . . . I'm sorry."

She felt as if the floor had suddenly opened and was about to swallow her. "What's wrong?"

He rolled off her and moved to the end of the bed. He sat there, hunched forward, holding his head in his hands. "I shouldn't have let this happen."

Willow stared at his back, at the tangle of *dermaglyphs* that were still writhing and swirling with vibrant colors all over his naked skin. "W-what did I do wrong? Is it because of what I said?"

"No." His reply came out sharp. "It's nothing you've done. Nothing you've said."

Abruptly, he got up and began to hastily put his clothes back on. Willow watched him in a state of confusion and concern. A terrible thought occurred to her. "Oh, God. Is it my blood? Please, tell me it hasn't harmed you—"

"It's nothing like that." He bit off the words and wheeled around to face her. She'd never seen him look so tormented, so furious. "You didn't do anything wrong. I'm the one at fault here. I should've had more control instead of taking something that can never be given back."

She recoiled, stung by the ferocity of his words.

His expression only darkened in reaction. "I'm only making this whole thing worse." He raked a hand through his mussed hair, then stared at her as if he could hardly stand to see her now. Even though he looked and sounded as if what they'd just shared had been the biggest mistake of his life, his amber gaze bore into her with unbridled heat. His fangs were still enormous behind his parted lips, her blood still slicking his sensual lips.

Glowering at her, he wiped the back of his hand across his mouth and swore again. "I need to get out of here for a while. Forgive me, Willow. I can't be near you right now."

Without waiting for her to answer, he grabbed his

flannel shirt off the floor then pivoted to stalk across the room to the door. He stepped out without a backward glance, as if he couldn't get away from her fast enough.

CHAPTER 23

Not only was he the biggest asshole to ever live, but also the biggest coward.

Tugging on his shirt and hastily buttoning it as he stormed down the attic steps, it was all he could do not to erupt with rage and loathing—all of it self-directed and well-deserved.

He'd thought Willow had given him the most precious gift when she allowed him to drink from her vein, but even that paled next to her tenderly spoken admission that she was in love with him.

A better man wouldn't have hesitated to tell her just how much she meant to him too. That she had become his light, his purpose, his everything. He should have gotten on his knees and told her in no uncertain terms that not only did he love her, but he didn't want to imagine a single moment of his life yet to come unless she was part of it.

Instead, he'd bolted like a heartless bastard.

He'd turned tail and run like a craven fucking coward.

The fact was he wanted nothing more than to complete the blood bond he'd initiated with Willow. If he had allowed himself to remain in the room with her for even another minute he wouldn't have been able to stop himself from giving her his own blood and binding her to him forever. Hell, he wanted that even now.

But it was bad enough that he took her gift while his secret still loomed between them. If he had also let her drink from him without her knowing the full circumstances of how their lives had intersected, it would be doubly unforgivable. As it was, he didn't think he'd likely ever be able to absolve himself for what he'd just done.

Knox and Leni were standing alone together in the kitchen as Razor stepped off the last stair from the attic. The couple were caught up in a sweet, private moment, their arms wrapped around each other, Leni's pregnant belly cradled between them. Knox had just dropped a tender kiss to his Breedmate's brow when Razor's abrupt arrival in the kitchen made them both glance his way.

"Sorry," he muttered. He waved his hand indistinctly. "Just passing through."

His voice sounded like hell, little better than a harsh, gravel scrape of sound in his throat. He probably didn't look much better than he sounded. Leni's eyes went a little wide at the sight of him. Knox's expression went dark with question.

"Everything okay?"

Razor scoffed by way of answer, continuing his trek

through the small kitchen. "Just fucking peachy."

Knox groaned. "What did you do?"

"I don't want to talk about it." Razor kept walking.

"Damn, brother." Knox released Leni and moved toward him. "How bad did you just fuck things up with her?"

Dark animosity—not for Knox, but for himself—brought Razor to a halt. His talons erupted from his fingertips before he could curb the combat instinct. He snapped his reply. "I said I don't want to talk about it."

Knox was a big Gen One male by any measurement, but even he stepped back at the sight of Razor's explosive fury. He moved himself into a protective stance with Leni behind him. "Keep your head, Raze. Especially when you're near my family."

"Sorry," Razor muttered, wrestling to put the beast in him back into its cage. He eyed Knox and his startled mate who peered around his shoulder. "Sorry, I . . . I shouldn't be around anyone right now."

"No shit," Knox said, still watching him as if he were a live grenade about to blow.

Razor thought back on the morning's events, and blew out a harsh sigh. It's true, he wasn't fit for company, but there were more important things than his black mood and his immediate need to continue punishing himself over his failings with Willow. He stared at his brother. "There's something you need to see."

"All right." With a meaningful look at Leni, Knox followed Razor out of the kitchen.

Walking through the living room where Riley and Shannon were on the sofa watching TV, they entered the den where the boy's laptop was still sitting on the coffee table. Knox closed the door, then took a seat on one of the chairs.

"Willow's sister recorded a video message for her," Razor said as he slipped the flash drive into the computer and opened the file. He sat back, watching as Laurel Townsend's stunning revelations began to play for Knox.

The big Hunter said nothing during the video, but with each moment he listened his face hardened with grim understanding—and barely banked anger.

By the time the video ended, his eyes were burning with amber fury. "Those fuckers. They were planning to eradicate our entire species."

"Still planning to do it," Razor said. "All they need is Laurel's formula."

"And some of her blood," Knox added. His mouth flattened. "Or her twin sister's."

Razor gave a sober nod. "Somewhere along the way, the decision must've come down that letting Laurel live was too great a risk to their operation. Now, they're after Willow."

"What does she want to do?"

"Willow wants to give the flash drive to the Order. She wants them to have Laurel's research and the formulas for Serenicure." He cleared his throat. "At least, that's what she wanted before I just fucked everything up with her."

Knox studied him. "Do I even want to guess?"

Razor scoffed under his breath. "I drank from her. I took her blood when I knew damned well I didn't have the right."

"Shit." Knox exhaled. "You still haven't told her about the drone surveillance?"

"I tried. I meant to explain it all before now, but I couldn't find the right time."

Knox grunted. "The right time would've been before you put your fangs in her neck."

Razor wanted to hit him with a sharp comeback, but he didn't have the words. He couldn't find anything humorous in the situation, knowing how confused and wounded he'd left her a few minutes ago. "It gets worse," he said, giving his brother a remorseful look. "After I drank from her, Willow told me that she loved me. I should've laid everything out then and there. Hell, I should've told her that I'm in love with her too. Instead, I walked out of the room letting her think she was the one who did something wrong."

Knox stared at him, not in recrimination, but with a cryptic kind of sympathy. "Yeah, you fucked up all right."

"Thanks for the vote of confidence."

"So, go fix it."

Razor nodded. "You think I can?"

He shrugged. "That's going to be up to her. All I know is, you've been half in love with that woman for the better part of a year. It's long past time you let her know it."

Knox was right on all counts. Razor only hoped he'd be able to persuade Willow to give him a chance to make things right.

"What about the flash drive?" Knox asked. "You going to reach out to your contacts at the Order?"

Razor considered, knowing time was of the essence. "I can contact them through private channels on the web. You got a secure phone I could borrow in case I need it for a callback?"

"Leni's got an old school land line in the basement."

Razor grinned. "Analog, even better. What's the number?"

Knox recited the digits, which Razor easily memorized. Going to an encrypted site controlled by Gideon at the Order's headquarters in Washington, D.C., he then typed in his message and left the number where he could be securely reached.

"It shouldn't take long before we hear back."

At that same moment, a soft rap sounded on the door. The two Breed males exchanged surprised looks until Leni's worried-sounding voice came through the thick wood panel.

"Is it okay if I come in?"

Knox was on his feet and at the opened door in less than a second. "What is it, sweetheart? Is it the baby?"

"No, no, we're both fine. The new freezer we ordered for the diner is here early. The driver's waiting to unload it over there now, so Shannon and I are going to run over and meet him."

"I'll go with you."

She frowned, looking at him as if he'd lost his mind. "It's nearly noon and broad daylight out there. Do you mind staying to watch Riley for a few minutes? Shannon and I can handle this."

Razor could practically feel his brother's reluctance to let his pregnant mate out of his sight, even at the risk of high noon UV burns.

"I'll be fine," Leni assured him. "Riley won't be any trouble, either. He's watching one of his favorite shows. Besides, you and Razor look like you've got things of your own you're dealing with here."

Although Knox didn't look pleased, he agreed with

a curt nod then dropped a tender kiss on Leni's mouth. He broke away on a low snarl. "If you're not home in twenty minutes, I'm heading over there."

She rolled her eyes, but smiled up at him with pure devotion. "Are you going to be this growly and protective over me once our son is born?"

"Baby, in case you haven't realized it yet, I'm going to be growly and protective for the rest of your life. I don't want to hear any complaints about it."

"Who's complaining?" She danced out of his reach on a smile and a giggle. "Let's go, Shan."

"I'll walk you two out," Knox said. He glanced back at Razor. "You good here?"

"Yeah. I'm just going to check a few more things."

Once his brother stepped out with Leni, Razor went back to the laptop. He brought up a new browser, then accessed one of his private servers. Out of habit, his fingers moved to the folder containing all of his months of drone surveillance footage.

He opened one of the video recordings, staring at the screen as the camera panned over the familiar Colorado landscape and small mountain cabin that once stood there. It was barely Spring in the video, snow still clinging to the rock and vegetation outside the cabin. The narrow dirt road was muddy and slick, but that didn't deter the black Jeep that steadily made the climb up from the village.

Razor's chest constricted as he watched the gorgeous brunette park the vehicle and hop out from behind the wheel. Not Laurel Townsend, but Willow Valcourt.

His woman.

His destined mate.

He'd known that in his heart even without her blood

living in his veins now.

After watching her head into the cabin, he closed the file and moved to another one. Still more drone footage, this one recorded later in the season. He fast-forwarded past the endless hours of inactivity outside the cabin, knowing precisely when Willow would appear in the frame.

How often had he played these recordings over the months of surveillance for Theo? How often had he dreamed of what it might be like to see his obsession in person, to talk to her, to touch her?

Now, she was right upstairs and all he wanted to do was avoid her. No, that wasn't true. All he wanted was to keep her at his side, in his life, for the rest of eternity. He wanted that dream to start now, and the only thing standing in his way was him. He needed to come clean with Willow and hope she'd find it in her heart to forgive him for not telling her the truth from the beginning.

As he rehearsed what he was going to say, Knox came back to the den at an urgent clip.

"Land line's ringing downstairs. Guess the Order got your message."

Razor closed the laptop and followed Knox to the basement to take the call.

CHAPTER 24

Willow stepped out of the bathroom freshly showered and dressed, her damp hair twisted into a loose, messy bun.

She thought the shower would help clear her thoughts but it was impossible to put Razor out of her mind when she could still feel him in every place he'd touched her. Every place he'd caressed, kissed, and dominated her body still thrummed with remembered pleasure . . . and longing.

She didn't want to know what that probably said about her. Razor hadn't been able to get away from her fast enough, calling what they'd shared a mistake. Even worse, he'd actually apologized for it, which only made her feel like an even bigger fool for believing there was something more between them than base desire.

He'd certainly made her think there was something real between them. He'd made her feel special.

Protected. Cherished. Had he said all those pretty things to her just so he could win over her trust enough to use her body? Her blood?

Something inside her balked at the idea that Razor could be so callous, despite the fact that he'd been born and raised as an emotionless killing machine. She'd believed in her heart that he was better than that, that he was a good man. Part of her still wanted to believe he was, but the part of her that was accustomed to being cast off and made to feel like an unwanted outsider whispered this wasn't the first time she'd been wrong about someone.

That didn't make it hurt any less, though.

To keep from getting lost in dark thoughts, she busied herself with straightening up the bed while trying to summon her dignity enough to leave the guest room. Humiliated or not, she couldn't stay holed up in the attic all day. As she began smoothing out the homespun quilt on the bed, a knock sounded on the closed door.

"Come in," she said, her voice sounding guarded even to her own ears.

The knob twisted and the panel began to creak open. Willow braced herself for the possibility that Razor had returned, but instead it was Riley who stepped into the room carrying his laptop under his arm.

"Well, hello," Willow said as the boy strolled in and plopped himself on the end of the bed. "What are you up to?"

His shrug seemed to involve his entire body. "I'm bored."

"Where's your mom?"

"She went to the diner with Aunt Leni."

"And where's . . . everyone else?" Willow hedged.

"I dunno."

Willow doubted Riley had been left alone in the house, and although she really wanted to ask about Razor, she refused to drag a child into her personal drama.

"Do you wanna play a game?" he asked, swinging his legs up onto the mattress as he opened the computer. He didn't wait for her to answer. Patting his little hand on the bed, he practically demanded she take a seat next to him.

Willow sat down and watched as the laptop screen woke up. An aerial view image of a tranquil, springtime mountainside filled the monitor. The view was strangely familiar.

The fine hairs at the back of her neck rose as she stared at the picture on the screen.

It was more than familiar. She would know that sloping mountain view anywhere.

"Where did you get this?"

Riley gave another of his full-body shrugs. "It's some dumb movie where nothing happens."

"May I have a look?" she asked, taking the laptop from him.

The still was actually a paused video. Some kind of surveillance footage, shot by an apparent drone. She tapped the play button and watched in confusion as the drone hovered high above the Colorado mountainside. When Laurel's cabin came into the frame, Willow couldn't hold back her shocked gasp.

"What's wrong?" Riley asked, peering up at her in concern.

She shook her head, incapable of words as she watched the drone footage of her sister's cabin. Hour upon hour of overhead surveillance footage, based on the playback timer at the bottom of the video.

"How did you get this, Riley?"

He held up his hands. "Maybe Razor was watching it. It was already open when I took my computer from the den."

Razor was watching this? Where would he have gotten video footage of Laurel's cabin?

She minimized the file and realized it was just one of many contained in the opened folder. Dates on the files tracked back well into last year. There had to be several months' of coverage.

Did they belong to Razor? What the hell was he doing with these?

She opened another video and watched it for a few moments. Then another. And another. Finally, she opened one that showed her Jeep rolling up to the cabin. Willow's breath seized in her lungs as she watched herself get out of the vehicle carrying a bag of groceries for Laurel.

The drone's camera zoomed in on her and held, following her every move.

"Hey, is that you?" Riley blurted, pointing at the screen.

Willow could only stare, confusion and a mounting sense of suspicion—of betrayal—rising inside her. What business did Razor have with months of drone footage of that mountain? Had he been watching Laurel? Was he involved with her killers somehow?

That last question seemed totally impossible, given all he'd done to protect Willow. Her mind rejected it almost as swiftly as her heart. Yet even if he wasn't connected to her twin's murder, that still didn't explain why he would have kept his surveillance a secret. Unless he was ashamed for some reason.

Willow watched the way the drone's camera seemed to tighten on her as she moved. It felt somehow intimate. A violation of her personal space, now that she was viewing the video months after the fact.

A corrosive thought seeped into her thoughts as she watched how obsessively the camera's eye tracked her. Razor hadn't known she existed when this video footage was taken. He must have believed she was Laurel all that time.

She opened another video and scrolled forward until she appeared onscreen. Just like before, the camera found her and closed in again, as it had on the previous surveillance footage. As if the drone's operator couldn't look away.

As if he were obsessed.

Not with her, but with her twin sister.

He had mistaken her for Laurel when they met at the base of the mountain. And now Willow recalled how tenderly he had treated her twin's body after she was killed, taking care to bury her as if Laurel had meant something personal to him. As if he had cared for her not as a stranger but as someone important to him.

Was that why Razor had bolted from the room the instant Willow had said she loved him? He said himself he'd made a mistake drinking her blood. Had it only taken one taste for him to realize Willow would never be the one he truly wanted?

Had Willow only been his consolation prize for the woman he had been obsessed with but could never have?

She felt sick with herself for the rush of jealousy and

bitterness that swelled inside her. A shaky breath leaked out of her as she closed the laptop and set it aside.

"Are we gonna play a game or what?" Riley asked, frowning at her as she got up and began to pace a tight path at the end of the bed.

Everything was pressing down on her suddenly.

Willow couldn't bear the idea of facing Razor after she'd made herself look like such a fool. After seeing how obviously infatuated he'd been with her sister, she didn't know how she could ever look him in the face again.

She couldn't stay here another minute.

She didn't belong here. Didn't belong with him.

He had the flash drive with Laurel's formulas and instructions. He could bring it to the Order on his own. As for Willow, she just wanted to get out of there.

"I'm sorry, Riley. Our game's going to have to wait." She was already stepping into her boots and grabbing her purse while she talked.

"Where are you going, Willow?"

"I don't know yet," she told him honestly. "I just have to go."

Taking her purse and the oversized hoodie, she hurried out of the guest room and rushed down the attic stairs as fast as her feet would carry her.

CHAPTER 25

Razor struggled to stay focused on the conversation as he spoke with Gideon from the Order's D.C. headquarters. His mind was on Willow.

The fact that she was still raw and hurting because of him was a distraction he could hardly ignore. Even if her blood wasn't living inside him through his bond to her, he'd carry the weight of her pain like it was his own.

"I'm sure I don't need to tell you that this is some explosive intel," Gideon was saying. "To say that you and Willow have the Order's gratitude is putting it mildly."

The warriors were obviously keenly interested in the flash drive's contents. After hearing everything about Laurel Townsend's murder and the events that had brought Razor and Willow from Colorado to their current remote location in the North Maine Woods, the Order was making arrangements to pick up the drive and get more information from both Razor and Willow.

"We've got a team in Montreal that can be in Parrish Falls tonight," Gideon said. "All of our daywalkers in that region are out on missions or I'd already have them en route to you."

"No worries," Razor said, rubbing at the persistent ache behind his sternum. "Everything's secure here. We'll be waiting for your team to arrive."

Standing at Razor's side in the basement, Knox inclined his head in grim agreement. The former Hunter hadn't been pleased to have Razor arrive unannounced on his doorstep bringing potential danger along with him, but he was all in on doing whatever he could to help Razor and Willow stay safe and deliver Laurel's formulas and research to the Order.

It had been a long time since Razor had needed to rely on anyone, and it buoyed him to know that Knox had his back. It felt good knowing he hadn't lost his decent standing with the Order too. After the mess he'd left for them to clean up at St. Anne's, he wasn't sure how his call today would be received.

Now, all he could do was hope Willow might give him another chance to make things right with her. The ache that had been building in his chest through the blood bond was worsening now—until it felt as though his heart might break apart.

"Something's wrong," he murmured. "It's Willow."

"What's going on?" Gideon asked on the other end of the line.

Razor didn't have words. Shoving the corded telephone receiver at Knox, he bolted up the basement stairs. Halfway up the attic steps his veins turned cold.

Willow wasn't up there. The blood bond would have

told him if she was near, but all he felt was the nearly empty farmhouse around him.

He called out to her anyway, refusing to believe what his instincts were telling him. "Willow!"

He flashed into the guest room at the full speed of his Breed genetics, but the only person inside was Riley. Seated on the end of the bed with the computer on his lap, the boy looked up from the screen. "She left."

"What are you talking about?" He couldn't curb the panic edging his tone. Quickly scanning the room, he noted her purse and hoodie were gone. "Where is she, Riley?"

He shrugged. "I dunno. We were watching your movies on the laptop and then she said she had to go."

Razor's stomach sank. "What movies?"

Ah, fuck. He knew the answer even before Riley turned the computer around and showed him the drone video of Laurel's cabin. Willow had seen his surveillance footage.

She'd realized he'd been watching her twin's cabin long before he showed up in Colorado . . . and now Willow was gone.

"Goddamn it."

Riley's eyes went wide. "Aunt Leni doesn't like it when people swear."

Razor wheeled around on his boot heel and left the room before he said anything worse in front of the boy. He had to find Willow. Where the hell did she think she could go in the middle of fucking nowhere?

Racing down the stairs, he nearly collided with Knox in the kitchen. "What's wrong?"

"Willow. She left."

Knox frowned. "Left . . . where?"

Cold worry shot through Razor, chilling him to the bone. "I don't fucking know, but I have to find her."

"Razor, you can't—"

Ignoring his brother's warning, he threw open the back door and headed outside—straight into the searing light of a cloudless, noontime sky. The UV rays nearly blinded him, sunlight burning everywhere it touched his uncovered skin.

He didn't care.

All he could feel was Willow's confused, broken heart and his own agony at knowing he was the one who caused it. That he might have prevented it if he hadn't been so afraid of losing her over the truth. Now, he'd lost her anyway, and he might never have the chance to explain.

He ran around the old farmhouse but Willow was nowhere to be found. He didn't sense her in the woods out back, and the only other place she could have gone was the long stretch of unpaved, two-lane highway that ran in front of the house in both directions.

If she was on foot, she couldn't have gotten very far.

He started running along the dirt road, his vision bleary from the scorching sunlight. As a Gen One Breed, he knew UV rays were deadlier to him than most. He had ten minutes before the burns would begin to eat away his skin and eyes. Half an hour at most before the sun consumed the rest of him.

He didn't know how far he'd run before he heard a vehicle rumbling up behind him. He could barely see anymore. His bare hands and forearms were blistered and red, his *glyphs* smoking as the sunlight continued to assault him.

An old Bronco rolled up beside him. Knox was

behind the wheel, his eyes shielded by dark sunglasses and his face covered in a knit ski mask. "Have you lost your fucking mind?"

"I have to . . . find her."

"You won't get far like this and you know it, Raze."

He growled and kept walking. Knox cursed and hit the gas, angling the vehicle across the two-lane so it blocked Razor's way.

"Get in the truck, brother. Before I have to scoop up your ashes and bring you back."

Razor seethed, but he knew Knox was right. He'd be no good to anyone in a few more minutes, including Willow.

He didn't want to accept that she had really left, but everything in him sensed that wherever she'd gone she had to be miles away already. Had she hitched a ride with someone? From what he'd observed since their arrival, the road wasn't exactly a bustling thoroughfare, except for occasional local traffic and the infrequent logging truck or semi rolling in or out of the North Maine Woods on its way to somewhere else.

"We'll figure it out," Knox said, his deep voice gentler now. "We'll find her, Raze. But first you need to get back inside so you can heal."

Razor took one last look up the seemingly endless stretch of roadway that cut through the dense forest. His only consolation was the fact that Willow was alive. And as long as she was, he would feel that certainty in his blood. In his heart and soul.

He *would* find her. He had to explain why he'd been so afraid to be honest with her, and he needed her to know he loved her more than anyone or anything in his life before her.

He had to make Willow understand she was, and would always be, the only woman for him. All he needed was the chance to say all the things he should have told her from the beginning.

"Okay," he said, his voice airless and dry as ash in his scorched throat.

Knox inclined his head in acknowledgment, then leaned over and popped open the passenger door for Razor to get in.

CHAPTER 26

"Thanks again for the ride," Willow told the delivery truck driver as he turned his rig in to the busy interstate truck stop nearly three hours east of Parrish Falls.

"It's no problem at all," the kind, older man reassured her. "I'm heading this way to deliver new appliances to the big resort, anyway. Was nice having company for a stretch, even if you're not much of a talker."

Willow gave him a weak smile. It had been all she could do to hold herself together for the long drive, never mind find the energy for a lot of conversation with a stranger. Besides, the less anyone knew about her or her problems, the better.

As harmless as the aged trucker seemed, she hadn't forgotten the fact that there were still bad men out there looking for her. It had only been two days since the attack at St. Anne's, and while she'd felt safe with Razor in Parrish Falls with Knox and Leni, she was well aware of how vulnerable she was out in public on her own.

The trucker, a grandfather named Lou with eight grandchildren and two great-grands on the way, as he'd been proud to tell her, glanced over at her as he brought the big truck to a stop to let her out. "Where you heading from here, Jenny?"

She had given him the fake name when he'd picked her up just outside Knox and Leni's house. When he asked why she was alone on the empty road through the North Maine Woods, she'd given him an equally fake story about wanting to hitchhike her way around the country for a few months. She didn't know if he believed her but he hadn't questioned anything she told him, and for that she was grateful.

"I'm not sure yet," she answered truthfully.

She couldn't go back to her place in Colorado anymore. Even if she didn't worry about Laurel's killers finding her there, she couldn't imagine trying to live anywhere near the place where her twin was murdered. It was time to start fresh again somewhere new.

Having spent most of her life by herself, she wasn't afraid of being alone. But somehow this time—without Razor—she felt lonely and adrift.

"Well, wherever you're going, you take care," the old man said, a solemn, sympathetic look in his eyes.

She nodded. "Thank you. Hug those grandbabies when you see them."

He chuckled. "Oh, no doubt about that. Goodbye, Jenny."

"Bye, Lou."

She climbed out of the truck and crossed the

pavement, hands in her pockets and her head tilted down inside the oversized hoodie. Lou had mentioned the Bangor airport was only about an hour south on the interstate. Maybe she could hitch a ride in that direction, then buy a plane ticket to somewhere warm and remote to hunker down for a while.

Guilt stabbed at her for the way she'd run out on Razor. She'd run out on her obligation to Laurel too. Willow had a duty to ensure her sister's death hadn't been for naught. Laurel's research into a true cure for Bloodlust could not be allowed to fall into her killers' hands. Those people had to be stopped from exploiting the formula into something horrific.

If she disappeared, at least no one would be able to use her blood to further their hideous plans to wipe out the entire population of the Breed.

As much as Razor's betrayal hurt her, she couldn't bear the thought of a world without him in it. Bad enough that he would no longer be in hers.

Rallying herself for what she had to do, Willow stepped into the truck stop convenience store and peered around for potential Good Samaritans who might be safe and willing to give her a ride.

Her options were sorely lacking. A sullen twenty-something man stood behind the cashier counter scrolling on his phone. He gave her a brief once-over as she entered, then went back to scrolling. The only other patrons included a couple of rough-looking truckers and an older man with a scraggly beard who gave her a greasy smile that lingered with too much interest on her face.

Tugging the hoodie farther over her head, she ducked into a snack aisle to gather some food in case this brief pitstop lasted longer than she hoped. Choosing a few things that would fit in her purse and not exceed the meager cash she had in her wallet, she attempted to look casual as she perused the store and prayed for a miracle to take her out of there.

Maybe the cashier would let her use his phone to call a rideshare service? She figured it was worth a shot to ask him.

With her small armload of snacks, she started heading toward the register—just in time to notice the police patrol car rolling into one of the parking spaces out front. Two uniformed cops got out and approached the entrance.

Shit. Willow quickly detoured, instead moving farther toward the back of the aisles as they came inside. There was nowhere to hide if they were looking for her. Nowhere to escape their notice, even if they weren't a threat to her. She crept back to the wall of glass-fronted refrigerators, turning her back to the front of the store and feigning interest in the dozens of sodas, juices, and bottled water.

"Got any of those roast beef sandwiches in the case?" one of the officers asked the cashier. "We're going to be eating lunch on the road today."

"Uh, I think we got some. Lemme check."

Willow watched the reflections in the refrigerator glass as the clerk shuffled over to assist the officer. The cop's partner headed for the chip racks. Meanwhile, another patron entered the store, a tall guy in a suit who was yammering about 'boneheaded accountants' and reports that were going to be filed late because of them. He paused to grab a bag of pretzels, still talking in the open as though everyone in the store needed to hear what a big, important deal he was.

Willow rolled her eyes, annoyed despite her anxiety over the police presence.

"Do you mind?" Suddenly, he was standing right next to her. "No, not you, Marcus. I'm talking to some kid blocking the soda cases."

Willow swung her head to look at him as she moved aside. Shrewd, dark brown eyes collided with her gaze for less than a second before flicking away without apology or interest. He opened the glass door and pulled out a Coke, letting the door close with a bang as he resumed his public conversation and walked to the cashier.

"So, how long am I going to have to wait on those commissions?"

Willow tuned him out, more focused on where the police officers were. The guy in the suit had distracted her long enough that she'd lost them in the store momentarily. She spotted them both in the chip aisle now, neither one looking her way.

Grabbing a bottled water, she tucked it under her arm and carried all of her selections up to the counter. As much as she wanted to ask the clerk to borrow his phone, she didn't dare linger inside any longer. She could try again after the police were gone.

She paid in cash as quickly as possible, then rushed out of the store.

She'd barely made it out the door before a heavy hand came to rest on her shoulder from behind. "Excuse me, miss."

Fuck. It was the cop who asked about sandwiches.

Dread arrowed through her as she debated whether to turn around and face whatever danger she'd just landed in or to make a run for it.

"You must be in an awful hurry to get somewhere," the officer said to the back of her head.

She slowly pivoted around . . . only to realize he was holding her bottle of water.

She let out a relieved breath and took the bottle from him. "Thank you."

He nodded, giving her a friendly smile. "Have a good day now."

Her anxiety released like an outgoing tide as she watched the two cops get into their patrol car and drive away. Her paranoia was just that. God, she was a bundle of nerves.

And she still had the challenge of finding a ride to Bangor, hopefully while it was still daylight.

The sound of swiftly approaching footsteps came from somewhere to her left. "Hey, can you tell me how to get to Medway from here?"

She swiveled her head to say she didn't know and was stunned to realize it was the man in the suit. He was smiling, but there was no warmth in his dark eyes. He came closer to her—too close—and abruptly brought his hand up.

Willow saw the gleam of a syringe needle flash in the sunlight before he jabbed it into the side of her neck. The world around her started going dark. Her legs gave out, but he held her up and started walking her toward his waiting vehicle.

"Yeah, it's her," he said in a low voice into his Bluetooth. "I've got her contained. I'm bringing her in now, sir."

CHAPTER 27

Razor peeled his eyes open with a groan.

Pain seared him over most of his body, although the worst of what he'd endured had passed. Skin that had felt as if it were being flayed off his bones had knit back together, healing faster than normal, no doubt because of the benefit of Willow's blood living inside him now.

The attic guest room where he lay was dark, the only light coming from the thin moon shining through the small window. He must have been unconscious and recuperating for hours. The last thing he recalled was Knox bringing him back to the house and helping him up the stairs after the ultraviolet rays had nearly smoked him on the road.

Now, the sounds of conversation downstairs—two deep male voices talking with Knox, and what sounded like a pair of females as well—helped shake off the last of his grogginess. He recognized one of the male voices. The Siberian-accented growl could belong to none other than Nikolai, a Breed warrior Razor had spoken with from time to time over the years and the leader of the Montreal command center.

The Order team was in Parrish Falls.

Razor sat up slowly on the bed, a move that sapped more of his strength than he wanted to admit. Swinging his legs over the edge of the mattress, he paused to simply focus on breathing.

His head pounded. The soft, pale moonlight felt as bright as a strobe to his scorched retinas. Everywhere his skin had been exposed to sunlight earlier that day felt as if it had been dipped in an acid bath.

But it was the unsettling, persistent silence in his heart—in his very being—that disturbed him the most. The internal quiet chilled him all the way to his marrow. Part of him felt almost untethered, as if a crucial piece of his soul had gone adrift while he was sleeping.

Ah, fuck.

"Willow."

He vaulted to his feet, ignoring the excruciating protests of his injured body. His steps dragged as he made his way out of the guest room, then shakily down the attic steps to the main floor of the house.

He found everyone gathered in the living room. Leni was seated on one of the cushioned chairs, Knox standing at her side. Nikolai and his leather-clad, ebony-haired Breedmate, Renata, sat on the sofa next to another couple from the Order. Although Razor had never met Order commander Sterling Chase or Tavia Fairchild, the rare Breed female Chase had taken as his mate, Razor knew enough about the Order's power couple from Boston to realize who they were.

As he approached, the group was talking about Serenicure and the doctor whose initial experimentations had been the basis for UWSI's newer, insidious purpose for the formula.

"As soon as we heard Henry Lewis's sick chemical cocktail was back in circulation, we wanted to see the flash drive for ourselves," Sterling Chase was saying, his hand locked around Tavia's. "Far as I'm concerned, that formula is a declaration of war. Lucan and the rest of the Order are in agreement too. We—"

The warrior's words cut short as he, along with everyone else in the room, saw Razor.

Based on the looks he was getting, he realized he had to look like death warmed over. Possibly not even that good.

"She's gone." The statement sounded flat in his scorched throat, but inside he was a tempest of exploding fury. "Something's happened to Willow. I can hardly feel her anymore."

Knox's face went grave with alarm. "You don't mean she's—"

"Not dead," Razor cut in. No, thank fuck, she hadn't been killed. But something had changed drastically in the time he'd been unconscious. "My bond with her . . . it's muffled. Something's dulling the connection."

The group from the Order exchanged confused, concerned glances. Nikolai stood up, staring at Razor in question. "You and this female are mated?"

"Long story," Razor growled. "I drank from Willow today even though I had no right."

Niko gave a somber nod, a grim sort of sympathy in his icy blue eyes. "Where is she?"

"As soon as she realized I'd been lying to her about something, she left."

"We don't know where she's gone," Knox added. "Near as we can guess, she hitched a ride with a freezer delivery truck driver. She could've been on the interstate within a couple of hours after leaving here."

"She's in danger," Razor snarled. "I can feel it. I have to find her."

The rest of the Order members rose, Chase glancing at Nikolai. "It's going to be a needle in a haystack, trying to locate her. She could be anywhere by now."

"I don't give a fuck how far I have to go," Razor muttered. "I'm not going to rest until she's safe."

Sterling Chase rested his hand lightly on Razor's shoulder. "I know. And you don't have to do it alone. Don't think any of us are unaware of how often you've lent a hand to the Order over the years without asking for anything in return. Whatever we can do to help now, you've got it."

"Me too, brother," Knox added. "We're all in this together."

The unexpected support shouldn't have hit him so hard, yet it did. After being born and bred for nothing but destruction and evil, he'd tried to live his life doing the right thing. Helping good people. Using his skills to make the world a little better. Now, feeling it come back to him like this at a time when he needed help the most was almost more than he could process.

He gave his friends a stiff, uncomfortable nod. It was all he could manage by way of expressing his profound gratitude. Everything in him was focused on the echoing silence in his veins. The cold dread that told him his woman, his mate, *his everything*, was in mortal danger.

"They've got her," he said, his voice scraping like gravel in his throat. "They've done something to her, I can feel it."

Nikolai glanced at Chase. "Too bad Lars and Simon Scrully are already dead. We could've shaken those trees for information."

It was Tavia who answered. "Then we go straight to UWSI instead." Her eyes flashed with amber light, and behind her lips the sharp points of her fangs gleamed. "I'd personally love to get my hands on the sick fucks who think they can profit off genocide against the Breed."

The other Order members nodded in agreement.

"I'll phone ahead to the command center and tell my team to suit up and be ready to roll when we get there," Niko said, already pulling his comm unit from his pocket to make the call.

Knox helped Leni up from her chair and gently pulled her into his embrace. "I'll be home as soon as I can. You going to be okay until then?"

She gave him a worried looking smile, but bobbed her head in the affirmative. "Be careful."

"Always." He gave her a tender kiss before stepping over to Razor.

"You don't have to do this, Knox. You should stay with your mate."

The former Hunter scoffed. "What's wrong? You think my skills got rusty living up here in the frozen north?"

Razor chuckled despite his pain and worry. "I guess what I'm trying to say is, thanks."

Knox inclined his head. "Let's go find your woman and bring her home, brother."

Although every movement was agony, Razor walked with Knox and the members of the Order out to the large black SUV parked in the driveway. They got situated inside the vehicle, Nikolai sliding behind the wheel.

Once on the road, he hit the gas and the SUV roared into motion.

Tavia pivoted around to look at Razor. "We're going to find her, no matter what it takes."

He nodded, but even as he did so he could feel his connection to Willow fading. Every minute that passed seemed to stretch his blood bond to her thinner and thinner.

Deep down, a sharp-edged panic began to settle into his veins. What if they were already too late to reach her in time to save her? What if he truly had lost her forever?

"Can this thing go any faster?" he muttered into the quiet of the SUV.

Niko met his gaze in the rearview mirror. The mood among everyone was too grim for humor now, even from him.

Without a word, the warrior floored the accelerator and the vehicle rocketed into the night.

CHAPTER 28

They made the drive to Montreal in record time, meeting up with the rest of Nikolai's warriors on a dark street about a block from a gleaming glass high-rise tower of UWSI headquarters.

The infiltration plan had been hatched and agreed upon while Razor and the others were en route. The team's objective was twofold, but of equal importance: Locate and rescue Willow; and confiscate every file, lab record, formula, and bit of information pertaining to Serenicure.

For Razor there was only one goal in tonight's mission, and he wasn't going to quit until he had Willow back in his arms. He clung to the fading vibration of his blood bond to her, which seemed to be diminishing by the minute.

He had to find her.

He had promised to keep her safe, to protect her

with his own life. He couldn't live with himself knowing he'd failed to uphold that pledge. It was hard enough knowing he'd also let her down in every other way that mattered.

"We'll need to split up to cover ground quickly," Chase instructed. "Tavia and I will take the east wing of the building with Razor and Knox."

Nikolai nodded. "My team will form two groups. Renata and I will cover the west side of the building, while the rest of my unit will sweep the lab and offices for any intel we can collect."

"Minimize casualties," Chase cautioned. "Most of the security detail and other employees in there are just trying to do their jobs. Use lethal force only if necessary. Stealth infiltration is key, especially until we can determine if they're holding Willow somewhere inside."

Knox glanced at Razor in concern. "You sure you're up for this?"

"Yeah. I'm good." The UV burns were almost healed now. Even if he'd still been scorched to within an inch of his life, nothing would stop him from his mission to find and rescue Willow. "I'm more than ready," he told his friend and the other warriors who were waiting for his answer. "Let's go."

Holstering the pair of semiautomatics given to him by the Order, he stalked ahead of everyone. The rest of the team moved stealthily too, their dark shapes vanishing into the night as the infiltration plan got under way.

Up ahead, the UWSI building gleamed like a beacon. Nearly every floor was lit up, the firm's employees apparently working around the clock. On the street level, armed security guards flanked the main entrance and roamed the lobby inside.

With the game plan being to secure and trance all onsite staff, they were going to have their hands full. Unfortunately, it was a necessary step in order to allow the warriors to turn the building inside out searching for Willow and confiscating everything related to the drug UWSI was working on.

While the Montreal team moved to the headquarters' west side, Razor and his three comrades slipped around to the underground garage without notice. Inside, they located a locked service door. Using a mental command to bypass the access code, they poured inside the building.

From what intel they had on the thirty-story building, the research labs were housed on the ninth and tenth floors. Meanwhile, Nikolai and his team should be sweeping through the administrative and computer rooms to secure those areas.

Razor raced up the stairwell with the others. Chase split off at the seventh floor. Tavia slipped through the door that opened onto the eighth. With a grim nod at Razor, Knox disappeared through the door leading to the research labs on nine.

Despite the fact that he was moving with all his Breed velocity and agility, to Razor everything felt too slow. Part of the feeling stemmed from the bone-deep dread that Willow was slipping further and further away from him. His bond to her was thinning, stretching, as fragile as a gossamer strand now . . . but it was still there.

She was still alive.

And unless his UV-scorched mind was playing tricks on him, she wasn't far from where he stood now. She was somewhere in this building.

"I'm coming for you," he whispered under his breath. "Hang on, baby. Don't give up. I'm going to find you."

He stepped onto the tenth floor from the stairwell door. Bright lights illuminated the hospital-like area full of white tile floors, stainless-steel medical equipment, and room after room of laboratory workers and humming electronics. The sterile, repulsive sight was so reminiscent of his own upbringing he could hardly contain his rage.

A security guard posted near the entrance spotted him and made the mistake of raising his service weapon at him. In a blur of motion Razor had his hands around the man's neck and poised to snap it. Recalling Chase's instructions about stealth and limited casualties, he tranced the guard instead and let his unconscious body slide to the tiled floor.

He stepped forward, cutting a swift line down the long hallway through the center of the research unit. Human lab workers in white coats scattered in every direction the second they saw him coming. Like rats on a sinking ship, they fled the floor in moments.

When another security guard came charging at him like a hero, Razor deflected the attack, breaking the man's weapon in two before knocking the guard into the far wall.

Several of the glass-windowed rooms had semiconscious occupants strapped to the beds. Breed males suffering Bloodlust and in various states of physical decline, all too weak or too heavily sedated to do more than lift their eyelids as he stalked by on his search for Willow.

She wasn't on this floor.

At the same time, Chase radioed in over the team's comm unit that he and Tavia had the seventh and eighth floors contained, but no sign of Willow there either.

"Nine is negative too," Knox reported.

Nikolai and his comrades advised they had tranced the staff in the west wing of the building and were in the process of downloading data off the UWSI servers. "We should have everything zipped up in about ten more minutes."

"I need more time," Razor snarled into his comm unit. "Willow is here somewhere. I can feel it."

He didn't wait for anyone's permission or agreement. The Order had the situation under control on their end, but he still had his own business to finish.

Stay alive, Willow. I need you to stay alive.

There were thirty floors in the building. If he had to search them all one by one to find Willow, he'd damn well better get started.

CHAPTER 29

Willow felt submerged in darkness, her body heavy and cold.

Her limbs were impossible weights that would not budge, even though her mind urged them to move. To fight. To escape whatever was holding her down, sapping every last ounce of strength she possessed.

Like a tide of thick tar, the world around her continued to close in. She swam and struggled against it, instinct warning her if she gave up and let it drag her under she would never emerge from it again.

And it wasn't only her own voice she heard demanding that she keep fighting, keep living. It was Razor's deep voice echoing in her head too. She heard him in her heart.

Don't give up . . .

I'm going to find you . . .

Stay alive, Willow. I need you to stay alive.

Even though she knew it had to be a trick of her suffocating mind, Razor's desperate, pleading words were like a beacon reaching out to her through the endless, black void that held her. She latched on to the ghost of his voice like a lifeline, holding fast and fighting to resurface.

Her eyelids slowly peeled open, feeling as leaden and uncooperative as the rest of her.

Blinding white light seared her vision from overhead lamps shining down on her from the ceiling of what appeared to be some kind of hospital room. A machine beeped softly from somewhere beside her. Its sluggish tempo began to increase in speed as she blinked and inhaled a rasping breath.

Her eyes were the only thing she could move. Glancing wildly at her foreign surroundings, she saw electronic monitors, wires, and slender tubes running from her body to several other machines positioned at her bedside.

A jolt of fear chased through her deadweight limbs. *Where the hell was she?*

Moving on pure adrenaline, she attempted to sit up. Tight restraints around her wrists and ankles kept her trapped on the hard hospital bed. The monitors attached to her began beeping rapidly in response to her rising panic.

Oh, God. What was happening?

She had to get up. She had to get out of there.

But she couldn't move. A dry moan escaped her parched lips.

"Shh, shh . . . Easy now," an emotionless male voice said from somewhere inside the room. "There's no cause for alarm, Miss Valcourt."

Like hell there wasn't.

She fought against her restraints now, using precious energy in a frantic, futile effort to break free. The man in the room with her moved closer to the bed, peering down at her with objective calm. Cocking his head, he studied her as though she were no more significant than an insect caught on the head of a pin.

"We're nearly finished now," he said pleasantly.

He was an older man, likely in his late forties. Beneath his white lab coat he wore an expensive looking suit and crisp white shirt. His dark hair was streaked with gray and thinning on top, his saggy jaw covered in a neatly trimmed salt-and-pepper beard.

There was nothing overtly sinister about his demeanor or his face, yet his brown eyes stared at her with total apathy even as hot tears leaked down her temples.

"I've kept you heavily sedated since you arrived," he told her. His cold gaze flicked to the monitors. "That shouldn't be necessary anymore. I trust you're not in any discomfort?"

She tried to curse at him but the sound that came out of her was pathetic, even to her own ears.

Who the fuck was he? Where was this place? How long had she been here?

Was there anyone else around to hear her even if she could manage to scream for help?

A shudder started in her bones and traveled the length of her body and limbs. The room seemed to be getting colder by the moment. Her teeth began to chatter behind her cracked, dry lips.

The man released a sigh as he gazed down at her on the bed. "You're cold because you've lost a great deal of blood. I'll fetch another blanket for you." He stepped away for a moment, returning to carefully cover her with a lightweight coverlet. "This should help," he said, tucking her in like a child. "Better?"

She couldn't answer. Couldn't make her mind make sense of anything she was seeing or hearing. All she knew for certain was the darkness still edging toward her, ready to pull her under so deep she would never get out. She wasn't so far gone that she was unable to recognize the madness of the man currently attending her.

Killing her, she had little doubt.

"Wh-who—"

He tilted his head. "Who am I? My name is Owen Lewis. I'm the president of the research institute where your sister, Laurel, was once employed."

The Unity for Wellness and Safety Institute, Willow's sluggish mind raced to recall. UWSI.

Why was this man's name somehow familiar?

She swallowed past the rawness in her throat. "You—you . . . killed her."

Lewis frowned and slowly shook his head. "It didn't have to be that way. She left me no choice, you see. Your sister couldn't understand the vision of UWSI's work. It's a shame, really. She was a brilliant chemist. As it turned out, her mind wasn't her only invaluable asset." He glanced up at the tubes running from Willow's arms to the machines collecting her blood. "I assume Laurel told you about her work on the Serenicure project? About the formula for Serenicure-L?"

Willow struggled against her restraints again, but the bindings held fast. "Let me—go."

He gave her a pitying smile. "Oh, I'm afraid it's too

late for that. You're almost drained now."

Fear seeped into her marrow at his chilling statement. Even though part of her realized what was happening to her, hearing him say the words was almost more than she could bear. She fought her restraints, but it only served to exhaust her.

"You know, as disappointed as I was with your sister, I didn't want to have her killed. I didn't particularly want to have Theo Collier killed either, but the two of them colluded together to sabotage the Serenicure project. They could have ruined everything, and that breach of trust could not go unmet."

Willow closed her eyes, appalled to hear her sister's murderer speak so casually about what he'd done to both Laurel and Theo.

"They thought they were so clever, the two of them. Stealing research, corrupting formulas. Destroying data that would take years to recreate." Lewis shook his head. "Your sister could have saved easily thousands of human lives through her formula for Serenicure-L. Her blood was the missing piece to a final cure for the global problem of the Breed. It's something we've been trying to develop for decades, starting with my father's work some twenty-odd years ago."

His father? And then it dawned on her—the reason his name sounded vaguely familiar.

Owen Lewis was Dr. Henry Lewis's son.

The same Dr. Lewis whose research Laurel had mentioned was the starting point for the Serenicure project. The same Dr. Lewis that Razor had said once served an even bigger monster named Dragos.

"My father never got the chance to develop his work to its fullest potential. If he had, he might have eradicated the Breed from existence long before now. Instead, it's my turn to make that dream a reality. I couldn't allow your sister or her boyfriend to stand in my way."

Willow's shallow breath raced as he spoke. Owen Lewis was mad, clearly. He was a homicidal lunatic and because of her stupid pride being wounded by Razor's rejection, she had walked right into this maniac's hands today.

What was worse, however—infinitely worse than her looming death—was the horror of realizing what he intended to do with all the blood he was draining from her veins.

"Laurel thought she had outsmarted me," he continued, reaching up to adjust a setting on one of the monitors above her head. "She thought she had destroyed all of the Serenicure-L specimens, but we still had a small sample in reserve. Enough that we didn't need to bother with a traitorous colleague who should've known better than to bite her master's hand. We were working to synthesize Laurel's blood so we could begin manufacturing the formula on a larger scale when it came to our attention that she had an identical twin." He smiled a serpent's smile. "Such a fortuitous discovery, don't you think? Your blood is about to save UWSI a great deal of effort, time, and money. Eventually, it will also return our planet to where it belongs—under human control. Your blood and Serenicure will finally mean the end of the Breed on Earth."

Rage erupted inside her. As futile as it was, she bucked and thrashed against the leather restraints pinning her down.

The monitors bleated in protest as her heart rate

spiked and adrenaline surged through her veins in what was likely a last burst of energy. Weakness from her blood loss left her sagging onto the hard mattress, her lungs burning with each hitching breath she took.

Lewis frowned at her now, looking agitated for the first time since she'd opened her eyes and saw his inhuman face.

"You've pulled some of the leads loose, you stupid girl." He was none too gentle as he fixed the problems, his brows furrowed over those cold eyes of his. Splashes of blood marred his white lab coat from where her IVs had come undone. "Perhaps I will sedate you for the remainder of our time together. We can't have any of your blood going to waste now, can we."

He made an adjustment to one of the monitors, and the room began to darken all around her.

CHAPTER 30

Razor's search of the building netted him floor after floor of frustration—and fear.

No sign of Willow, despite his bone-deep certainty that she was there . . . somewhere.

His bond to her had been fading by the minute but as he raced through some empty offices on the twenty-third floor, he felt a surge of life flood into his veins. The sensation was short and sharp, a jab of panic laced with the bitter tang of adrenaline. *Hers.*

Goddamn them. What were they doing to her?

Focusing his senses on the feel of Willow in his blood, he honed in with everything he had. The bond was weakening, but he wasn't about to let it slip out of his grasp.

And then, he knew.

Willow was on one of the higher floors.

Holy hell. He could only be moments away from her.

"Hey!" A deep male voice called out from behind him. "I'm talking to you, asshole."

Razor swiveled his head as a tall, menacing looking guy in a dark suit stepped out of the open elevator to approach him at an aggressive pace. He carried himself like a military man, with a wireless communication device in one ear and an assortment of weapons barely concealed under his unbuttoned jacket.

Private security, no doubt.

"What the fuck are you doing up here?" the guard demanded.

The man's eyes widened when he realized what Razor was. If he'd been smart he would have pivoted right around and got the hell out of there. Instead, he reached for one of the semiautomatic pistols holstered on his hip.

Razor leapt at him.

His rage over whatever was happening to Willow left him with no mercy. The guard tried to scramble back into the elevator, but his human reflexes were too slow. Razor took him down halfway inside the lift, grasping his head between his taloned hands and twisting the muscled neck as though it were nothing but a twig.

Rising up off the corpse, he was about to step off the elevator when his gaze caught on the numbered panel near the doors. There were buttons for all twenty-nine floors, with the top floor designated with the letters PH.

Penthouse.

Son of a bitch. That had to be where Willow was being held. Every instinct he had lit with cold, murderous certainty.

He jabbed the button but it did nothing. Protected by some kind of access code. Razor hit the panel with a mental command, blasting through the feeble electronic security system with the power of his mind.

Shoving the dead guard out of the elevator car with his boot, he stood back and waited for the doors to close and the lift to begin ascending to the top floor.

He sensed the presence of more armed security personnel even before the elevator opened into the foyer of a lavish penthouse. Two hulking guards gaped with shock as they spotted him.

Like their comrade, they grabbed for their weapons as if bullets would stop him. The fact that he was Breed was enough to render the pair walking dead men; his determination to reach Willow made Razor something far worse than lethal.

With fangs bared and talons out, he took down both guards in less than seconds. His boots moved silently over the polished wood and tile of the penthouse. Whoever it belonged to must have felt he was secure enough with just a handful of heavily armed men to safeguard him in his massive private office and living space at the top of the corporate tower.

It would have taken more than a full-scale army to keep Razor from Willow.

He was so close to her location now, his veins throbbed.

Rounding a corner in the art-lined corridor of the sprawling residence, he came upon a closed steel door at the far end of the hallway. He stalked toward it, rage building like an inferno inside him.

A state-of-the-art retina scanner lock was mounted into the thick concrete wall outside the door. Razor didn't even bother to short-circuit the panel. Seizing the door handle, he tore the reinforced steel panel from its hinges with his bare hands and tossed it behind him.

A man stood inside what appeared to be a private hospital examination room. He was wearing a blood-spattered white lab coat, a look of utter disbelief on his face as Razor took a step through the gaping hole.

But for all the man's shock, he was still managing to hold a scalpel against Willow's neck as she lay semiconscious on a hospital bed near where he stood.

"Don't come any closer," the middle-aged human warned. The sharp edge of his blade gleamed under the cold white light shining down on Willow's diminished form.

Razor growled, flexing his talon-tipped fingers. He could move faster than any man, but one slip of that scalpel and Willow's throat would be slashed wide open.

She must have sensed he was near. Her eyelids lifted lethargically, and those beautiful green eyes of hers locked on him through her obviously drugged haze. "Razor . . ."

With horror, he realized it wasn't only sedatives sapping her strength. All the medical tubes and beeping monitors hooked up to her—all the lines carrying her blood from her body to the collection machines situated around her bedside—the sick bastard standing next to her had nearly drained her dry.

Willow was dying right before his eyes.

"You son of a bitch," Razor snarled, his voice low, utterly inhuman. "You're killing her."

He started to lunge forward, but her captor pushed the scalpel even tighter against her throat. So tight, beads of blood began to gather against the glittering steel.

The man holding the blade shook his head. "I said, stay back. You may have stormed your way in here, but this is my domain. You and your kind have had your reign for long enough. Tonight, I've taken back the control that has always, rightfully, belonged to us. To mankind. What my father was prevented from completing, finally, I have finished."

Insanity crackled in the man's gaze, but his words started fitting together like a jigsaw puzzle in Razor's mind. "Your father was Henry Lewis."

"Dr. Henry Lewis," he corrected with a jut of his bearded chin. "He was a great man. A brilliant physician whose work would've changed this world for the better—"

"Your father was a genocidal piece of shit who deserved to die. So are you."

He laughed at the threat. "Even if you kill me, you can't stop my work. UWSI—"

"UWSI is finished," Razor informed him. "Your labs downstairs, your computers, all of your research and formulas. It's all gone now. You've lost control of your entire operation tonight. Serenicure will never see the light of day. Neither will you."

Finally, a crack in the man's veneer of confidence. He flinched, and the momentary inattention to the scalpel he held was all the opportunity Razor needed.

Moving so fast he was nothing but a blur of motion, he pounced on Willow's captor. Talons flashing like black blades, he tore the human apart and flung his shredded corpse to the other side of the room, as far away from Willow as possible.

Going her bedside, all his focus—all his concern—was centered on her. Retracting his talons, he tenderly stroked her clammy brow. "Love, can you hear me? You're safe now, Willow."

He wasn't sure he believed that, though he desperately wanted to.

She looked so weak, so pale.

Fuck, her skin was so damned cold beneath his blood-stained fingertips.

"Willow? Sweetheart, please, open your eyes."

Moaning softly, she did as he implored, though it clearly wasn't easy for her. "Razor . . ."

"That's right, it's me. I've got you now." He started unfastening the restraints on her ankles. "I'm going to get you out of here, baby. I'm going to make this right, I promise."

Moving to the leather straps shackled around her wrists, he worked impatiently to free them. Next, he got to work disconnecting all of the medical machinery.

Emotion swamped him as he unhooked her from the wires and tubes and leads. He didn't know he was capable of the kind of raw anguish he felt seeing her like this—or the terror he knew at the idea that even after all of this, he could still lose her.

"Don't you leave me, Willow," he told her urgently. "It nearly killed me when I realized you had left earlier today. When I realized I was to blame—"

"N-no," she whispered, her head moving side to side on the pillow. Her eyes were open, but only barely. Yet he could not mistake the ferocity shining in them. "Not your fault."

"Yes, it was." He bent his head toward hers, gently caressing the side of her face. "I know why you left. I know you saw that drone footage of Laurel's cabin. I know what you must've thought." He cursed under his breath. "I should've told you Theo had asked me to watch over the cabin for him. I should have explained everything to you right upfront—including the fact that I fell in love with you from the moment I first saw you drive up that mountain. *You*, Willow. There was never anyone else for me in all the time since. Only you."

A sob caught in her throat as she looked up at him. "I thought . . ."

"I know what you must've thought," he said, still loathing himself for the pain he caused her. "What you need to know is I love you, Willow. I always will."

She sighed softly, her eyes drifting closed. A peace settled over her, but all it stirred in Razor was bone-chilling alarm. Her color was fading toward a terrifying shade of blue. He took her hand between his and tried to rub some warmth into her. "Willow?"

She didn't respond. Carefully, he lifted her toward him and held her close. She was limp in his arms, slipping away with every shallow breath she took.

Ah, fuck. He couldn't let it happen.

He didn't know if she would welcome the gift he was about to give her. It should be her choice to make, not his. He had already taken her bond when it hadn't truly belonged to him. Now, he was about to bind her to him for the rest of eternity.

It was either that or feel her die in his arms.

A dark, desperate curse exploded off his tongue. Razor lifted his wrist to his mouth and bit down hard with his fangs. As soon as the blood began to pulse from his wounds, he pressed them to Willow's slack lips.

"Drink," he whispered fiercely. "Please, Willow . . . drink."

Her tongue swept lightly against his wrist. Then again. She took a deeper breath, a quiet moan vibrating her body. When her tongue came back for another taste of him, her lips fastened over his punctures. She drank. One small sip, then a bigger one.

Relief surged through him as she began to feed from him in great, hungry gulps.

"Yes," he coaxed her. "That's it, love. Drink some more. Drink as much as you need."

CHAPTER 31

At the first taste of Razor's blood, the thick black tide that had been clawing at her so determinedly recoiled, shrinking back under the power surging into her as she drank.

Like a scuttling thing made of shadows, insubstantial and cowering, that drowning darkness was no match at all for the roar of Razor's blood now filling her depleted body. His strength was hers, feeding her cells and organs, replenishing the life force that had been drained from her.

Razor's words in the moments before he gave her his wrist continued to echo through her senses. He didn't long for her sister or anyone else. He loved her. He had from the start. He loved her now and always would.

His words had been such a balm to her, she'd clung to them as he'd said them, ready to give in to the black tide of a sleep she knew she'd never wake from. Instead she felt herself coming back to life stronger than ever before.

All because of him.

Because of the blood bond that now connected him to her mind, body, and soul.

She felt his love for her through the bond, a force even more immense than the vitality she felt surging into every cell and fiber of her being.

Razor loved her with the same fathomless depth of caring she felt for him.

It was unbreakable . . . eternal.

Willow opened her eyes and found his golden gaze locked on her, filled not only with that love, but with deep concern and regret. "You're going to be all right now," he told her softly, his voice low and raspy with emotion. "You're alive, Willow. You're safe."

She wanted to say something to him, too. She was overcome with the need to tell him how sorry she was for doubting him. She needed him to know she'd heard everything he said to her and that she would never doubt him again.

He smiled tenderly as all the things she wanted to tell him grew nearly to bursting in her heart. "I'm sorry too," he reassured her as though he heard them all now through their bond. "I'm sorry for letting Henry Lewis's bastard of a son get his hands on you."

He caressed her cheek as he gently withdrew his wrist and sealed the punctures with his tongue. "I'm sorry for the misunderstandings and doubt I caused. I thought I'd be sorry for forcing my bond on you, but I can't regret that now. You're alive, and I would've done anything in my power to save you."

The rawness of his admission brought tears to the

backs of her eyes. She could never regret their bond, either. Licking her lips to savor every last drop of his life-giving blood, she slowly shook her head.

Her strength returning tenfold, she sat up on the bed and held his remorseful gaze. "You saved my life Razor. Not just a few moments ago, or back in Colorado, or at St. Anne's." She reached up to him, tracing the hard line of his jaw. "I never realized I'd spent my whole life hiding and running, not from any one person, but from life. From feeling anything for anyone, from allowing myself to love."

He cursed reverently under his breath. "I'd been living the same way. Then I saw you for the first time on my surveillance feed. Nothing was the same for me after that moment."

She smiled, nearly overcome by her feelings. "When I found that drone footage, all my old fears came pouring back in again. I thought it proved I was a fool for opening my heart to you. I did the only thing I knew how to do . . . I ran away from it. I should've believed in you, Razor. I should have believed what I knew in my heart to be true about you. You're a good man. I'm the one who's sorry. Sorry I didn't trust you. Sorry my actions might have allowed Owen Lewis and UWSI to carry out their awful plans."

Razor cupped her face in his strong yet infinitely gentle hands. "Neither he nor UWSI will ever hurt anyone now. The only thing that matters to me is that I'm holding you in my arms again. I love you so damn much, Willow. You're my everything."

A sob broke from her throat. "I love you too."

Drawing her into his embrace, Razor kissed her with all the devotion she could feel flowing between them through their blood bond. She didn't want to let go, not ever. She didn't want this hard-won kiss to end after everything they'd had to fight through in order to have it.

They were still wrapped in each other's arms when the sounds of fast-approaching footfalls filtered in from the corridor outside the breached examination room.

Razor drew away from her at once and pivoted to face the disruption, ever the warrior prepared to defend what was his. His stance relaxed almost immediately as two large Breed males in black combat gear appeared on the other side of the hole he'd made in the doorway.

"So much for stealth and limited casualties," the big male with short blond hair and a Russian-sounding accent remarked with an ironic grin, stepping inside and glancing at Owen Lewis's savaged corpse. "Looks like that asshole had it coming."

"He did," Razor replied.

The other male approached them, glancing at Willow as Razor helped her to her feet. "You must be Willow. I'm Sterling Chase, and this is my mate, Tavia," he said, gesturing to the beautiful Breed female who now entered the room behind him.

"We're so glad you're okay," Tavia said, placing a hand on Willow's arm.

More Breed warriors, male and female, arrived from the corridor. Knox was with them too. They were all dressed for battle and armed to the teeth, a rescue team like nothing Willow had ever seen before.

"You brought your brother and the Order with you?" she asked Razor, astonished.

It was Tavia who answered. "I believe he would've moved heaven and earth to find you."

"Hell too," Razor added, bringing Willow under his protective arm. "Now that I've found her, I'm never letting her go."

Lifting her chin on his fingertips, he bent his head and kissed her again, not letting up until Sterling Chase cleared his throat.

"So, what the fuck happened in here? We've got dead guys all over the place out there, not to mention this one who looks like a meat grinder chewed him up and spit him out."

Razor smirked, but his focus never left Willow's face. "I'll fill you in later. Right now, I just want to get my mate out of this place."

Tavia smiled. "That sounds good to me, too."

Sterling Chase rested his hand on Razor's shoulder. "Lucan Thorne is going to want a debrief from all of us, the two of you as well. I can't overstress how grateful the Order is to have Laurel's flash drive under our protection. We've also confiscated everything on site related to Serenicure. No part of that project will ever be used to hurt anyone now."

Willow exhaled, relieved to her marrow. None of this would bring her sister back, but there was some measure of peace in knowing that Laurel's death hadn't been in vain after all. Willow and Razor—along with these warriors from the Order—had avenged her twin and Theo in the best way possible.

Sterling Chase's approving gaze moved from Razor to her now. "There's no telling the number of lives that have been spared tonight. I'm sorry it came at the cost of your sister, but I know I can speak for Lucan Thorne and the rest of my brethren when I say that you will always have family in the Order."

"Thank you," she whispered, humbled at the thought.

"That goes for you as well, Razor." Chase extended his hand to him with a solemn smile.

As the two Breed males shook hands, a chorus of voices from the other warriors, male and female, joined together all around them. "You honor us well."

One by one, the warriors and Knox each approached to offer praise and kind words. Willow had never felt so showered with warm regard, all of it made even sweeter because of the love she and Razor were finally brave enough to express to each other.

She didn't know what the future held for them now, or where it might take them. She only knew she wanted to spend that future at Razor's side. He was her family now. He was her home, the only true north she would ever need.

And in her heart—down to her marrow—she knew that she was that true north for him too.

With hands linked and their blood bond glowing with power between them, she and Razor walked out alongside their friends, leaving the night's horror and carnage behind them forever.

EPILOGUE

Six months later . . .

"It's almost time," Razor called out to Willow, glancing at the big antique grandfather clock in the foyer of the little farmhouse.

The sweater she had convinced him to put on tonight scratched at his neck and was a hell of a lot less comfortable than the black t-shirts and leather he preferred, but he wasn't about to complain. If seeing him wear it brought Willow joy, then he was happy to oblige.

Well, maybe "happy" was a bit of a stretch.

Pacing as he waited for her, he ran his finger inside the collar and tried to avoid catching his reflection in the large mirror in the hallway. Just because he agreed to wear it didn't mean he wanted to see himself in it.

Careful footsteps on the stairs leading down from the bedrooms on the second floor drew his attention as

Willow descended. The instant he saw her, all the breath in his lungs leaked out of him on a stunned sigh.

Not that he should ever be surprised by his Breedmate's beauty, but tonight she looked particularly gorgeous. Everything male in him ignited with approval.

"Holy hell."

She stepped off the last stair and did a little spin for him. "Do I look all right?"

He could hardly speak for what the sight of her was doing to him. "You look incredible."

She wore a red satin dress that had tiny gold beads and sparkly embroidery sewn onto it. The skirt was short and full, topped by a form-fitting bodice that accentuated her small waist and delectable breasts. Although she usually favored cowgirl boots, tonight she wore towering high heels that made her legs seem to go on forever.

Her thick dark hair was gathered into a soft updo with random, loose tendrils that curled along her face and the smooth column of her neck. The only jewelry she wore was the half-heart pendant necklace she never took off. Laurel's matching charm joined hers on the chain that hung suspended between Willow's breasts.

Anxiously, she reached up to her naked earlobes. "I have earrings upstairs. Do you think I should put them on?"

Razor slowly shook his head and walked toward her. "You look absolutely perfect just the way you are."

She beamed, then her gaze drifted to what he was wearing and she let out a small giggle. "You look . . . so amazing."

He frowned. "I think you mean ridiculous."

Holding his arms out, he let her see the full spectacle

of the hideous red-and-green Christmas sweater. As if the colors weren't bad enough, it also had a giant Santa head appliquéd on the front, accented with sequined snowflakes and "Ho-ho-ho!" embroidered across the top.

Willow's giggle became a brief fit of laughter. Throwing her arms around his neck, she rose up on her toes and kissed him. "Don't worry, you won't be the only one in a Christmas sweater. Leni convinced Knox to wear one too."

Razor chuckled at the thought. "Now that is something I need to see."

His brother and Leni were bringing their two-month old baby boy, Caleb, along with Shannon and Riley. Several couples from the Order had accepted their invitation to Parrish Falls tonight too, as had his Hunter brothers from Florida and their mates.

Now that it was actually happening at any minute, Razor wasn't sure he was ready for the merging of his former life and this new one he was making with Willow. Never mind the fact that he would be doing so dressed in a Santa sweater.

Willow smiled at him. "Would it help if I tell you I also think you look totally sexy?"

"It might," he grumbled. "Maybe you should show me what you think instead."

"We have guests on the way," she playfully reminded him.

When he groaned in protest, she kissed him again then took him by the hand and led him into the living room. Like the rest of their cozy home, this room was decked in full holiday style too.

Decorated greenery draped the fireplace mantel and

window frames. The large pine Razor had chopped down from the wooded acreage behind the house a couple nights ago stood as the centerpiece of the room. Now, it was full of glittering ornaments, garlands, and tiny lights. Underneath the tree were beautifully wrapped gifts—handcrafted pottery Willow had made for everyone who was coming to celebrate with them tonight.

And outside a light snowfall had kicked up a couple hours ago, delicate flakes pattering against the window and swirling merrily in the cold of the North Maine Woods.

It was all like something out of a festive dream, all of it Willow's doing.

She'd never had a proper Christmas, and Razor was glad he could be part of the magic he saw dancing in her eyes as she drank it in with him.

She turned to him, a watery smile in her eyes. "Isn't it beautiful?"

He nodded, his gaze trained only on her.

His woman.

His mate.

And, in six more months, the mother of his child.

"I've never seen anything more beautiful in my life." Razor gathered her into his arms, dropping a kiss on the top of her head.

If he'd had his way he'd like to hold her like this all night, just feeling her breathing against him, her joy and contentment bringing him a peace he'd never dreamed could exist—at least not for someone like him.

The decision to start their life together in Parrish Falls had been an easy one, even before they'd spotted the *For Sale* sign in the front yard of a quaint gentleman's farm less than a mile up the road from Knox and Leni's place. Willow loved having horses, goats, and chickens to care for, and Razor loved that he was able to convert one of the heated barns out back into a dedicated pottery studio for her.

He supposed he might get the itch to return to action one day, but if Knox had been able to find his own rhythm living off the grid in the North Maine Woods, Razor probably could too.

Besides, come spring the two of them would be keeping busy installing a white picket fence around Razor and Willow's front yard.

Razor smiled to himself and held her a little closer, both of them watching the twinkling lights on the tree and the snow falling outside while they waited for their friends and family to arrive.

Willow had told him that he'd saved her, not only physically but saved her from a life of hiding and running from her emotions. The truth was she had saved him. She had healed him far more than his blood had healed her that awful night in Montreal.

She had made him whole.

She had given him a place in her heart, somewhere he finally felt safe too.

She had given him the only home he would ever need.

Right here, with Willow beside him . . . forever.

~ * ~

ABOUT THE AUTHOR

LARA ADRIAN is a *New York Times* and #1 international best-selling author, with nearly 4 million books in print and digital worldwide and translations licensed to more than 20 countries. Her books have regularly appeared in the top spots of all the major bestseller lists including the *New York Times*, USA Today, Publishers Weekly, Wall Street Journal, Amazon.com, Barnes & Noble, etc. Reviewers have called Lara's books "addictively readable" (Chicago Tribune), "strikingly original" (Booklist), "extraordinary" (Fresh Fiction), and "one of the consistently best" (Romance Novel News).

Visit the author's website at
www.LaraAdrian.com

Find Lara on Facebook at
www.facebook.com/LaraAdrianBooks

Hunter Legacy Series

Thrilling standalone vampire romances from Lara Adrian
set in the Midnight Breed story universe.

AVAILABLE NOW!

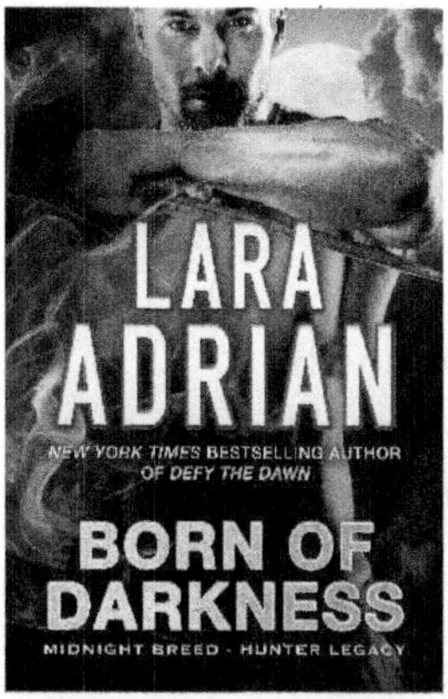

Thirsty for more Midnight Breed?

Read the complete series!

A Touch of Midnight (prequel novella)
Kiss of Midnight
Kiss of Crimson
Midnight Awakening
Midnight Rising
Veil of Midnight
Ashes of Midnight
Shades of Midnight
Taken by Midnight
Deeper Than Midnight
A Taste of Midnight (ebook novella)
Darker After Midnight
The Midnight Breed Series Companion
Edge of Dawn
Marked by Midnight (novella)
Crave the Night
Tempted by Midnight (novella)
Bound to Darkness
Stroke of Midnight (novella)
Defy the Dawn
Midnight Untamed (novella)
Midnight Unbound (novella)
Midnight Unleashed (novella)
Claimed in Shadows
Break the Day
Fall of Night
King of Midnight

Go behind the scenes of the Midnight Breed series with the ultimate insider's guide!

The Midnight Breed Series Companion

Available Now

Look for it in eBook and Paperback at major retailers.

If you enjoy sizzling contemporary romance, don't miss this hot series from Lara Adrian!

For 100 Days

The 100 Series: Book 1

"I wish I could give this more than 5 stars! Lara Adrian not only dips her toe into this genre with flare, she will take it over . . . I have found my new addiction, this series." —The Sub Club Books

All available now in ebook, trade paperback and unabridged audiobook.

Award-winning medieval romances from Lara Adrian!

Dragon Chalice Series

(Paranormal Medieval Romance)

"Brilliant . . . bewitching medieval paranormal series." –Booklist

Warrior Trilogy

(Medieval Romance)

"The romance is pure gold." –All About Romance

Connect with Lara online at:

www.LaraAdrian.com

www.facebook.com/LaraAdrianBooks

www.goodreads.com/lara_adrian

www.instagram.com/laraadrianbooks

www.pinterest.com/LaraAdrian

Printed in Great Britain
by Amazon

33951246R00169